THE
ROCKFORD
FILES

Forge Books by Stuart M. Kaminsky

THE ROCKFORD FILES
The Green Bottle
Devil on My Doorstep

THE ROCKFORD FILES

Devil on My Doorstep

STUART M. KAMINSKY

A TOM DOHERTY ASSOCIATES BOOK

NEW YORK

THE ROCKFORD FILES: DEVIL ON MY DOORSTEP

This book is printed on acid-free paper.

A Forge Book
Published by Tom Doherty Associates, Inc.
175 Fifth Avenue
New York, NY 10010

Forge® is a registered trademark of Tom Doherty Associates, Inc.

Library of Congress Cataloging-in-Publication Data

Kaminsky, Stuart M.
    Devil on my doorstep / Stuart M. Kaminsky.—1st. ed.
       p.   cm.—(The Rockford Files)
    "A Tom Doherty Associates book."
    ISBN 0-312-86444-2
    I. Rockford files (Television program)   II. Title.   III. Series:
Kaminsky, Stuart M.   Rockford files.
PS3561.A43D5   1998
813'.54—dc21   97-29851
                                            CIP

First Edition: March 1998

Printed in the United States of America

0 9 8 7 6 5 4 3 2 1

FOR EMILY LAZARUS,
JOSIE LAZARUS, AND
MAX HECKARD

PROLOGUE

Answering machine of Jim Rockford.

—*This is Jim Rockford. Please leave a message after the beep.*

—*Jimbo, this is Dennis. Weather looks great for tomorrow. Andy and I will be standing at the door, rods in hand, waiting when the sun comes up. I called Babe Wosentwozen and he says they're biting. We'll bring the night crawlers. Where the hell are you?*

—*Mr. Rockford, this is Madison Torvall. I am a patient man. I don't even mind making these daily calls to you and talking to your machine, but the powers above really would like me to collect the $321.11 you owe on your sofa. They have the distinct, reasonable and unshakable belief that since I sold you the couch, it is my responsibility to collect the payment. Please call or, better yet, stop by with a check or cash.*

—*Jim, Angel. Can't talk about it on the phone, but I've got a sweet deal going. You've got my Malibu address and number. I could use a friend with your talents.*

—This is Beatrice Wallace. We have surveyed and assessed the contents of the trunk you found in the crawl space of your father's house as you requested. There are a few items of interest—primarily the old coins, some of the collectables, etc. We are prepared to offer you $450 for the entire contents, including the trunk itself. We will not charge the $75 normal charge for the assessment should you choose to sell.

—Who was the secretary of state under President Martin Van Buren? If you know the answer, call Mr. Robertson at 1-800-QUIK and win a two-day all-expenses-paid vacation at the Mountain Lakes Retirement Homes where you'll see the most beautiful scenery in the United States and attend seminars on living at Mountain Lakes or training as a Mountain Lakes trainee. Call now with your answer. This is a limited offer. The law requires that we inform you that your name was given to us by a Mr. Angel Martin for a nominal fee, which he will receive if you win this free trip to Arkansas.

—Jim, Jim, if you're there pick up. This is Jenny. Did I leave my earrings at your place Monday night? I need 'em. Wait, forget it, I know where I left them.

—Jim, this is Beanie Stutz. Remember me? Got the permanent bump over my eye. Rocky and me used to camp out back in the old days before my hip went. Just found out about Rocky. Sorry I missed the funeral. I'm not leavin' a number, just my sympathy and if you get a chance, throw a purple flower on Rocky's grave for me. He'd understand.

—I need a detective. Now, not a week from now. My name is Karen Potter-Mills. This is my second call today. If I don't reach you by the end of the day, though you've been recommended as being

relatively inexpensive and discreet, I'll have to seek help elsewhere. I'll keep calling. I can't leave my number.

—*You owe it to your family to provide the maximum security when accidental or natural death comes, as it does to us all. Please call me, Sylvan Foxx, at 454-3434 for a pennies-a-day life insurance policy you can't afford to pass up. I don't wish to alarm you, but one day, on your bed of final rest or the instant before the truck bearing down on you strikes, you'll feel an instant of guilt unless you make this call.*

—*Rockford, this is Morry Weinstock. I'll make it simple. You want your Firebird fixed so it runs like new, $345. You want it fixed so it runs like always, $210. I can do either job in four hours. Cash only.*

—*Who is Jim Rockford? Where is Juanita? What is Juanita doing giving me this number? I'm checkin' the phone book and comin' there. Juanita better be packed and . . . Wait, I think I dialed the wrong number. Sorry about that.*

—*You may not remember me, but I'm Stu Preswell. Few years back you said if I ever came across a Benson Six rod with an original reel in good shape, I should give you a call. Got one. You've got my number. If not, I'm in the Van Nuys book.*

CHAPTER ONE

THE sun was just about to come up and I was late. I must have hit the snooze button on the alarm clock without knowing it. I turned on the Weather Channel and heated some of yesterday's—or was it the day before's—coffee in the microwave while I drank a glass of orange juice. The coffee was awful, but it was coffee.

I showered, shaved, dressed fast in fishing trip clothes, red flannel shirt, jeans, boots, Rocky's baseball hat, the faded one that says EZRA'S DIESEL FUEL in red letters. I checked my fishing gear, drank my coffee and discovered that it was going to be a perfect day for fishing with Dennis and his son Andy.

I turned off the television, looked around the trailer, hoisted my fishing gear and tackle box and went out the front door into the dim morning light, locking the door behind me. There really wasn't too much point in locking the door. Hard-core beach bums or collection agency flat-noses could get in with a rock or a toothpick.

If someone did come when I was gone, the Travises, Fred and his wife, in the trailer across the lot would let me know. It was their sacred retirees' duty to take turns protecting the property by spying on the few of us who lived on or owned property on the Cove. A family named Webster had lived in the third trailer on the cracked concrete lot. They had recently sold out to an old black woman named Bailey. Mrs. Bailey liked to spend her time under the awning of her trailer, sitting in a chair, listening to her portable radio and looking through her half glasses at the notebook in which she was always writing.

When I meet people who ask me where I live, I tell them on Covina Cove in Santa Monica. If pressed, I tell them I'm on the beach. In truth, I have a trailer in need of constant repair on a cracked concrete lot by a beach that was getting to be more of a hangout for dangerous, lost and often drunk tan boys and girls and those who tried to pass as the tanned boys and girls they had been a decade earlier.

I heard the waves washing in on the beach about a hundred yards away and smiled. It wasn't perfect, but it was home. The smile passed quickly.

She was huddled in one of the white plastic chairs on my narrow porch. People were always walking away with the chairs, and I was always picking up new ones at garage sales. The good folding deck chairs and a folding small plastic table I kept inside the trailer. Next to the girl was a cloth suitcase.

She was huddled under a dew-covered lightweight jacket in a near-fetal position. She couldn't have been comfortable even though she was asleep. I wondered for a second if she was having a bad dream. Her hair was dark, straight, cut short. Her face was very young, her skin near white and clear, and she was making a sort of strained humming sound as if she were dreaming. I'd had a dream last night too. I was in the living room of an old girlfriend. Maybe a wife. I couldn't make out her face. There was a huge glass tank filled with large tropical fish. The glass suddenly burst, sending fish, glass and a torrent of water over me. I think that's when I woke up.

"Miss," I said gently, touching her shoulder.

It wasn't unusual to find on or near the deck or even in the back of Rocky's pickup truck a runaway or a kid or old man or woman who had gotten drunk or high or just plain lost or broke.

"Miss," I said, putting down my fishing gear and shaking her just a bit harder. "It's morning. You can't sleep here."

The girl's eyes opened. They were large and brown and she was definitely pretty, though when the jacket slid down I could tell she could use a few weeks of grilled steaks, a lot of milk and regular meals.

When she let the jacket slide forward into her lap, I noticed a small suitcase next to the chair, one of those suitcases with pink flowers on it. It didn't look cheap.

She looked around as if she had awakened in Oz, and her eyes turned to the beach and the ocean as she ran her fingers through her hair.

Now that I could see what she was wearing I knew she wasn't one of the homeless kids who head for the beaches of Malibu. She wore washed blue jeans and a pink short-sleeved polo-style shirt that looked like silk and definitely wrinkled.

She sat up, blinked, looked at me and said, "James Rockford."

"Jim'll do," I said.

There was something familiar about the girl. Maybe I had seen her on the beach or having breakfast at Harry's Grill. It would come to me if I worked at it. I didn't feel like working at it. I felt like going fishing and I didn't like the fact that she knew my name.

She looked at me, studied my face. I couldn't have looked like the ideal she might be searching for. My cap, advertising Ezra's Diesel Fuel in red letters, was tilted forward. My pants were baggy, held up by suspenders, and my shirt was my favorite plaid fishing shirt that had seen better days. Hell, it had seen better years, but so had I.

"Look," I said, fishing into my pocket. "Here's a few dollars and some change. You want to make a phone call for someone to pick you up, there's a phone outside the bar down the beach."

The girl didn't speak.

I sighed deeply and dramatically, tilting my cap back on my head and trying to remember if I packed the sunscreen.

"Okay," I said. "I'll drive you to Los Angeles. I'm going that way, but I'm going and now. Some people are waiting for me."

She looked at the bills and coins I had given her as if they were rocks from Mars and then looked at me while I checked my watch. I was already going to be late, and Dennis was not a patient man. Dennis had been a cop about twice as long as the girl in front of me had been on this planet. Cops are either born impatient or learn to be. The crimes keep getting worse and piling up higher. You can't help wanting to make the pile smaller as fast as you can before it falls over and smothers you. And you spend most of your days listening to lies.

"Your father is Joseph Rockford," the girl said.

She had my attention now.

" 'Was,' " I said. "He died a few years ago."

"I'm sorry," she said, and she sounded as if she meant it, meant it more than just someone giving stale sympathy.

"Thanks," I said. "Now . . ."

"He was called Rocky," she said.

"Yes, he was," I was wary.

"You used to be a confidence man," she said. "Now you're a private detective. You went to prison once."

I folded my arms, waiting for the punch line, knowing the exasperated look that was on my face. It always came when I thought someone was going to try to take me in. I had dealt with the best. Old women and kids were among the best. I had spent five years in San Quentin on an armed robbery conviction. I had been a kid confidence man running scams and making a living when I went to prison. I had never been arrested for any con, but I had made it to Quentin for something I hadn't done. The real robber was eventually caught. I got a full pardon from the governor of California and after doing some legwork for the lawyer who had helped find the guy who did the robbery, I got my private investigator's license and started a successful career, which left me with a few hundred dollars in the bank, a trailer home that ate money, a tender back, bad knees and a few friends.

She reached down, put the small suitcase on her lap, zipped open an outer pocket and pulled out a crumpled envelope.

"My mother said if anything ever happened I should find you and give you this."

She handed me the envelope. I didn't want it, but I took it. There was probably an angle here, but the fish were biting thirty miles away on my dad's favorite fishing river and I had spent a rough week feeling sorry for myself.

My address was on the envelope. So was my name. They were written in ink, a woman's writing, clear, slightly slanted to the right.

"Who are you?" I asked.

"Melisa Conforti," she said, fishing out a small brush from her suitcase and working on her hair. "Conforti is my stepfather's name."

I didn't ask why.

"You know what's in this letter?" I asked.

"My mother told me to bring it to you if something happened," she said again.

"And something happened?"

"Yes," she said softly, looking back at the ocean.

"Something bad," I said.

The girl nodded.

I carefully opened the envelope with my pocket knife and pulled out the single sheet inside. It was brief and written by the same woman who had addressed the envelope. The sheet was wrapped around a photograph. I looked at the photograph.

There was a younger, grinning Jim Rockford on the beach in a bathing suit. I didn't look half bad without a shirt. But that was long ago. In the photograph, I had my arm around a beautiful young woman with long dark hair. She was wearing a bikini, an iridescent blue bikini. She was smiling, but there was something sad and distant in the smile. I wondered who had taken the photograph. I couldn't remember. But I remembered her, and when I looked at the bottom of the sheet I saw the name, Rene.

I read the letter. I read it twice. I looked at the girl, who said,

"I'm hungry. Do you have something to eat? I like cereal."

I didn't answer. I read the letter again.

"You know what's in this letter, don't you?" I said.

She was silent.

Rene and I had been close, very close, for almost four months. I had gotten beyond serious and then one day I woke up, reached over and found an envelope with my name on it not much different from the envelope I held in my hands. I still had the note somewhere: "Dear Jim, I love you, but I have to go. I can't explain. Don't hate me."

The note in my hand told a different tale.

"Your mother's maiden name?" I asked the girl.

"Henley," she said. "And your lawyer is a pretty woman named Beth Davenport."

"She's a famous author now," I said. "She doesn't do much legal work anymore."

"I read one of her books," the girl said. "I think you're Carter Wilson in *Dancing on the Beach.*"

"I haven't read it," I said. "How old are you?"

"Seventeen," she said, stretching and rubbing her stiff shoulder.

The shoulder was fine in about two seconds. If I had slept outside, my shoulder would be out of business and in need of deep massage and heat for at least a week.

"Birth date?"

She gave me her birth date. I handed her the letter and asked her to read it out loud.

" 'Dear Jim,' " she began. " 'Melisa is your daughter. When I became pregnant, I wanted the baby but I had to leave. I didn't think you were ready for a family. I don't think you'll ever be. I may be wrong. If you are reading this, something bad has happened and Melissa needs your help. You wouldn't be reading this if it weren't absolutely necessary. I loved you. I still do. Help her.' "

The girl put the letter in her lap and added,

"It's signed 'Rene.' "

I handed her the photograph.

"She was beautiful," she said softly.

"Does that mean 'she's not beautiful anymore' or . . ."

"I think she's dead," the girl said, looking up at me and folding her hands as if she were in class. "I think he killed her."

"He?"

"My stepfather," she said. "Michael Conforti."

The phone was ringing. I knew who it was.

"You keep the photograph," she said, handing it back to me. "She must have wanted you to have it."

I took the photograph back.

"Let's go inside," I said, opening the door, picking up my fishing gear and letting Melisa Conforti walk in ahead of me with her suitcase. Now that she was standing I could see that she was tall for her age, tall and walking with the slight sway I remembered in Rene.

"Have a seat," I said, pushing the door closed and heading for the phone on my desk before the answering machine could pick up. My machine was set for seven rings so someone could hang up before the machine came on if they wanted to and I could get from the bedroom to the phone no matter how stiff my knees might be.

"Hello," I said, looking at the girl as she walked over to the refrigerator.

I was finding it hard to believe that this girl on my doorstep might really be my daughter. It was hard to believe, but it was possible. I was sure as hell going to find out.

"Jim," Dennis said in exasperation. "Where the hell are you? What are you still doing home?"

"Something came up, Dennis," I said. "I can't go today."

"You can't . . . Jim. We've got the campsite. The tent's packed. The grill's packed. The gear's packed and the weather is perfect. Andy had to find someone to take his shift tomorrow. I don't know when he can get off again."

Dennis's son Andy was a rookie cop. There had been a time when Andy was younger, blamed his father and mother for everything and got into trouble. That time was long gone. Dennis had his son back. Did I have a daughter?

"If it weren't an emergency, I wouldn't be doing this, Dennis. I need this fishing trip as much as you do," I said, watching Melissa, who looked at me. I nodded at her that it was all right to open the refrigerator, which she did.

"What's the emergency, Jim?" Dennis said suspiciously.

"Remember Rene Henley?" I asked.

"Rene . . . No. Wait. Yes. The one who walked out on you."

"Delicately put, Dennis," I said.

"She's back?"

"No," I said, "but this is about her. She's in trouble."

"I liked her," said Dennis. "Thought you and she were . . . you know."

"I know."

"She's in trouble?"

"Maybe big trouble," I said.

"And you just found out?"

"I walked out the door, all ready to get into the pickup, and it was waiting for me on the deck."

"It?"

"I'll explain later. Why don't you go fishing? Give my apologies to Andy?"

"I don't know," Dennis said.

"Give you some quality time alone with your son," I said as Melisa opened the cupboard next to the refrigerator and found four boxes of cereal.

"I don't know," he said, definitely disappointed. "Maybe I'll call and change the reservation, ask Andy if we can do next week. I wanted you, me and Andy to catch a few and talk about his future. When you've got a kid it never stops, Jim."

I looked at Melissa and said,

"I'll take your word for it. I'm sorry, Dennis."

"Next week okay?" he asked.

"I hope so," I said.

"You sound funny, Jimbo. Need some help?"

"Not yet," I said. "But I may take you up on that."

"I'll talk to you later," he said. "If you change your mind in the next half hour, give me a call. Andy and I'll wait."

"Okay," I said and hung up. I placed the photograph of me and Rene on my desk, looked at it for more than a few seconds, and then looked at Melisa.

She picked out Cheerios, which was fine with me. I didn't like them. I bought them on sale as backup if I ran out of Cap'n Crunch or Frosted Wheaties. While she ate, I searched for and found the gray steel box in the lower right-hand drawer of my desk. My papers—birth certificate, private investigator's license, Rocky's papers and some memories. I found the note Rene had left for me more than eighteen years earlier. I put the photograph of her and me on the beach inside, closed the box and put it back in the drawer.

I served Melissa and offered her juice and coffee. She said yes to both and I worked on getting the coffee while we talked.

"Mind if I look at that note again?" I asked.

She handed it to me and kept eating. I compared the two notes. It was Rene's writing on both. No doubt.

"Tell me your story," I said.

"You don't believe I'm your daughter, do you?" she asked, seated at my small table, a spoonful of little doughnut-shaped pieces of cereal on the way to her mouth.

"It's hard," I said. "And it's sudden."

"I know how you feel," she said. "This is news to me too."

"The dates are right," I said, leaning against the counter, my arms folded. "It's possible."

"Why didn't you marry her?" she asked as the coffee brewed and bubbled behind me.

"I was willing," I said. "She took off. There was always something secret about your mother."

"I know what you mean," the girl said, showing me the empty bowl. I refilled it. "But she did tell me about you and Rocky. There was something sad in her voice when she talked about you."

"I've got to tell you you're right. I'm not convinced I'm your father," I said, watching her dig into her second bowl of cereal. "Too sudden. Too convenient. Too late. But I'll keep an open mind, or try to."

"My mother talked about you every once in a while from the time I was about fourteen," she said, pausing to sip some coffee. "She said you were a friend, a good friend. She told me about Rocky, Beth and someone named Angie."

"Angel," I said. "Evelyn Angelo Martinez, Angel Martin."

"That's it," she said, pointing her spoon at me. "Angel. I didn't know you were my father till the letter, but I sort of suspected, I think."

"We'll leave the father business out of this for now," I said, sitting in the chair across from her at the small table. I drank my coffee and looked at her. There was definitely a lot of Rene about her. I was looking for something Rockford. Maybe it was there. I hadn't started to give serious thought to what it might mean if this was my daughter. "Tell me your story. And your mother's. What you know of it."

"Well," she said, "I think she was originally from somewhere in California. North, I think. San Francisco. She knew a lot about San Francisco. Berkeley. Oakland. Palo Alto. Richmond. Places like that. Before she had me, before she was even showing, she went to Florida. Sarasota. I think she had a friend there. She met Michael there. He was big, good looking, treated her fine and had plenty of money. At least that's what she told me. He knew about me coming but asked her to marry him anyway. She did. Things were okay,

I think. I seem to remember fights when I was a little kid. I know I remember them when I was nine or ten. I never saw him hit her, but he yelled and broke things. She never raised her voice but she never backed down. At least that's the way I remember it."

"What did they fight about, Melisa?" I asked.

She shrugged.

"What did they fight about, Melisa?" I repeated.

"Lots of things," she said, pushing her empty bowl away and pulling her coffee to her. She took the cup in both hands and rolled it slightly, looking into the now-tepid dark brown.

"You?" I asked.

"How did you know?"

"I'm a detective," I said. "You're a pretty girl."

"He made, like, moves on me," she said. "Mostly in the last couple of years. He always pretended he was a little drunk. I never let him touch me and I didn't tell my mother, but she found out."

"And then?"

"About a month ago," she said, "Michael came in one afternoon. He managed a Toyota car place. He came in one afternoon just after I came home from school. He told my mother and me to pack fast. He didn't ask us. He didn't listen. He looked scared. He wouldn't tell us what was happening or where we were going. He said we had an hour to pack. No more. I got almost everything I had in the suitcases I got for my last birthday. We put everything in a van parked in the driveway."

"And your mother didn't ask questions?"

"Nope," Melisa said. "She seemed to understand what was going on without being told. I thought we were going away for a few days. We drove all day and stayed at a motel at night. I got a look at the card he filled out. He wrote in the name Walter Plunket or something like that and he paid cash. We got about five hours' sleep and then he drove all night and the next day. Mom and I slept in the back. She never complained and nobody talked much except me asking where we were going and why. I didn't get any answers."

"And then?" I prompted as she drank the last of her coffee.

"And then. Pasadena. I was told that we were now the Jacobs family. There was a house waiting for us to move in. Small. Nice. I was just two months from graduating from high school. I . . . what do I call you?"

"Call me Jim," I said. I wasn't ready for 'Dad' yet, not by a long shot, and I don't think she was either.

"Michael wouldn't let me enroll in the high school," she said. "I don't know why."

I knew why. If Melisa enrolled, the new school would want the records from her past school. Conforti, or whoever he was, didn't want anyone to be able to pick up his trail through Melisa.

"I knew we were hiding," she said. "So did Mom. But from what or who . . ."

"Last night?" I asked.

"Last night," she said with a deep sigh, her eyes going moist and looking down. "Or really sort of late in the afternoon, I heard them arguing downstairs. It was worse than usual. I went down and he was dragging her out the front door by her hair. I tried to stop him. He hit me and Mom shouted at me to get out, run away. He didn't even pay any attention. I guess I was crying. He pulled her out of the door, left it open. Mom was screaming for help. The houses are kind of far apart, but a few people came out, mostly older people. I just stood in the doorway. Nobody wanted to mess with Michael. He's big."

"I know. You told me."

"And he was acting crazy. He pushed her in the car. He had sold the van the day after we got to Los Angeles."

"You know what kind of car he pulled your mother into? The license number?"

"It's a dark green, two-door, two-year-old GEO Metro. License number is 353-267. I packed fast. Remembered the letter, grabbed it, packed a few things and by the time I found you, it was late so I went to sleep on your deck. I've got two hundred and eighty dollars, but I hitched rides here. I didn't know when I could go home or how long the money would have to last me. Mom . . ."

And then it broke. She put her head in her arms on the table and began to cry, her shoulders rocking. I'm not great at situations like this, but my shoulders are broad. I remembered Rene, and there was a distinct possibility this girl was my daughter. I got up, took the step to her and helped her out of the chair and into my arms. She put her head on my shoulder and her arms around my neck.

Someone knocked at the door and I shouted, "Come in."

Over Melisa's shoulder I watched Fred Travis, president of the Covina Cove Homeowners Association, step inside. The association consisted of Fred and Connie Travis's trailer, another trailer that had belonged to a family named Webster who had sold out a few months ago to the old black woman, and my trailer. There was a bar down the beach where they dealt mostly in beer and simple sandwiches, but the owner was hardly ever there and he refused to pay dues.

Fred and Connie were in their seventies. Fred is almost as tall as I am. He stood, the door wide open, looking at me and Melisa. Fred's eyes were covered by the brim of his tan cowboy hat so I couldn't see his eyes. At first the hat wasn't due to a desire to feel like Clint Eastwood. Fred and Connie liked the sun. They had moved from a place in the East where the sun was a rarity. Fred had started to get small skin cancers. They were removed by a doctor and he looked leathery and fine, like an old cowboy, but he had to use gallons of sunscreen and wear a hat that kept the sun off his face.

Fred was wearing his jeans and a blue polo shirt. He took off his hat and revealed his fine head of white hair.

Now that I could see his eyes, I could see what he was thinking. Melisa looked no more than her seventeen years and I was . . . well, at least old enough to be her father or even her grandfather if we cut the dates close.

"What is it, Fred?" I asked over Melisa's sobbing. She didn't look up.

"Connie logged the girl sleeping on your deck," he said. "Girl came at 0100 hours."

"One in the morning," I told the ex-Marine.

"If you want to put it that way," he said. "You know her?"

"My niece," I said. "Ran away from my brother and his wife in Tacoma. Had a fight over a boyfriend. They'll come down and pick her up."

Fred looked relieved.

"Just checking," he said. "Two of those surfer kids knocked on the your door earlier yesterday. Then they went away."

"Thanks, Fred," I said.

He nodded, looked at us, not sure how suspicious he should be, and then backed out and closed the door.

When Melisa had stopped the heavy crying, which was after about five minutes, I asked her if she was all right. She pulled back, eyes red, and nodded that she was all right. It was the right question to ask, but I knew she'd give me the answer I wanted rather than the truth. I had to admit to myself that holding her had felt good. It had felt as if I might really be her father.

I got her seated on the sofa near the window, where she could watch me go behind my desk. I asked her some questions, The last one was whether she had a recent photograph of herself. She did. She took it out of a green wallet in her pocket, removed it from the celluloid pocket and handed it to me. It was one of those photographs you take in a machine in a mall. The picture was small. Melisa was smiling and in spite of the bright flash, she looked pretty and very young.

"Mind if I hold on to this for a while?" I asked.

"You can keep it," she said. "I have the other ones I took at the same time as that one. You've got the second-best one. I gave Mom the one I thought was best."

I called Dennis back. He was still there.

"Jim, we going?" he asked.

"No, Dennis," I said. "Go with Andy."

"I'm calling the guy who owns the site and changing the date," said Dennis in disappointment. "Andy'll check his schedule. I'll tell you when it'll be and you better make it."

"Give me a few days, Dennis. Make that a week."

"Whatever."

"Dennis?"

The pause on his end was long.

"You want a favor," he said.

"It's important."

"Ask."

I asked him to check the house in Pasadena and tell me what he could find out about the owner, who called himself Michael Jacobs but was also known as Michael Conforti. I told him Conforti had moved here from Florida a couple of months earlier. I described the car and gave him the license number.

"This about Rene?" he asked.

"Yes."

"I'll get back to you," Dennis said.

I picked up Melisa's suitcase. It wasn't very heavy. Then I guided her to the bedroom in the back of the trailer. I showed her where the small bathroom was and suggested that she take a shower and get some sleep. She nodded obediently and I told her I'd work on finding her mother. I got a change of clothes out of my closet.

I went back to my desk, wondering where to begin. I knew. The house in Pasadena. The shower started and I changed clothes. I wrote a note for her saying that she shouldn't answer the phone and that I'd be back in about three hours.

My guess was that she'd still be sleeping when I got back.

Before I left I went to the bedroom door and opened it a crack. She was curled up pretty much the same way she had been on the deck, and she was breathing evenly, sound asleep. She wore a Tampa Bay Buc's extralarge T-shirt and a pair of orange shorts. In her arms was a beat-up Raggedy Ann doll. I closed the door and headed for Pasadena.

CHAPTER TWO

IT was still early, but I caught some of the Inquisition torture of rush hour on the Long Beach Freeway.

On the way, I thought about Rene. I had met her in the small library in Burbank. I had been coming to the library for more than a week wearing serious glasses with glass in them in place of lenses, trying to look like a scholar doing research. Actually, I was watching a librarian who couldn't have been less than fifty and looked her age and profession. Her husband, a bartender at Nifty's near the Burbank airport, was sure she was cheating on him. He hired me through a friend and I parked myself every day in the library at a six-seat table pretending to take notes while I read mystery novels. Eventually, I found out that the model of a librarian had another interest, but it wasn't men. It was pornographic movies. She made excuses to her husband, the head librarian and anyone who needed them, and went regularly to XXX-rated places all the way back in the city.

Before I found that out, I met Rene. She wandered into the library one afternoon. She was wearing a plain brown dress and her hair was tied back. She wore no makeup and she was the most beautiful woman I had ever seen. She was also the saddest. Melisa had that look.

Rene picked out a book, a big coffee-table-sized one, sat near the window with it open in front of her while she looked out the window at an empty street.

We were the only two patrons in the reading room.

She sat for almost two hours with that book, never looking at it. And I looked over the top of my fake glasses and fell in love. At the end of the two hours, I got up, took off the glasses, went over to her and said,

"Pardon me, my name is Jim Rockford. You are both the most beautiful and saddest-looking woman I've ever seen."

She looked up at me in fear. I smiled.

"My name really is Jim Rockford," I said. "I'm in the phone book if you want to check, and you can have my wallet and the forty-two dollars in it as an act of good faith."

She still wasn't buying it. She started to get up.

"Can I help?" I said.

"Why?" she asked with undisguised suspicion, looking at the front door and escape from the intruder on her life.

"I help people for a living," I said. "Really, I'm harmless. Would you like a cup of coffee?"

She thought for a while, looked at my face and made the decision.

"All right," she said. "Someplace with lots of people."

"I know just the place," I said, ready to abandon my librarian-watching post. "You have a car?"

"No," she said.

"I do," I said, not touching her but taking a step toward the library door.

My supposedly wandering librarian with the bartender husband watched the pickup blankly. Later I wondered what fantasy she came up with about me and Rene.

Rene was reluctant to get into my car, but it was drizzling and she couldn't take much time to think about it without getting soaked. When she got in, she tightened as if waiting for me to attack.

I didn't attack. I drove to a place I knew that wasn't far away. We had coffee. We talked. She said she'd been in Los Angeles a few weeks, was living in a rented room in a house a few blocks from the library and was running out of money, though she thought she had a job lined up in the park district as a day-camp counselor and swimming teacher. She said she had been a swimmer, made it to the Olympic trials, lost out by a few tenths of a second. She stayed in shape and . . . then she suddenly stopped talking and asked about me. I told her, even about my doing time.

We spent an hour drinking coffee and eating croissants. I like the ones with chocolate inside. So did she. By the time we decided to leave, I had the feeling that she was beginning to trust me, that she hadn't talked to anyone for a long time and I was a good listener.

I dropped her off at the house where she had a room. The drizzle was gone, and I had a library to get back to.

"Thanks," she said before she got out.

"You know the next question," I said.

"Will you be at the library tomorrow?" she asked.

"Promise," I said.

"I'll stop by."

She got out of the car and walked into the house. She did come to the library the next day, and it began. I didn't touch her till the third time we went out, and then it was just to hold her hand. I didn't kiss her till the fourth time, and I didn't get a full smile till the fifth time. The sixth time was magic and, possibly, the night Melisa was conceived. Gradually, Rene met my friends, Rocky, Rocky's friends. We spent time on the beach by my trailer and time in my bed. I didn't mind the long trips back to Burbank, where she did get the job in the park.

She told me she was from Delaware and that she had once been married but her husband died. That was why she was in California. That was why she had that sad look the day I first saw her. She could swim better than anyone I knew. She knew more about current events and history than I knew, and she knew English literature like the college major she had been. Later, I realized that her story lacked details. I didn't even know what college she went to. I marked that up to not wanting to talk about her past, and I respected it.

After a month, she spent more nights with me on weekends when she wasn't working, and I was no more than a day away from asking her to marry me when she left the note and disappeared.

I checked the house where she lived. The old woman who owned it said that Rene had come home in a cab, run into her room, thrown things in a bag, given the old woman a month's rent in cash, and left. The park district wasn't more help. She had done her job. She had been good at it. She wasn't really friendly with anybody she worked with.

I did what a detective should be able to do and tried to find her, but there were no leads and I knew so little about her life before Burbank that I didn't know where to start. Eventually, reluctantly, I gave up, let the memory of her out of my life.

Now she was back.

It took me less time than I had figured, and I found the house in Pasadena on Paloma Street without much trouble. I parked the Firebird half a block away and walked to the house next door to the address Melisa had given me. It was modest by neighborhood standards, two-story, brick, including brick steps to the white wooden door. Bricks and door were as clean and well trimmed as the grass on the front lawn, which put to shame a lot of golf-course greens I had been on.

I knocked, waited. There was a car in the driveway, which may or may not have meant that someone was home. As it turned out, someone was home. He opened the door and looked at me as if I were an uninvited magazine salesman.

The man was probably close to seventy, tall, bald with brown age or sun spots on top of his head. He was wearing a sweat suit with GRINNELL COLLEGE in green letters across the front.

"Go west, young man," I said with my most winning smile.

The man did not respond.

"That's what Horace Greeley told Grinnell, who took his advice and—"

"I know," the man interrupted. "I taught at Grinnell for more than twenty-five years. Did you know that Gary Cooper went to Grinnell?"

" 'Fraid not," I said, still smiling.

"He did," the old man said, holding the door and looking down at me one step below him. "So did Harry Hopkins, Hallie Flanagan and a lot of others. Who are you?"

"Name's Gristoperman," I said. "Running a credit check for the First Centennial Bank."

"I don't have any credit cards and I don't do my banking at the First Centennial Bank. I've never even heard of the First Centennial Bank."

I laughed, the laugh of a patient man who has been misunderstood.

"No, the credit check is on your neighbor, Mr. Jacobs."

The tall old man sighed a put-upon sigh.

"I didn't even know their names. We barely exchanged

pleasantries, though the girl smiled at me the few times I saw her."

"Did you hear a disturbance at the Jacobs' house yesterday in the afternoon?"

"I did," he said. "What has that to do with credit cards?"

"Mr. Jacobs is now considered a high-risk client and we have reason to believe he may have fled to avoid payment of not only ours but many credit card and other debts."

"Not surprised," said the man. "Mr. . . ."

"Gristoperman," I supplied and held out my hand, showing my white teeth.

He took my hand warily. He had a decent grip.

"My name is Glazer," he said. "Gerald Glazer. I was working at my computer—I am writing the definitive biography of Chester Allen Arthur, a vastly underappreciated president—when I heard the screaming. The window in my office faces out to the driveway next door. I saw a large man dragging a woman by the hair and throwing her in a car."

"The girl?"

"Girl?"

"The one who smiled at you a few times," I reminded him.

"I didn't see her. You might ask the people across the street. They were standing on their lawn watching."

He was pointing at the house directly across the street from the Jacobs'.

"No one tried to help her?" I asked.

"Mr. . . . I am an emeritus professor with a far-from-perfect heart. My goal is to pamper it till I finish my book. Four university presses are extremely interested. I have completed eleven hundred and twelve pages and have only about five hundred more. It will probably be published in three volumes, and I hope it will receive recognition I will

THE ROCKFORD FILES: DEVIL ON MY DOORSTEP

be around for and well enough to appreciate. If I suffer a heart attack, the book will never be finished, and President Arthur, who deserves to be ranked among the upper echelon of American presidents, and I might never receive the documented credit we deserve."

"I understand fully," I said.

"Good," Professor Glazer said. "Now if you'll excuse me, you knocked right in the middle of a sentence and it has become increasingly difficult for me to hold complex ideas and data for extended periods."

"Sorry to have bothered you," I said with a smile.

He started to close the door and paused.

"I would like to know if the girl is all right," he said. "She was . . ."

"I know, though I can't reveal our sources, that the girl is safe and with a close relative."

"Good," he said again, and closed the door.

I crossed the street and looked back at the Jacobs' house. It fit in perfectly, not too big, not too small, clean, two-story, neat with a newish roof. The door was closed and there was no car in the driveway.

I rang the bell at the door of the house across the street. There was a car in the driveway, a Bentley, probably a few decades old but looking as if it had just come out of the white-gloved hands of the artists who made it.

A woman came to the door. She was well built, in her forties, not bad looking and obviously, because of the briefcase in her hand, on the way out.

"Yes?" she asked warily.

"A few questions about what happened yesterday afternoon," I said, taking out my notebook. "I understand you witnessed the abuse."

"We told the policeman last night everything," she said. "Really, I'm very late. Why don't you ask him?"

"I'm really sorry," I said, still holding my notebook, "but there's a difference between a police officer on patrol and a detective."

I opened my wallet and flashed my PI license, hoping she wouldn't look too closely. She didn't look at all.

"Please be quick," she said. "I'm due in surgery in about an hour."

"You're a nurse?" I said. "So is my sister."

"I'm a thoracic surgeon," she said. "Questions, please. I'm sorry I can't invite you in."

"That's all right, Doc," I said. "What did you see?"

"That hulking son of a bitch dragging his wife out of the house while their daughter watched, just stood there in the doorway crying. Her mother was shouting something to her. I didn't understand the words, but we did hear what the girl shouted."

"Which was?"

"I'll kill you."

"Kill him?"

"I assume she meant him," the woman said. "But she just stood in the doorway instead of going after him."

"She probably wouldn't have done much good," I said. "I understand Mr. Jacobs is a big man."

"But the girl did have a very large kitchen knife in her hand," said the woman. "In any case, the man drove away with the woman next to him and the girl went back in the house. My husband called nine-one-one."

"Your husband at home?"

"No," she said. "He has an art gallery in a suite at the Fairbriar Hotel, a very private gallery. He is showing a Holbein this morning. Now, I've really got to get going."

She moved toward the Bentley and I followed her, notebook still out.

"Other neighbors see any of this?"

"If you were a police officer, which I doubt, you would have had this information from the man who talked to us yesterday," she said, moving to the driver's side. "If you're a burglar, which I doubt, our cleaning lady is inside. Her name is Ceisla. She speaks almost no English and would match Mr. Jacobs pound for pound and is probably twice as strong."

"I'm not a thief," I said, putting the notebook away.

She stood with the car door half open and said, "Three things. First, you didn't ask me my name. Second, you scribbled a few things in that notebook but you didn't take a real note. Third, you should have that left knee taken care of."

"Accident a few years back," I said. "I've already had surgery on it."

"You need more," she said. "You're helping the girl, aren't you?"

"I'm a relative," I said. "I didn't think I'd get answers if I said I was Melisa's . . . uncle. I'm really in the construction business."

She shook her head and said, "No. Too smooth and bold with the lies. I don't know what you are, but I think you want to help the girl. I think she needs help. My name is Amelia Gottlieb. My husband is Irwin Gottlieb. If the police come back, I'm probably going to have to tell them about you."

"Fair enough," I said with a shrug.

Then she got in the car and drove away. The Bentley barely hummed. She drove right past my Firebird, whose headlights caught the sun and the reflection of the Bentley. I imagined the Firebird was blinking with envy.

I could have knocked at more doors, had more people see me, tell more lies. Instead, I crossed the street again, went past Professor Glazer's house and, without turning my head, checked as well as I could to see if anyone was watching me. I didn't see anyone. That didn't necessarily mean anything. With a stride of great confidence as if I knew what I was doing and why, I took out my notebook, made a scribble and walked behind Glazer's house, hoping anyone who might be peeping through curtains would think I was a city inspector, a landscaper or something official.

It took me about a minute to get to the back of the Jacobs' house after I was sure Professor Glazer didn't see me. From behind the corner of the house I could see the top of his flecked bald head through his office window as he chronicled the distinguished career of Chester A. Arthur and imagined himself on some podium humbly receiving a large, gold plaque.

There wasn't much of a backyard at the Jacobs' house, and what there was was surrounded by high green bushes, which suited me fine. There was a small, stone fish pond with a little bronze statue of a cupid peeing water. There weren't any fish.

I tried the back door. Locked. I didn't see any signs of an alarm system, but there might be one inside. I moved to a window. It was unlocked. I slid it open slowly, climbed in awkwardly with as few grunts as I could make. Curtains brushed me gently in the face as I hit the floor.

I sat on the kitchen floor for a few seconds, listening for an alarm, and then got up as quickly as I could to look for an alarm box. Usually the turn-off system gave the homeowner whatever time they wanted to take before it went into action. I made my way quickly through a living room, den and office, not taking time to look at the mess around me. No alarm box. A system could also be wired through the phone. Punch in a code and the alarm didn't go off. I found two phones and turned them over. People sometimes forget their codes and write them somewhere nearby that they think is safe, usually the underside of a phone or in a nearby drawer or vase. Nothing.

I had taken too much time already.

I decided to take five minutes, no more. I wasn't sure I could talk my way out of this, though I probably could. What decided me to make the search quick was the fact that every room in the house had been tossed, taken apart and the pieces left all over the place by a real professional. I concluded that whoever had made the search hadn't found what he or she was looking for. I could have been wrong, but once someone finds what they're looking for, they leave. They don't just destroy the rest of the rooms in an apartment or house for the fun of it. But I had nothing much to lose by looking, and I might get lucky.

The thing that struck me was that in no room of the house, including Melisa's, could I find a note, a letter, a diary, unpaid or paid bills. There were no photographs and no books. The person who had stripped the house had either taken everything or Conforti/Jacobs had destroyed everything before he took off.

I did find one of those big green plastic garbage bags and filled it with clothes, shoes and other things from Melisa's bedroom that she hadn't been able to fit into her suitcase, plus the contents of the medicine cabinet in her bathroom and whatever was on top of the sink that hadn't been smashed.

Feeling like a second-story Santa Claus with a bag of crumpled goodies in the sack over my shoulder, I paused to go back into what I was sure was Rene and Jacobs' room. I thought I smelled her, faint but there. A mood like this could get me caught.

Bad knees, heavy sack and a clock ticking in my head, I

went back to the window I had come through at the rear of
the house. I parted the curtains and looked out before
climbing, which turned out to be a good idea.

Two men stood next to each other on the small patch of
backyard lawn. They were both big, one in his thirties, the
other closer to fifty. They both wore dark suits and darker
sunglasses. I recognized the bulges under their jackets. Both
men were armed.

"Climb out slowly," one of them said. He was the older of
the two.

I calculated, made what could have been a dumb decision
and, instead of climbing out, slammed the window closed,
picked up the loaded garbage bag and hurried back into the
house. I was almost at the front door when I heard them
scrambling in through the window. They weren't worrying
about noise and they were a lot more agile than I was. I
opened the front door, threw some of Melisa's clothes out on
the brick path and ducked into the entry area closet, closing it quietly behind me.

It took them about ten seconds to climb in, probably
pull out their weapons and get through the house to the
front door a few feet from where I was hiding. They could
see Melisa's clothes now.

"You go left. I'll go right," I heard the older one say and
then I heard the front door close.

I came out of the closet quickly and relatively quietly. I
took a quick glance out one of the front windows and saw
them running down the street, no weapons showing. There
was no way in hell I could have run far enough and fast
enough to be out of their sight, but they didn't know that.
For all they knew, I had finished with a bronze medal in the
Olympics back in the sixties. I went for the rear window,
opened it, ignored my knees and got out fast. I could see
Professor Glazer looking out of his window at the front door

of the Jacobs' house as I made my way across his lawn and behind his house. I wonder what he made of what he saw—someone throwing clothes out the door and two men coming out and running down the street. He'd probably call 911. The historical appreciation of Chester A. Arthur would be set back another hour or two.

I made it back to the Firebird without seeing the guys with sunglasses. I didn't bother with the trunk. I threw the loaded bag in the backseat, got in and made a U-turn as quietly as I could. I scanned the street for the two who were after me and spotted one of them more than halfway down the block glancing toward backyards and into parked cars. He had already passed my Firebird.

I put on my Greek fishing cap, pulling it down over my eyes, opened the window and turned the radio on loud. I drove slowly and pretended I was singing to the horror of heavy metal that came through my speakers.

The guy with the sunglasses and gun looked in my direction. I had my arm resting on the open window and he did what I hoped he would do. He assumed I was a local on my way to pick up a new CD or check with my stockbroker. The Firebird was antique material. Still, though he was about fifty yards behind me, he stepped into the street, pulled out a notebook and took off his glasses to write my license number. I was probably too far for him to see much more than that the car was in-state, but he might have gotten a number or two. I sped up just a bit in the hope of getting out of his even remotely possible visual range.

An hour later I was back in my trailer. Melisa was still asleep. I put the green garbage bag of her things next to the bedroom door and then I checked my messages. There was only one, from Dennis Becker.

I found the last can of my last six-pack and sat behind my desk, rolled it against my forehead and drank slowly while

I called Dennis. A young voice answered and I said I wanted
to talk to Lieutenant Becker. I gave my name. I could hear
Dennis growl in the background, "I don't have time to talk
to him. Hang up."

The phone went dead.

I watched a soccer game with a Spanish-language an-
nouncer, finished my beer and considered my next move.
Ten minutes later and one sliced turkey sandwich with mustard down, the phone rang.

"Jim," Dennis said. "I'm sorry. I couldn't talk before.
Diehl was having a fit of male menopause."

"Careful, Dennis, my phone might be bugged."

"Not by us, at least not yet, but things are happening."

There was something about his voice I didn't like. I
clicked off the television. Tasco was well ahead by four goals.

"Rene is dead," he said.

I didn't answer. I looked toward the bedroom door and
felt sorry I had drunk the beer. My stomach went sour.

"You there, Jim?"

"I'm here."

"You all right?"

"No," I said.

"It gets worse," he said gently. "She was found in Jacobs'
car, a kitchen knife in her chest. Pasadena called in the state
police. They aren't sure, but they think the prints on the
knife are a woman's, probably a young woman's. They're
checking to see if they match Rene's daughter's prints."

"Jacobs?" I asked.

"No sign of him," said Dennis. "Pasadena police. L.A.
police in the valley and here have been told it's going to
the FBI."

"The FBI?" I asked.

"I didn't get the why, Jim, but the federal witness protection program is involved," he whispered. "They've got

people out looking for Jacobs and Rene's daughter, Melisa. There's at least one witness who says the girl had a knife in her hand when her mother was dragged away, and she shouted, 'I'll kill you.' "

"Dennis," I said, "isn't it obvious she was talking about Jacobs, not Rene."

"How did you know something had happened at the Jacobses' house?" he asked.

"Can't say," I answered.

"Client?"

"Sort of," I answered.

"You've got the girl or know where she is," he guessed.

"Where are you calling from?"

"Pay phone in the lobby," he said.

"I'll get back to you," I said.

"Bring her in, Jim, and tell me what the hell is going on."

"As soon as I have something, I'll call you. Promise."

"The FBI, U.S. Marshals and homicide cops are already all over this, Jim. Bring her in."

"Thanks, Dennis," I said. "I've got to go now."

"Sure," he said. "Jim, I'm sorry about Rene."

"Someone's going to be a lot sorrier, Dennis," I said, and hung up the phone.

I looked up. Melisa stood in the bedroom doorway. She almost tripped over her green garbage bag of goodies.

"I heard you on the phone," she said. "Couldn't sleep anymore."

She yawned, rubbed the corners of her eyes and ran the fingers of both hands through her hair.

"Melisa," I said. "Put something on fast. We've got some things we've got to talk about and I've got some things I have to tell you. We'll talk in the car. I brought everything I could carry of yours from the house. In the green bag. I

think the police'll be here in a little while and I don't think
you should be here when they knock at the door."

She looked as if she were going to ask a question, but I
said,

"Hurry."

God, she looked like Rene.

It took her a few seconds and I grabbed the green bag. I
knew the Travises were watching. I knew the police would
question them about seeing a young girl with me. I knew I
would have to come up with a story when I came back, but
now we were running. There must have been something in
the way I looked and talked that got Melisa moving. Her
shoes were untied and her blouse wasn't tucked in. She carried the garbage bag over her shoulder. I took her suitcase,
and we were on our way.

I took the Firebird. For the first five minutes, driving
north up the coast on the Pacific Coast Highway, I said
nothing and neither did Melisa. Once in a while, when the
view was clear of houses on our left, she looked past me out
at the ocean. Once in a while she looked out her window at
the rough cliffs of rocks and the open lawns of estates and
high-priced developments.

"We're going to stop at a place along the way for coffee,"
I said. "They make great doughnuts."

"You've got something bad to tell me," she said, looking
down at her lap. "Please just tell me."

"In a minute," I said, pulling into the parking lot of a
clapboard truck stop. There were a few cars getting gas and
a few cars parked in front of the diner. I led her in. A couple of truckers were eating pancakes at a booth and telling
jokes. A family, two small kids and two large parents, were
in another booth arguing. One person was at the counter, a
uniformed cop. There had been no police car in the lot. The
guy was probably on his way to or from his shift. He was in

his late twenties, well built and kidding with Karen, the plump, smiling waitress behind the counter. I led Melissa to a booth. We sat across from each other and Karen called, "Long time, Jim."

"Long time, Karen," I agreed. "We'll have two coffees and four doughnuts. Two chocolate frosted and . . ."

"I don't care," Melisa said.

"And two peanut," I said.

"Got it," said Karen.

When Karen came with the doughnuts and coffee, I looked across at Melisa and said.

"Melisa, I'm sorry. Rene is dead."

She looked at me blankly as if I hadn't spoken.

"Your mother is dead," I said, touching her shoulder.

Her head was shaking no but I don't think she knew it. And then she broke. I moved out of my seat and slid in next to her. She leaned against me and cried, not the loud, wailing wet kind of cry, but a private, gentle weeping that shivered her small body. Her face was buried against my shoulder, and I found myself stroking her hair.

The young cop turned to look at us, his mouth full of something and a cup in his hands.

"My daughter," I explained. "We've had some bad news."

The young cop nodded in understanding and went back to his meal.

Melisa and I sat like that for about five minutes. Then she pulled away slowly.

"He killed her," she said, her voice distant. "He killed her, didn't he?"

"Who?"

"Mike," she said, a touch of anger seething through the word, an anger I thought she could use as a temporary floating log in the river of her grief. Hell, I was getting into a poetic mood and I'm not good at it. I was grieving too, for a

woman I had loved, for the woman who may have been the
mother of my daughter.

"Could be," I said, handing her a doughnut, one with
chocolate. "Melisa, when he took your mother away, you
came to the door with a knife in your hand and shouted, 'I'll
kill you.' "

"I think so," she said, nibbling at the doughnut absently.

"I'm sorry. Your mother was killed by a knife, a kitchen
knife, and it looks like it has your fingerprints on it."

She may have been a smart kid, but I was throwing a lot
at her.

"My mother was stabbed? Oh God. And are you saying
the police think I killed her?"

"Let's keep it down," I said, looking at the young cop's
back as the quarreling family quartet paid their bill and
left. "Maybe they think you killed her. That's why I had to
get you away from the trailer."

"I wasn't talking about Mom when I had that knife,"
she almost pleaded. "I was talking about him. Did they
ask him?"

"They can't find him," I said.

We sat silently for a few minutes. She started to cry again,
but this time she didn't come to me and few tears came
from her closed eyes. I guessed she was praying or starting
to grieve for her mother. I didn't know her well enough to
guess.

"Finish your coffee and doughnut. We've got to go now,"
I said. "The highway patrol's going to be looking for us and
a red and white Firebird is not all that hard to spot."

I left a tip, went to the counter, paid Karen and looked
at the cop, who was just finishing. He nodded, acknowledging Melisa's and my grief.

"Drop by once in a while to let me know you're still
alive," Karen said.

"I will," I answered.

I went back to the booth, helped Melisa up and got out of the diner and back to the car.

I pulled back on the Coast Highway and continued north.

"Can you tell me anything that might help?" I asked.

"Help what?"

"Help me find who killed your mother? Help me clear you from suspicion. Help nail your stepfather if he killed her. I'm a private detective, remember?"

She opened her eyes and looked at me. She was either a great actress or the most truly helpless person I had seen since I visited one of Rocky's friends in the Veterans Administration hospital six months earlier.

"Are you any good?" she asked.

"Since there's no time for modesty," I said, taking a slight chance and passing a Ralph's Market truck, "I'd say I'm pretty good. Better at some things than others."

"Finding killers?" she asked, turning in her seat to face me and brushing her hair back with her hand.

"I've done some of that," I said. "I'm taking you somewhere where you'll be okay while I try to find out what's going on. Meanwhile, give me a dollar."

"A . . . ?"

"You're hiring me," I said. "There's a certain amount of client privilege. Not quite like a lawyer or a psychiatrist, but enough for me to fall back on if I have to, and I've got a great lawyer."

She rummaged around in the suitcase at her feet, came up with a blue wallet and fished out a dollar while I drove. I took the dollar and stuffed it in my pocket.

Melisa said nothing more and looked straight out the window. The look was blank. I knew the first shock of finding out someone you love is dead. The idea of "never" takes a long time to accept, and some people never do. Melisa wasn't even dealing with the first stage, the stage of initial realization that she wouldn't be seeing her mother again.

It took me half an hour of semi-reckless driving to get to the house in Pacific Palisades. It was about two hundred yards back from the highway, and there was a spot behind an outcrop of rocks where I could park and not be spotted unless helicopters were looking for us, which I doubted. The house itself was one of those lunatic expensive things built into a high hill and held in place on stilts. Good view of the ocean. Bad bet in case of even a pipsqueak earthquake. And certainly deep trouble in a mud slide. But this one, I knew, had been up at least a dozen years. I'd passed it and noted it, along with a lot of others like it.

We got out of the car. I carried the green garbage bag. Melisa carried her small suitcase. We climbed the wooden stairs to the high deck. The ocean view was great, but neither of us was in the mood for admiring natural wonders. I pushed the button next to the white door and heard chimes inside playing the opening of Beethoven's "Ode to Joy."

No answer. I played a little more music and the door finally opened to reveal Angel in a knee-length blue smock covered with paint. His jeans and shoes also were more than dabbed with splotches of blue, white and yellow.

Angel himself had undergone one of his many transformations. His curly dark hair with traces of gray was long, and his beard was trimmed short and neat. There was a small blotch of almost rust-colored paint in the beard.

Angel and I go way back. Back to being cell mates when I was sent up. When Angel got out we stayed something like friends and even worked a few scams together for the sake of clients or to get me or one of our mutual friends out of a jam. I knew Angel's main concern in life was Angel Martin, born Evelyn Angelo Martinez. He'd take my last dollar and swear he was innocent of the theft. In a pinch, he couldn't be counted on, but something held us together. I tolerated a lot from Angel and, in turn, he owed me a lot, sometimes money, sometimes loyalty.

"Jimmy," he whispered, looking at me, Melisa, the green garbage bag and the suitcase in her hand. "I've got a client in there. I can't talk now. Come back in an hour."

"This is Melisa," I said, ignoring what Angel said. "She needs a place to stay for a while. That place is here."

"No way," Angel whispered emphatically. "I've got the scheme of my life going here. I can't baby-sit."

"Melisa can take care of herself," I said, looking at her.

She was staring at Angel, who looked a little wild-eyed.

"Can't do it, Jimmy. You know I'd do anything—" he started, but I stopped him with,

"You remember Rene?"

Angel closed his mouth. The name rang a bell.

"I remember her," he said.

"This is Rene's daughter," I said. "Rene died yesterday. She was murdered. The police want to talk to Melisa about it. I don't want the police to talk to Melisa about it for a while."

Angel looked at Melisa and back over his shoulder into the house.

"Come in," he said, "follow me. Be quiet."

The house was filled with modern Scandinavian furniture, taut leather and shining metal. I hated the stuff. Angel probably didn't care much one way or the other. It wasn't his house. He was house-sitting for a retired movie studio executive who was away with his wife in Europe for at least six months. Angel had lied and produced false letters of recommendation to get the house-sitting job. He took great pride in his success.

He led us to an office complete with a black-topped desk

with shining steel legs, a computer complete with everything, a VCR and laser disc player and some chairs. I motioned for Melisa to sit. She did, still lost somewhere in the
first stages of her grief. I motioned for Angel to sit. He did
it reluctantly.

"There is a good chance that Melisa is my daughter,
Angel," I said.

"Daughter?" Angel repeated.

He took a long look at Melisa, searching for signs of
Rockford.

"Oh Jimmy." He wailed. "I've got a great deal goin' on
here. I'm using my own name. It's almost legal. I do portraits. Actually, I don't do them. My cousin Diego. You remember him?"

"Two years for forgery," I said.

"That's the one," Angel said with a smile. "Anyway, I
have the client sit for me for a week while I do sketches and
paint. They can't see what I've done till it's finished. Diego
does the painting from a Polaroid. Makes the subject look
good. Uses the style of Velasquez. You see Jimmy, that's the
in. I'm the great-great-great-grandsomething of Velasquez
and I've inherited his talent. I tell the marks I was born in
Toledo, Spain not Ohio. I use my Spanish accent and the
beauty part is I can actually speak the language."

"You talk Spanish with an East L.A. accent even *I* can
spot," I said.

Angel nodded his head tolerantly and said,

"You know it. My relatives know it. People on the streets
and cops know it, but these people don't. They're happy to
pay big bucks to have an Angel Velasquez Martinez portrait
hanging over their fireplaces. The bigger the picture, the
more I charge. You wouldn't believe what some of these
people are willing to pay. About half of them figure they've

made an investment that'll pay off later or something they can donate to an art museum when they get tired of it and need a really big tax write-off. You see the picture, Jimmy?"

"She stays here, Angel," I said.

"Oh, Jimmy," he said, putting his head in his hands.

"I'll try to keep it down to a week, maybe less," I said. "But it might be more. And remember she just lost her mother, Rene, and she might be my daughter. Also, she is only seventeen."

He took his hands from his face and looked at me with a good imitation of pain.

"What are telling me, Jimmy?"

"Keep your hands off of her. Treat her like a treasured niece."

"Jimmy, Jimmy, Jimmy, Jimmy."

"Angel, Angel, Angel, Angel. Now, we've got that over, show Melisa her room and I'll get to work."

"You have to go?" Melisa said.

I'd become her raft, her family. I stepped in front of her, helped her up and looked into her eyes.

"I'm going to find out what's going on," I said. "I'm going to see to it that you're taken care of. And don't worry about Angel. He's cunning, dishonest and untrustworthy, but he owes me and he knows me and he knew your mother. He'll take care of you. Right, Angel?"

"Right," said Angel with a sigh of resignation.

He got up and added,

"Now I've got to spend about ten more minutes with Mrs. Palmer. And I don't want her getting any ideas about taking a peek at what I've done so far. Just sit here and I'll be back."

He hurried out of the door, Joseph's dream coat of a smock trailing after him.

"You'll be all right here," I said. "I'll call you. I'll come when I can and I'll get this taken care of as fast as I can. You going to be all right?"

"Yes," she said, moving into my arms.

I hugged her and she stepped back.

"It's okay to cry a lot more," I said. "I did it for Rocky when no one was around. It helps to remember the good times. I'll see what I can do about hurrying Angel up in getting you to a room."

I left Melisa standing in the office and moved toward Angel's voice. Now I owed him one. I wanted to pay it back as fast as I could. I followed the voice till I came to an open door. Angel was painting on a canvas. It was a mess. Fortunately, the woman, thin, serious and wearing a necklace that should have been in a vault, sat motionless as the master worked and spoke nonsense.

As I entered the room, Angel was saying,

"Azul, the blue. Not siempre an . . . how do you say . . . not an ordinary blue, but your own mood of the color. It dominates. It controls my hands. I am hopelessly lost in the inspiration of your color."

The woman remained rigid. Angel spotted me and a look of fear crossed his face.

"Mr. Martinez," I said in my best Billy Bob Texas accent, flashing a huge smile. I assumed the woman with the necklace had heard the door chimes earlier and that my appearance wasn't a shock. "I really can't stay, but I just want to tell you again how pleased Jean Mary and I are with her portrait. We've got it in the house in Santa Barbara, but we may move it to Connecticut with us for the summer. I left you a little bonus check on your desk."

Angel came out from behind the easel and canvas and smiled humbly.

"It was a pleasure to paint your wife's portrait," he said. "She is a lovely woman, a woman of greens and reds."

"Danged if you're not right," I said with a grin, looking at the woman, who allowed her eyes to turn in my direction. She'd probably be too stiff to move when Angel finished the sitting. "Well, *adiós*."

I headed for the door.

"*Adiós*," said Angel, waving at me with his brush.

I didn't go back into the office to see Melisa. She would be all right with Angel, for a few days at least. I drove back to the trailer. I wasn't in a hurry this time. I wasn't worried about the Firebird being spotted. Besides, I knew what was waiting for me when I got home, and when I got there I was sure of it.

The blue four-door was parked right next to the pickup. There was no one in it. I didn't even bother to sigh. My home might as well have been the wash room at a mall.

I went in expecting to see Diehl, Dennis or someone I didn't know. But I knew these two. They were standing in front of my desk. They had heard me pull up, probably watched me. It was the two guys I had gotten away from at the Jacobs' house in Pasadena.

They didn't look happy to see me.

CHAPTER THREE

"JAMES Rockford," the older one said. It wasn't a question so I didn't answer. I did say with indignation,

"You police? If you are, can I see your warrant for entering my home?"

I admit it. I was surprised when the older one produced a warrant to search my premises.

"You're U.S. Marshals," I said.

"Says so right there on the paper in your hand," said the older one, who was well on the way to being bald.

Neither was wearing sunglasses now. The older one had blue-gray eyes. The younger one's eyes were brown. I didn't see much possibility of understanding, sympathy or compassion in either set of eyes.

"What's going on?" I said, trying to regain my indignation.

The older one nodded and the younger one began to search the trailer.

"The gun's in the cookie jar," I said. "It's registered."

The younger guy immediately went to the cookie jar, opened it, took out a notebook and recorded the serial number. He put the .38 back and closed the lid.

"I'm having coffee," I said. "Either of you want some?" The younger one didn't answer. The older one said, "Brewed or instant?"

"Brewed," I said. "I grind my own beans."

He nodded approvingly.

"What have you got brewed?" he asked as I watched his partner move furniture, dig under pillows, go through my desk and file drawers.

"Colombian. With caffeine."

"I don't like that flavored stuff," he said, making a face of disapproval, "but Colombian sounds okay."

"I'm glad the Rockford House of Coffee can serve you," I said, heading for the day-old coffee that was warm on my small counter.

I poured him a cup and one for myself. He glanced at his partner, who nodded no and continued working.

I handed the guy with blue-gray eyes a white cup that had a full-color picture of a smiling Mickey Mouse. My cup was a black one with red letters saying GENTLE DENTISTRY CENTER OF ENCINO.

"Coffee's good," the guy said as his partner headed toward the rear of the trailer. I had to admit the searcher knew his job. He moved fast. Checked everything and left things just the way they were.

"Thanks," I said. "Is this going to be one of those multi-part coffee commercials or are you going to tell me what's going on?"

"We're federal marshals," he said. "I'm Anthony Donahue. Partner's Lew Troy."

"Troy and Donahue," I said, smiling.

"We've got a section chief with what he considers a sense of humor," Donahue said. "He teamed us. Actually, it's turned out fine. We've been together for four years now."

"That's nice," I said, moving to my desk now that Mar-

shal Troy was in my bedroom. Donahue turned and faced
me and kept drinking.

"What were you doing at the Jacobs' house?" he asked.
"And what were you looking for?"

"The place was tossed when I got there," I said. "I'm not
sure what I was looking for, but I didn't find it."

"You left with a stuffed green garbage bag," Donahue
said calmly. "Two neighbors saw you. You told one of those
neighbors that you were an insurance investigator."

Donahue was good. Share a cup of coffee. Chat a little
and then hit me with a big one. I had the uneasy feeling that
there was about to be an even bigger one. But I'd tackle this
one first.

"Bag contained garbage," I said. "When I saw you two
guys coming for me, I grabbed it, thinking there might be
something in it to help me find Mrs. Jacobs."

"And?" he said.

"Nothing in it but garbage," I said with a shrug. "I threw
it away."

"Where?"

He was damn good.

I gave him my sympathetic smile.

"Don't remember. One of those garbage Dumpsters behind a restaurant on the way back here. I can tell you
which—"

"Rockford," Donahue interrupted. "No bullshit, please.
I'll show you respect. You show me respect. If not . . ."

"Rene Jacobs is an old friend," I said. "I heard she was
back in town. I tracked her down and found out she'd been
dragged out of her house by her husband. I was mad. I almost married Rene a long time ago. I wanted to find her
and probably warn her husband to keep his hands off of
her. Maybe I'd even hit him in the mouth or knee him

where it would hurt. Maybe I'd tell Rene she should leave him. I don't know what I was going to do, but I didn't want her hurt."

"She's dead," Donahue said, looking at me.

I tried to look surprised. I found the best way to do that was simply to go blank as if the information was too much for me to take.

Donahue was looking at me. I was mustering a vague image of Rene smiling on the beach in her two-piece blue bathing suit. I suddenly realized that this man telling me what I already knew had actually brought the memory of Rene back to me in a blast of loss.

"You're good, Rockford," Donahue said. "Mind if I have another cup?"

"My house is your house," I said as he poured himself more coffee.

"You knew she was dead," he said.

"How would I know?" I said, covering my eyes with my hand.

"I think your old friend Rene Jacobs' daughter may have told you," he said. "Neighbors say a young girl fitting her description spent the day here and you left with her about an hour and a half ago."

"You mean Travis?" I said.

Donahue just watched me over the top of his cup.

"I'm not married," I said. "Sometimes a lady will spend time with me. In this case, it was a client."

"This was a kid," Donahue said. "Young enough to be your daughter, maybe even your granddaughter. You spent some close time with an underage girl, Rockford? That's against the dirty-old-man law."

"I thought we were getting to be friends," I said.

"This is the way it works," he said. "And you know it."

"Okay," I said, putting my hands on the table and looking at him sincerely, forcing myself not to blink. "Melissa was here. She slept in the chair on my deck and I found her there this morning. I'm sure the Travises told you that too. She said her mother told her to come to me if something happened. I told you, I'm an old friend and I'm a private detective. Melisa wants to find her mother. Well, her mother's been found."

Troy came out of my bedroom, one hand at his side, one hand holding up a pair of small women's pink panties.

"In the bed," said Troy.

"The dirty-old-man law, Rockford," Donahue said.

"She took a nap. She was tired. She hadn't slept well on the deck and she looked like she needed some nap time. Donahue, my neighborhood spy will tell you I went out less than half an hour after she came in here. You saw me in Pasadena. I wouldn't have had time—"

"Half hour's plenty of time," said Troy, putting the panties in his pocket.

"You don't need the threats," I said. "And you couldn't make the story stick even if you wanted to waste the time. Melisa was here. I said I'd go back and see if I could find her mother. She was worried about her. There had been violent arguments. She had seen Jacobs or Conforti or whatever his real name is drag Rene out. Neighbors saw it."

"You have Coke or something?" asked Troy.

"Help yourself," I said, pointing at the small refrigerator. He got himself a Cherry Coke, popped the cap and leaned against the refrigerator.

"Where did you take her, Rockford?" asked Donahue.

He was broad in the shoulders, hair almost red and cut short. He looked strong. He looked sincere.

"Why?" I asked.

"We want to talk to her," he went on.

"Why?" I repeated.

The two marshals looked at each other and came to an agreement with simple eye contact.

"Suspicion of murder," said Donahue. "Witnesses saw her standing in the doorway when Jacobs dragged his wife out. The girl was holding a knife. She shouted, 'I'll kill you.' "

I shook my head in disbelief and said,

"Donahue, she was talking to her stepfather, not her mother who was being dragged away kicking and screaming. What sense does it make that she was threatening her mother?"

"Not much," Donahue admitted, putting his cup on the counter. "But Rene Jacobs was shot with a gun and on that gun were her daughter's fingerprints."

Dennis had said Rene was stabbed. Donahue was close to the best I'd ever faced. I didn't answer.

"Why didn't you ask how Rene Jacobs died?" said Donahue.

"I don't know," I said. "I . . . it was enough that you told me she was dead. I guess I assumed Jacobs killed her."

"Rene Jacobs was stabbed," said Troy.

I turned toward him.

"You're really good, Rockford," said Donahue with a smile. "I think you knew that."

"How could I?" I said.

"The girl," he said. "Her fingerprints are on the knife. There's a kitchen knife missing from the Jacobs' house."

"How do you know?" I said.

"Brilliant detective work," said Donahue. "There's one of those wooden knife holders in the kitchen, the kind where you stick them in slots. One slot's empty. The murder weapon matches the others and fits just fine in the empty slot. Where did you take her?"

"She's my client," I said. "I don't think I have to answer that until I see an arrest warrant."

I half expected him to come up with one, but he didn't. He folded his arms and looked at me blandly. I was on a small roll so I went on.

"And even if you come up with a warrant or haul me in for obstructing justice," I said, "I call my lawyer. Time passes. Melisa is somewhere else. Why don't you spend your time looking for Jacobs or Conforti or whoever he is? He's probably the one who killed Rene. You know what I think?"

"Tell us," said Troy.

"I think," I said, "our wife killer is in a federal witness protection program. U.S. Marshals don't get involved in murder cases just for the fun and blood. I think Melisa's being set up. I think Rene's husband is in witness protection and has been for years, but whoever you guys are protecting him from found him and he ran and got a new name. Now he's murdered Rene and you're still protecting him. After all these years does he still have anything he could tell you, or are you afraid to have him testify at a grand jury hearing? I think, maybe, Conforti-Jacobs has something on your department your bosses don't want made public."

Donahue sighed, scratched the side of his nose. Troy, having finished the Cherry Coke, crushed the can in his hand.

"You have a recycle bin?" he asked.

"I thought you looked at everything in the place," I said with weary sarcasm. "Box under the sink."

He opened the door and dropped the can in the box for recycling.

"You don't have very much right," Donahue said to me. "A few things maybe. Let's say we agree she was set up. Let's say we think she needs protection."

"I'm protecting her," I said.

"You're Howdy Doody up against Godzilla," Troy said.

Donahue frowned at the lousy comparison, but it was a small frown. Troy shrugged, acknowledging the weakness of his comparison. But he had made his point. He had added to the suggestion that organized crime was after Jacobs and had spent a lot of years trying to find him. Getting Melisa might be a high priority for them.

"I'll think about it," I said.

"Do that," said Donahue, nodding at his partner, who moved toward the door. "If something happened to her, you wouldn't want to think that you could have turned her over to us and saved her."

"I'll think about it," I repeated.

"Maybe," said Donahue, reaching into his pocket and coming out with his sunglasses. Troy did the same. "What I think you're planning to do is look for Mr. Jacobs. Don't do it."

"Donahue," I said. "I've got a client. Client wants me to find her mother and stepfather. Looks like we found her mother. Now I plan to look for her stepfather."

"Suit yourself," Donahue said. "You've been warned."

They left, closing the door behind them. I didn't bother to reach for my phone. If they had a warrant to search, they probably had a warrant to tap my phone or maybe even bug the trailer. I heard them drive away and then I spent twenty minutes looking for bugs. Nothing. The phone was a different matter. I went outside. The sun was on the way down. The concrete lot had a reddish look. There was no sign of my neighbors and there were only a handful of people in the water. Their voices carried. One kid with a tan that invited skin cancer screamed at a swimmer,

"Let's go, dogface."

The swimmer either didn't hear or chose to ignore him. The tanned screamer laughed and yelled,

"Since when did you pass up some easy ass. You suddenly go gay, dogface?"

I kept walking, enlightened by the conversation that was

going on between two probably brain-affected kids who thought they would live healthy and forever. I knew where I had to start. I wasn't sure whether it or what I would do next would get me anywhere.

The public phone was on the beach near the rusting pier a few hundred yards down the beach. About half the time the phone was missing. This time it was there. The Pacific made a late afternoon series of incoming waves, loud waves. I called Beth at home. She still had a small office but she never went there. Beth Davenport had married. For a while I had thought she and I were going to get married, but we both knew I wasn't right for her. She had made a good choice. I had tried marriage a little while after Beth went for it. Married a lawyer. It lasted long enough to convince me I shouldn't marry anyone, for their own good. Since my ex-wife made a hell of a lot more money than I did, alimony wasn't an issue. Money wasn't the investment we'd lost.

I dialed. The phone rang and Beth finally answered.

Since getting married, she had written a novel, joined the other members of the bar in writing a book based on her experiences. The book had done very well and was going to be a movie. She was working on her second book.

"Hello," she said.

It was an unlisted number, but her voice was still wary.

"Jim," I said.

"Can I call you back in an hour or two?" she said. "I'm at the computer and for the first time in a week, the book is really moving."

"I'm calling from the pay phone on the beach," I said, holding out the phone so she could hear the waves. "You can't call me at home. I'm pretty sure my phone is tapped. These guys are so good they may even have this phone tapped."

"These guys?"

"United States Marshals," I said.

"What do they want from you?" she asked, getting interested.

Beth had only a few clients now, old friends like me. She liked to keep her contact with the profession but she didn't want more than minimal contact.

"They want me to tell them where a young girl is, a client. They had a warrant to search my place. I think they may get the L.A. cops to pull me in on obstruction."

I told her the whole tale and she listened quietly till I was finished.

"What have you left out, Jim?" she asked.

I looked at the ocean, watched a big whitecap roll in and saw Dogface coming out of the water down the beach.

"The girl may be my daughter," I said. "You ever meet Rene Henley?"

"I met her," Beth said.

"Melisa's mother," I said.

"How sure are you this Jacobs or Conforti was in witness protection?"

"I wasn't sure until the visit I just had from the U.S. Marshals. Now I'm pretty sure. I'm gonna need you to keep me out of jail and see to it that I have the best lawyer in Los Angeles with me if I'm questioned."

"I accept your flattery," she said. "If they pull you in, call me. Leave a message if I'm not here. Say nothing till I show up but be sure to tell me where they take you."

"The usual routine," I said.

"It's worked up till now," she said. "Jim, I'm sorry about Rene."

"Thanks," I said. "Now let's do something so we don't have to be sorry about her daughter."

I hung up and walked back along the sand, avoiding the concrete drive as much as I could. My knees seemed to do

better on the sand. Dogface and Overtan were gone by the
time I got back to the trailer.

I passed Mrs. Bailey sitting in front of her trailer under
her aluminum awning. She, the Travises and I were the
neighborhood.

Mrs. Bailey was old. I don't know how old. Her hair was
gray. Her body heavy and her smile real. She had saved for
a lifetime and raised at least two families to live and die in
Santa Monica on the beach. Mrs. Bailey, wearing a yellow
dress with purple flowers, was listening to a talk show and
arguing with a caller and the host. At the same time she was
writing in her big school notebook, looking down at the
page through her half glasses.

"Man's a fool," she said, squinting up at me over the
glasses.

"That a general observation or only for the guy on the
radio?" I said, standing in front of her.

"I guess it could go either way," she said. "Guess I believe
it both ways.

"Care for some lemonade?" she said. "That's what old
ladies are supposed to offer rare callers."

"No, thanks," I said. "Not today. Today I've got problems
I've got to go home and think about."

"Mrs. Travis says you're a detective like on television," she
said.

"I'm a private investigator," I said.

She nodded in understanding.

"That explains all the different kinds of people come to
your place and walk right in even if you're not there," she
said.

I didn't see how it explained it, but she had sat back with
a smile that suggested she had just solved a problem that
had been bothering her.

"I've got to go," I said.

She nodded.

"Friend died," I explained. "A good friend."

Again, she nodded.

"Most everyone I know, friends, family, even some children, are dead," she said. "Used to hurt a lot. It's the price you pay when you live to be old as I am. I'm sorry you're hurtin', Mr. Rockford. Beyond that, unless you're a good Christian, there's nothing I can say that'll help you."

"Thank you, Mrs. Bailey," I said.

"You could help me with something, though," she said, taking off her glasses.

"What?"

"What's the legal penalty for stealing a dog for ransom?"

"I don't know," I said. "Petty theft. Might depend on the dog. If it's a show dog . . . I can find out."

"Makes no matter," she said. "Just something I was thinkin' of putting in my script."

"You're writing a script?"

"Movie script," she said with a smile, patting her notebook. "Wanted to for years and now I've got time and the rights."

"Rights?"

"Rights to write a movie about the life of Marcus Garvey," she said. "You know Marcus Garvey?"

I kept looking at my trailer, waiting for trouble to drive up, get out and come for me.

"Garvey was the leader of a back-to-Africa movement in the twenties," I said.

"Close," she said. "Well, I got the rights."

"Who gave you the rights?" I asked.

She opened the notebook, thick with three-hole sheets of lined paper, to the back. Taped to the back cover of the notebook was an envelope. She pulled a sheet of paper from the envelope and handed it to me and then folded her arms.

The sheet of paper was from something called Pemberton Enterprises. The letter said that Mrs. Gwen Bailey had their full and complete permission to write a screenplay about Marcus Garvey. The letter also had two paragraphs of legal jumbo that said nothing.

"Where did you hear about Pemberton Enterprises?" I asked.

"Ad in a writers' magazine," she said. "I read 'em all. Little ad said they could obtain the right to produce a novel or screenplay on the life of any famous or historical person or event. I remember those words. Got the ad in the trailer if you want to look at it."

"What did they charge you for these rights?" I asked.

"Five hundred dollars. Not much. I'm budgeted pretty tight. But it was worth it," she said, patting the script she was working on.

I asked if it was all right if I jotted down the address and phone number of Pemberton Enterprises.

"Might want to write a book about General Custer," I said. "I think we have a lot in common, me and George Armstrong."

"Help yourself," Gwen Bailey said.

I jotted the address and phone number in my notebook. Pemberton Enterprises was in Tarzana.

"Thanks," I said.

She nodded and turned up the volume on the radio.

"I don't care," came an angry voice. "I know I promised to keep my mouth shut and listen to any crap that came in, but this bonehead is too much. Sue me for breaking my word, but I've got to tell Mr. Bonehead and anyone who agrees with him that the way to take care of serious crime in this country is to line up convicted felons and shoot them. Read the damn Constitution."

"Amen to that," said Mrs. Bailey. "Amen."

I went back home and changed into an old pair of chinos and a pullover shirt, put Rocky's baseball cap on my head and made myself a sliced turkey sandwich on white bread with tomato and onion. I put my dinner on my white bamboo tray along with a wedge of lettuce and a glass of white wine I poured from a bottle that had been at the back of the refrigerator too long. I took the tray carefully out on the deck and moved to where I could watch the sun go down. I went back in, got my folding beach chair covered in faded yellow canvas and got back just in time to shoo away a seagull with sandwich theft on his mind. I had a spray somewhere that was supposed to keep gulls away, but it didn't seem to work. You weren't supposed to feed gulls. They just wanted more, and though their brains only had two sections as far as I was concerned—one larger part in constant search of food and one smaller part that stored information on where food had been scrounged in the past— I didn't want them swooping down on me like Hitchcock's birds every time I went out on the deck.

I leaned back, tray on my lap, and remembered Rocky and me sitting back here at sunset and him saying, with a smile, "This is the life, Sonny."

Before I ate the sandwich and the wedge of lettuce, I looked out at the ocean streaked with sun red, and toasted, first to Rocky and then to Rene.

My plan was to call Dennis at home and see if he had anything more I could go on. If that failed . . . well, I'd come up with something. But I'd do it in the morning.

As it turned out, I didn't have to wait till morning.

THE car pulled up next to my trailer. I gave it a few seconds and then looked back over my shoulder. I'd finished eating and the sun was hovering right above the horizon. The front of Rocky's baseball cap was tilted over my eyes now. Mrs.

Bailey had turned off her radio, folded her chair for the night and gone inside.

The man walked slowly up the stairs at the end of the deck, glancing at me and looking at the last of the sunset. He was young, probably in his late twenties, but he could have been a little older. The closer he came, the older he looked. He was a well-groomed natural blond dressed in a very light tan suit with a multicolored designer shirt under his jacket. As he got closer, I was ready to bet that the suit and tie were silk.

He said nothing, just stood next to my chair, hands folded in front of him, watching the sun and water.

When the sun was all but gone, the blond man in the tan silk suit kept looking out at the water and said, in a smooth, soft voice,

> "O'er all that leaps, and runs, and shouts, and sings,
>   Or beats the gladsome air, o'er all that glides
> Beneath the wave, yea, in the wave itself
> And mighty depth of waters. Wonder not
> If such my transports were; for in all things
> I saw one life, and felt that it was joy."

"Nice," I said.

"Wordsworth, *The Prelude*. School days memories," he said. "I was an English major at Northwestern. Hated the classes, loved the poetry."

"What can I do for you Mr. . . . ?" I asked, getting out of the chair with some difficulty and picking up the tray.

"Let me help you with that," he said, taking the tray helpfully.

"Thanks," I said.

"You are Jim Rockford?"

"I am," I said. "And you're a wandering poet, making a

good enough living so you can both dress well and preserve a dying art form."

"Not quite," he said with a smile. "You can call me Wright."

He held the tray in one hand and extended his right. We shook and I led him into the trailer, where he placed the tray on the counter near the sink.

"Want me to clean this up?" he said, looking back over his shoulder at me.

"Wouldn't want you to get water on your silk," I said. "And there's not much there. I'll take care of it later. Now, what can I do for you, Mr. Wright? I've had a long, hard day and I think I'd like to see if I can find a few innings of a baseball game on television and then get some sleep."

We were facing each other now and his hands were folded in front of him again.

"I would really appreciate your coming with me to see a man who is anxious to speak to you," he said. "It won't take long and it could mean an eager client for you."

I didn't like the way he was invading my space. I took off my cap, said, "Call me in the morning," and turned on the television.

He turned it off.

"He'd really like to see you now," Wright said almost apologetically.

"Not now," I said.

"If you don't want to come, I've been instructed to bring you," he said as if he regretted it.

I turned the television back on. He took a step and moved his hand so fast that I barely saw it. The screen of the television exploded just as a polar bear holding a can of Coke appeared.

My mouth opened and I looked at him standing calmly.

"Mr. Rockford, I can hurt you. I can hurt you badly. You

are considering hitting me. It won't happen and you'll be injured trying. I have a weapon, but I rarely need more than my hands."

I looked at the television set, its insides still sputtering electrically, and I considered what I could hit this guy with. He looked at his watch and said,

"It's getting late and I'm supposed to have you there within the hour. This should all be painless and possibly beneficial. I can, if you make it necessary, force you to come, which would embarrass you and make me a bit sorry."

"Look, Wright," I said, pointing a finger at his face.

Before I could say more, he had the pointed finger in his hand, and the other hand leaped out like a snake and caught me, fingers under my rib cage. It hurt like hell and I couldn't move because my finger hurt just as much. I considered throwing a punch with my free hand. Wright nodded no and smiled sadly, understandingly.

"Where are we going?" I asked.

"Not far," he said, letting me go. "Would you like to change quickly?"

"No," I said. "I'll just grab a cookie for dessert and we can be on our way. Want one?"

I headed for the cookie jar. Wright stepped in front of me, opened the jar and pulled out my .38. He put the gun back in the jar, pointed to the door and said.

"Nothing is more outwardly visible than the secrets of the heart, nothing more obvious than what one attempts to conceal. Hence, the man of true breed looks straight into his heart even when he is alone."

"Shakespeare?" I guessed.

"Confucius," he said. "At least as was liberally translated by Ezra Pound."

I turned off the lights, went into the night and got passively and angrily in the passenger seat of his red Porsche. The car smelled new. Wright found a classical music station on FM. It sounded like an opera.

"German," he said as we drove. "I can't take German opera. You?"

"I don't know much about opera," I said.

"Ponderous," he said. "Wagner may have been a genius, but it takes a saint to sit through *Parsifal.* French opera is too fluffy. Czech and Russian opera tend to be repetitious. No, opera was created for Italians and Mozart."

"If you say so," I said, trying to think of a way to get away from the well-dressed demon.

"Well," he said, changing the station, "believe what you like. There are exceptions like *Carmen,* and Beethoven's lone operatic work is damned good. Do you know we're being followed?"

"Yes," I said, looking out the window.

"Whoever it is, is good," he said with admiration, "but . . ."

He turned into a road leading into the hills and we played tag with the car following us at what it considered a safe distance. Wright was better than the people in the car behind us. Besides, it's easier to get rid of a tail than to be one.

He found a talk show on the AM band. I think the host was the same guy Mrs. Bailey had been listening to. The host was insulting his callers over the issue of a gay rights parade in Topanga. When we pulled back onto the road at the foot of the hills, the car behind us was gone, probably wandering the narrow gravel streets above with its headlights off, checking each small driveway for Wright's car.

Wright smiled, shook his head and said,

"You seem like a likable guy, Rockford. You watch the sunset. You're polite. Take my advice. Give the man you're

going to see what he wants right away. He'll make an offer.
You take it. Believe me. You'll give him what he wants
eventually and eventually won't be very long."

"You mean you'll hurt me?" I said.

He pursed his lips and shook his head in the affirmative.

"He'll have you hurt. Could be more than simple pain
and a break here and there," he said. "You could be dead."

"And you'd be the one to kill me?"

"Probably," he said.

"The maimed may pause and breathe," he continued,
turning off the radio,

> "And glance securely round.
> The deer invites no longer
> Than it eludes the hound."

There was a long silence. I folded my arms and looked as
angry as I felt.

"Emily Dickinson," he said. "Morbid woman. Great
poet."

I didn't answer. We drove in silence back to Los Angeles
and into Beverly Hills. We went past the neon and the
young and old moving in and out of shops. We passed the
Mondrian and the comedy clubs and into the darker part of
Sunset Boulevard where offices upstairs of closed and not
very chic shops were crowded together and rented for more
than they would have been worth if they didn't have the
Sunset Boulevard address.

We parked and he motioned me out onto the sidewalk. I
got out. He was at my side almost instantly. There were a
few parked cars, a few people walking down the street not
wanting to make eye contact at this hour and on this part
of Sunset.

Wright guided me across the street through the light

traffic going by, and we went into an office-building entrance wedged between a tourist electronics shop and a small restaurant called the Emerson Diner. The elevator door was open. We got in and Wright pressed a button. He stood behind me and motioned for me to face front. There are a lot of things I don't like. I don't like Irish corned beef. I don't like child molesters. I don't like flat-out cowards, and I surely don't like feeling like a kid being escorted by the school disciplinarian to be punished by the principal.

The elevator stopped at the fourth floor and we got out. There was no real hallway, just four doors. All were wood. All were marked: THOROBRED PRODUCTIONS, SCRIPTS INTERNATIONAL, CONRAD ECU—PHOTOGRAPHER TO THE STARS, CONESTI EXPORTS.

We went in the door marked Conesti Exports.

The lights were on, and we were standing in a single room large enough for a small conference table and a desk. Behind the desk was a window looking out into the darkness. There weren't any pictures on the wall. There was nothing on the desk but a telephone. It looked like someone had just moved out or was about to move in. The someone sat at the conference table with six chairs. No one sat behind the desk.

He was hefty, a bull of a man with gray hair. He was wearing a blue suit much too heavy for California. His tie, however, was great, stylish blue and red thin stripes at a slight angle.

He watched us step in. It was cozy. Just the three of us.

"Someone followed us," said Wright. "I lost him."

The hefty man nodded.

"Sit," the man at the table said, pointing to a chair across from him.

I sat. Wright stood at the door, hands folded. I looked at the man and waited.

"You know who I am," he said. It wasn't a question.

"I read the papers, watch some television, at least I did when I had one," I said, looking at Wright, who was impassively watching.

"This meeting is not taking place," John Barini said. "You understand?"

I nodded.

"Good," Barini went on. "I want to tell you a story."

"Great," I said with the biggest false smile I could muster. "I like having my property destroyed and being kidnapped by people who want to tell me stories."

"Don't be wise," Barini said impatiently, indicating that this was going to take longer than he had wished. "You can get hurt being wise to the wrong people. I've got thick skin, but it's still skin. You understand?"

"I understand," I said, folding my arms to show I was ready and reluctant to hear his story.

"You know, you dress like shit," he said.

"Mr. Wright didn't give me time to change," I said.

"I got a feeling you'd still dress like shit. Maybe we can do something about that."

This time I shut up. Barini was on television, in magazines and in the papers every year or so because he was the "reputed" leader of a powerful crime family in New Jersey, a family that had grown to the point where its leader, Frank Corlis, was reputed to head the council of criminal families in the Northeast. The only problem was that Corlis was in jail and had been for about fifteen years. By now he must be seventy. Barini had taken over making frequent trips to see his friend Frankie Corlis. I was sitting in Godfather territory. I listened.

"Long time ago," Barini said, "a friend, a good man, a father to me, more than my own father, got a bad rap and went to the pen. You know what I'm telling you?"

"I know," I said.

"Good," he went on. "There was only one witness to the crime my mentor was supposed to have committed. Since my friend had a bad reputation, the jury believed the witness. A couple of things have come up, some new information, a couple of witnesses have stepped forward, witnesses with A-one reputations. A hearing for my friend is coming up. Then maybe a new trial. The witness who put him away has to be found and persuaded to tell the truth. You're with me so far?"

"Still with you," I said.

"Story's over. Where is Irv Grazzo?"

"Irv Grazzo?" I repeated.

"Grazzo, Conforti, Jacobs," Barini said, putting his hands on the table. He wore two rings. One was a simple white gold wedding band. The other had a ruby about the size of Australia. His fingers were manicured and stubby.

"I want you to tell me where he is, where his wife is, where her kid is," Barini said conversationally. "You talk and you tell the truth, you get cash in an envelope, a lot of cash, more than you make in two years."

"And if I don't talk?"

"*That* is not an option," Barini said, shaking his head. "The harder the time you give me, the less is in that envelope. And if we somehow got to the point where I didn't get what I want from you, the envelope would be empty and you'd see your old man sooner than you expected. I understand you loved your father. That's good. That's the way I love Frank Corlis. I don't want him dying in a cell."

"I'm looking for your Irv Grazzo," I said. "I already have a client for that. When I find him, I think he's going to have his own problems and he won't make such a good witness."

Barini looked at Wright, who shrugged slightly to indicate he didn't know what I was talking about.

"Grazzo's wife is dead," I said. "It's a pretty good bet he killed her. My plan is to find him and prove it. He tried to pin it on his stepdaughter, but that's pretty thin and getting thinner."

"She's dead?" Barini said, trying hard not to show whatever he was feeling.

"And," I repeated, "I think Grazzo's going to have a nice, quick trial unless he confesses. The girl is safe and the one place where I think we might have some trouble is that I don't intend to tell you where she is. She's my client."

Barini smiled. I smiled back. Barini smiled at Wright. He smiled too, but his smile was smaller.

"So you're trying to nail Grazzo?" Barini said.

"If he killed his wife," I said. "Which is a pretty good bet."

Barini looked up at Wright and said,

"How come we didn't know about this? We pay fair to get this kind of information. How come?"

"I don't know," said Wright.

"Get Larry, Eddie and Steve to bring our source in for a meet tomorrow morning, eight. The other address."

Wright nodded, indicating that he understood and it would be done.

"Go, Rockford," said Barini. "Do your job. You need help, Mr. Wright will be calling on you. You find Grazzo. You got four days. You nail him for his wife's murder and that envelope comes to you, a birthday present. You can get up. Mr. Wright'll take you home."

I moved to the door.

"Oh," said Barini, still seated and looking pleased, "don't bother to come back here. This'll be an empty office for rent by morning."

It was my turn to nod. The conversation was over. Wright drove me home and listened to classical music. He didn't say a word until he pulled up in front of my trailer, and then he said,

> "In *vengence*, and eternal justice, thus
> Made manifest. 'Come now ye golden times,'
> Said I, forth-breathing on those open sands
> A hymn of triumph as the morning comes
> Out of the bosom of the night."

"I don't get it," I said, feeling more than a little disgruntled.

"It's by William Wordsworth."

"I hadn't noticed," I said, opening the door.

"Think about it," he said. "'Come now ye golden times.'"

He looked like a model from the Neiman Marcus Christmas catalog and his smile was full of white, even teeth.

I got out, leaving the door open and turned my back on the Porsche. He closed the door and drove off.

I went inside to my broken television set, playing over feelings of anger, fear, determination and confusion. Then I got it, or thought I did. If Grazzo got nailed for Rene's murder, he would be a discredited witness against old man Corlis. That was clear. Men who murder their wives with kitchen knives don't have a lot of credibility. What hit me next was that if Grazzo was guilty, Barini and Corlis's friends wouldn't be under suspicion of killing a witness's innocent wife.

I cleaned my dinner tray, swept up the glass from the broken television, carried the broken television out to the Dumpster, dropped it in and thought I'd be doing a lot of reading for a while.

I went back to the trailer, brushed my teeth and went to bed. I planned to lie there thinking for a while and then change into a clean pair of shorts. I didn't have a decent thought that would help, and I fell asleep wearing what I had worn most of the day.

One of my last thoughts before I fell asleep was that whether I liked it or not, I was working for the mob. "And in these dreams will be strangers we did not know together." Maybe I did understand.

CHAPTER FOUR

It was after nine when I woke in the morning. The phone had rung several times within the last hour or so, and I was dimly aware of the ringing. I covered my head with a pillow so I couldn't hear the messages.

When I got up, I showered, shaved, brushed my teeth and hair and dressed for jail. I was surprised they hadn't come already. I had some coffee, listened to my messages, which weren't important, and went outside, where a thin drizzle was keeping the kids, their surfboards and their brilliant patter out of the water. Mrs. Bailey was sitting in front of her trailer under her aluminum awning, writing. The drizzle pinged against it. She looked up, smiled at me and pointed to the sky. I smiled and nodded and then waved. I wasn't sure how good her eyesight was.

There were no cars parked in the area that I didn't recognize. I wasn't trying to hide, and I figured the car that had followed Wright and me last night was the U.S. Marshals or the L.A. police, and it wasn't Wright they were following.

I went back in the trailer and got my kind of ratty, thin raincoat with the hood before heading back out and down

the beach to the pay phone. It was still working. I called
Beth. No answer. I told her machine what was going on.
Then I called Dennis at his office.

"Dennis, I need to talk to you," I said.

"Rockford," he said. "We've got both a federal and a
county warrant for your arrest for withholding evidence and
suspicion of murder."

"Suspicion of . . ." I blundered.

"Rene Jacobs," he said.

"Grazzo," I corrected. "Didn't Troy and Donahue tell you
that?"

"No," he said with some irritation.

"Look, Dennis, I'm coming in by myself. I've asked Beth
to meet me at your office. I have a deal to make. The marshals can be present."

"That's nice of you, Jim," Dennis said.

"It's a good deal," I said. "Can you stop them from serv-
ing the warrant if I'm there in an hour?"

"I don't know," he said. "I'll try. One hour."

The car that followed me to Dennis's office was probably
the same one that had been lost by Wright the night before,
or maybe one of Barini's friends was on my tail to report on
my progress in finding Grazzo. The car was midsized, very
dark blue with tinted windows. I think it was a Toyota
Camry. This time it was a dreary daylight and I wasn't trying to lose whoever was behind me. He stayed close, knowing that I saw him.

By the time I found a downtown meter, dropped the
coins in and headed for the police station, the rain had gotten worse. With my head covered and with some protection
from my raincoat, I did a kind of fast walk. When I got to
the entrance, I saw the car that was following me parked
across the street in a no-parking zone. A man in the pas-

senger seat was looking at me through the wet window. I couldn't make out his face through the tinted glass.

I went inside, waved at some of the officers I knew and one bookie named Mohana, a black stick of a man, who was cuffed and alone on one of the wooden benches. He was dressed for the day in sport clothes and he looked as if he didn't have a care in this world and probably in the next. He slouched with his eyes half closed and didn't notice me.

Dennis Becker met me at his desk. He was a lieutenant but he didn't have his own office. The reason was simple. Diehl was a captain. He had his own office. He didn't like me and so he didn't like Dennis, even if he did recognize that Becker was the best he had and honest.

Dennis reminded me more of a balding bull dog every day. He had the good, slightly bulky look and face of a tough cop. He came out from behind his desk looking serious, his collar open. The new chief of police had ordered collars and ties. He hadn't said the ties couldn't be loose and the collars open. It was only a matter of time, though, before a memo came down on that, providing the new chief of police lasted long enough in his job to issue it.

"Beth here?" I asked as he motioned for me to follow him.

I had a good idea of where we were heading.

"No," he said.

"You and Andy go fishing?"

"No," he said, looking straight ahead.

"Well, maybe next week . . ."

"You may be singing 'Swing Low, Sweet Chariot' behind bars next week, Jim," he said, pausing to look at me and stopping in front of the interrogation room door.

"I could be out on bail," I said.

"What you have better be good," he said, reaching for the

door. "There are three bastards in there who want to nail you with railroad spikes."

We went in and Dennis closed the door. The three bastards were Troy, Donahue and Diehl. They were seated at the end of the table. Two seats were open at the other end. I took one. Dennis moved toward the corner, but Diehl waved him back toward the door.

Dennis glanced at me and started to leave the room.

"Lieutenant Becker leaves and I don't deal," I said.

Diehl laughed.

"You are in no position to make demands," Diehl said.

He was narrow, perfectly dressed to code, with a recent haircut. His hair was definitely growing more and more gray. I wondered how long he had to go to retirement. It couldn't be too long.

"But I'm making the offer," I said with a smile, folding my hands on the table. "Becker goes and I don't talk."

"Then we lock you up," said Diehl.

"My lawyer will be here soon," I answered.

"Let the lieutenant stay," said Donahue, the older Marshal.

Diehl looked at the marshal as if he were going to say something, changed his mind and motioned Dennis to the corner.

"I want a witness I trust," I said, glancing at Dennis.

"What's your deal?" asked Donahue.

"When my lawyer gets here," I said.

"We're not waiting," said Diehl.

"Then I'm not talking," I said.

There was a knock on the door and an older, worn-out cop named Riordon who I had met for five-second conversations over the years came in. He was wearing a-little-better-than-shabby slacks and jacket.

"Mr. Rockford's lawyer is here," he said.

"Send Mr. Rockford's lawyer in," Donahue said.

The door remained open and a lanky black kid in jeans, a white pullover and thick glasses came in, a briefcase in his hand. He was under thirty but I wasn't sure how much.

"This your lawyer?" Diehl asked, watching the slightly confused looking young man with the briefcase look around at us.

"Miss Davenport had to leave town," the young man said nervously. "Emergency. She got her messages, briefed me and told me to get here fast. I'm Fred Archer."

Archer decided I was his client and sat next to me. Diehl was smiling openly.

Archer and I shook hands and he placed his briefcase on the table.

"Your client was about to offer us a deal," said Donahue. "I don't know what kind, but there are warrants in the next room for your client on counts ranging from abetting a murder suspect to suspicion of murder. Now, we want his offer and we want it now."

"I'll have to talk to Mr. Rockford privately first," Archer said in a reedy voice.

"Out of the question," said Diehl. "We've been jerked around enough on this."

"I talk to my client privately," said Archer. "If I do not have that opportunity, you are in violation of the law of the State of California."

"We're U.S. Marshals," said Troy.

"Then you'll be in violation of federal law if you arrest my client," said Archer, adjusting his glasses and fishing for something in his briefcase, which he was having great difficulty finding. "If you want to talk to my client without giving him the opportunity to discuss the allegations with me, we may have a situation which could give me my first Supreme Court case and make the newspapers happy to

have a little filler story for page three. Who knows, one or
two television reporters might even want to report this
breach of law."

"Oh crap," said Diehl.

"Find them a place to talk," said Donahue. "Ten minutes?"

"Should be fine," said Archer. "I'll tell you if we need
more."

Diehl nodded to Dennis, who led Archer and me out of
the room and toward the end of the hall. People bustled by
us, a few mumbling complaints, one woman humming
something I think was the theme from *Friday the 13th.*

"In here," said Dennis.

He opened the door to an office and we stepped in.

"Thanks for insisting that I stay," said Dennis sarcastically. "I'm sure my love ratings are going to go up with
Diehl."

"They couldn't be much lower, Dennis," I said. "Besides,
I think you're going to come out of this two steps up and
maybe with your own office."

He snorted and closed the door. Archer, his back to me,
stood in front of the desk. I stood watching as he put his
briefcase down, opened it and continued to search for something. Then he found it, turned to me with a smile. He was
holding one of those cardboard containers of juice, apple
juice in this case. He removed the straw attached to the
side and inserted it in the carton, which he placed on the
desk.

"I . . ." I began, but he put his fingers to his lips to
stop me.

He made the fastest bug search I've ever seen, missing
nothing, taking no more than three minutes of our ten. He
found one bug, tore off the plastic-and-metal top and then
sat down to listen to me and drink.

"They can't use anything they hear," he said, "and, legally, they can't bug a lawyer and his client even with a warrant, but they could learn whatever it is I'm going to learn. Which is?"

I told him my story. I told it fast. I didn't leave anything out. He nodded, adjusted his glasses, took notes, sipped at his apple juice and nodded occasionally. He asked no questions.

The door opened and Dennis said, "Time."

"I do all the talking," whispered Archer, throwing his empty apple juice carton into a wastebasket near the door, "unless I tell you to say something, in which case you say as little as possible."

"I know the routine," I said.

We returned to the interrogation room, where Archer, having finished his apple juice, unfolded his notebook and sat next to me facing the trio. Dennis stood behind them against the wall, looking decidedly uncomfortable.

"We tape this?" asked Donahue, pointing to the black box on the table.

"We prefer it," said Archer, pulling out his own little silver battery recorder from his briefcase. "So there'll be no question about what's being said."

Both recorders were pressed on, like dueling compact weapons.

"My client committed no crimes," said Archer. "He is a licensed private investigator. On the matter concerned, he was given reason to believe that something had taken place at a certain house in Pasadena. Mr. Rockford's client, who lives at the address in question, gave him full permission to go to the house and attempt to find her mother. As for murdering Rene Grazzo, my client has no idea where the crime took place or when. If it took place as we can assume between the late afternoon of the fourteenth and sometime later in that day, Mr. Rockford has stand-up good citizens to vouch for every minute of his time."

"The girl," said Donahue. "She's wanted on suspicion."

"She's not my client, at least not yet," said Archer. "But since Mr. Rockford is and is working for her, I feel it is clearly within my right to point out that her mother is the one who was killed and that when she appeared at the door with the knife she was clearly saying, 'I'll kill you' to Grazzo, not to her mother. What sense would it make, gentlemen, for the girl, knife in hand, to threaten her mother, who was being dragged away against her will by her husband?"

We have three neighbors who will testify to the nature of Mrs. Grazzo's abduction by her husband and their belief that daughter was definitely speaking to her stepfather."

"We have fingerprints," said Diehl.

"Do you have Grazzo?" asked Archer.

"None of your——" Diehl began and then stopped when Donahue put a hand on the captain's shoulder.

"How did your client find out that Jacob's real name is Grazzo?" Donahue asked. "The girl tell your client?"

"Part of the deal," Archer said, taking off his glasses and exploring them through squinting eyes to see why they weren't working to his satisfaction.

"No promises," said Donahue, who nudged Diehl.

"No promises," echoed Diehl.

"If the offer is satisfactory to you or to the district attorney, who should, as a matter of fact, have a representative here . . ." Archer continued, putting his glasses back on. "Does the district attorney even know about this meeting?"

Diehl shifted uncomfortably. The marshals were impassive.

"Let's talk," said Donahue.

Archer nodded at me and I said,

"Last night a poetry-quoting blond with a lethal body took me for a ride into town. I assume it was either L.A. detectives or a U.S. Marshal who tried to follow us. The blond guy, who said his name was Wright, lost you and took me to an office on Sunset, far down on Sunset. I'll give you the address and tell you the office, but you'll find it empty. You might find fingerprints, particularly on the table, but they might have wiped the place before they left."

"Whose fingerprints will we find?" asked Troy.

"John Barini," I said.

"Barini's in Los Angeles?" asked Donahue skeptically.

"In the ample flesh," I said.

"Good so far?" asked Archer.

"So far," said Donahue. "What did he want from you?"

"To find Grazzo," he said. "Find him before you do and, if possible, find evidence to prove he killed Rene."

Donahue shook his head. I think the shake was in admiration of the New Jersey gang boss.

"You know why he wants this?" asked Donahue.

"Frank Corlis is pushing for a new hearing, new evidence," I said. "I figure Grazzo was the primary eyewitness against Corlis and was in witness protection. Barini is looking hard for Grazzo, finds him in Florida. Grazzo grabs Rene and Melisa, lets you guys know, and runs to California. By now maybe he knows about a possible new trial for Corlis. He's nervous. Hell, he's out of his mind. He's been hiding and looking over his shoulder for about twenty years. Maybe Rene had enough of it. They fought. He pulled her out of the house by the hair and killed her. And you want to find Grazzo and a patsy for Rene's killer because if he did it, he'll be one lousy witness if Corlis gets a new trial."

"The girl's prints are on the knife," said Diehl.

I looked at Archer, who thought about it for a few seconds and said,

"My client considers that one possibility is that someone who doesn't want Grazzo on trial for murdering his wife removed the knife from Mrs. Grazzo's body and substituted the kitchen knife with Melisa Henley's fingerprints on it. In addition, the knife, if it did come from the Jacobs' kitchen, might not be the one the girl had in her hand. In any case, it would be very natural for every knife in the house to have the girl's fingerprints on it. She lived there."

"That's crazy," said Diehl.

"Are Grazzo's prints on the knife?" asked Archer.

No answer and then Donahue said,

"No."

"Are the victim's fingerprints on the knife?" Archer asked.

"No," said Donahue.

"Are any fingerprints besides the girl's on the knife?"

"No," said Donahue.

"You find that odd?" Archer said, leaning forward on his now-closed briefcase. "The knife is from the kitchen and it bears no prints of two of the people who were almost certain to have used it. The only prints are the girl's. Think, gentlemen. I think that would make a grand jury pause and a jury of her peers think deeply."

Now Archer shrugged and pulled a large, black ring-binder notebook with a few dozen sheets in it from his briefcase. He opened the notebook, looked at it as he flipped pages and said,

"*Goodfield versus the U.S.,* a Georgia case. Same situation. Knife switch to frame a known felon. Federal officer was fingered by his own partner. Officer was charged and pleaded guilty. Then there's *Goldblatt versus the United States,* just six months ago. That time the knife—"

"You can't get that kind of information introduced into a trial," Donahue said.

"Maybe not," said Archer, "but I think CNN, ABC, the

L.A. and *New York Times* might be interested. We haven't even discussed the possibility that Corlis's friends found Mrs. Grazzo's body and made the knife switch hoping you'd figure it out and help put Grazzo behind bars and waiting for a trial for murder."

"What do you want and what do we get?" asked Donahue.

Diehl was definitely sulking now. This was not going the way he had imagined.

"Mr. Rockford wants his client cleared of all charges," he said. "He also wants the opportunity to find Grazzo. Of course it is likely you will find him first, but my client might have resources you do not. If Grazzo committed this murder, and we have evidence, we meet again. Lieutenant Becker serves as Mr. Rockford's contact with both the police and the U.S. Marshal's office. Meanwhile, we want a copy of the autopsy report on Rene Grazzo's body, specifically to find if the wound that killed her came from the knife with the fingerprints of Mr. Rockford's client or if that knife was inserted in the corpse after death."

"You've got no right to . . ." Diehl began, looked at Donahue and went quiet and red faced.

"Your client, the victim's daughter, can make a request for the autopsy report," said Donahue, "but not you or Rockford. So . . ."

"Do we have an agreement?" Archer asked.

"You want Rockford to walk and collect from the mob," said Diehl.

"My client will not accept money from organized crime. His only legal client is Melisa Conforti," said Archer.

"Why?" asked Diehl. "Why are you so damned interested in this case, Rockford? Why are you sticking your . . ." He remembered the tape recorders, looked at them and changed his tone. "Why?"

"Mr. Rockford knew Rene Henley a long time ago," said Archer. "There is a good chance that Melisa Grazzo is Mr. Rockford's daughter."

The room went silent. The tapes rolled. Dennis, arms folded and leaning in the corner, closed his eyes.

"No deal," said Captain Diehl.

"How much time does your client want?" asked Donahue, ignoring Diehl.

Archer handed me a fountain pen and a pad of paper. I wrote, *at least a week.*

"My client wants two weeks," said Archer. "He will not leave California and he will keep Lieutenant Becker informed about his movements related to this investigation."

"If Grazzo killed Rene," I said, "I don't want it covered up so he can testify against Corlis. If Grazzo didn't do it, I want to know who did."

Troy touched his partner's shoulder and the two whispered, leaving Diehl out of the discussion.

"One week," said Donahue. "Then we arrest your client for harboring a murder suspect."

"His daughter," said Archer.

"Maybe," said Donahue. "Meeting's over."

"Wait a second here," said Diehl. "We're just going to let Rockford walk?"

"I said the meeting's over," Donahue said firmly, standing up. "We'll talk in your office."

"Then my client and I are free to go?" asked Archer.

"Go," said Donahue, reaching over to turn off the tape recorder.

Archer kept his going and in his hand as he ushered me out of the interrogation room, down the stairs and into a gray but no longer drizzly day. I carried my raincoat over my arm. Only when we were outside did Archer turn off his minirecorder, awkwardly open his briefcase and put the recorder away.

"You're good," I said. "Thanks."

We shook hands and he said,

"I wouldn't have gone to law school if it hadn't been for Beth Davenport," he said. "I'd probably be in training for store manager for a supermarket back in Akron. Beth knows my mother. You know how it goes."

"Somewhat," I said. "How do I reach you?"

He pulled a card out of his wallet and handed it to me.

"You've been doing this long?" I asked as people passed us on the street.

The dark car with the tinted windows was parked in the same place it had been. There was a man seated inside, but the tinted and probably bulletproof glass protected him.

"Got to Los Angeles three days ago," Archer said. "You're my first case. I'm a member of the Ohio bar and I'll be taking the California bar next time it's offered. To tell you the truth, Rockford, I don't know if half of the stuff I said in there about the law is true, and those cases I quoted—"

"You made them up?" I said.

He nodded and adjusted his glasses again.

"I'm safe," he said. "We weren't under oath and nobody confessed to anything. They're not going to check me out and if they do, what have they got?"

"I don't know," I said.

"A situation that's getting deeper and deeper in mud. A situation that our marshal wants to keep simple and get over with fast."

"If Beth ever decides she can't handle me as a client," I said, "I'd be pleased to have you representing me, Mr. Archer."

James Archer smiled and looked around and said,

"I was pretty good in there, wasn't I?"

"You were great," I said.

"You can't imagine how scared I was," he said. "But it was the biggest high I've had since I won the state Scrabble championship of Ohio."

"What about graduating law school?"

"Piece of candy compared to Scrabble," he said with a grin.

He turned and hurried down the street. I went the opposite way, to my car. I had to find Grazzo and I had to have some place to start.

THE dark car followed me home. I didn't pull into the Cove. Wright's red Porsche was parked in front of my door. I didn't need poetry or a good beating. I kept driving and spent fifteen minutes losing the car with the tinted windows. When I was sure I had succeeded, I drove to the house on stilts Angel was supposed to be taking care of.

Angel answered the door. He was wearing tan chinos and an open-necked shirt with a gold chain around his neck.

"You come to get the girl?" he asked hopefully.

"I've come to talk to her," I said.

"I've got a client coming for a sitting in a little over an hour," he said, checking his watch. "I'm giving her and her husband a finished portrait. It looks great. We're talking big bucks. Don't flush it on me, Jimmy."

We were inside now and he was ahead of me, looking back.

"Didn't I help you with my Billy Bob yesterday?"

"Yeah," said Angel. "I'll give you that. But I'm baby-sitting for you."

"And I appreciate it, Angel."

Melisa was on a second-floor deck in a flowered sundress and a matching floppy hat. She was wearing sunglasses, and a book lay in her lap. She was facing the ocean. Given the gray sky, the glasses weren't necessary, at least not to ward off the ultraviolet rays.

"Melisa," I said, "I need your help."

"I gotta go get ready, Jimmy," Angel whispered. "You know, suit, tie, the whole schmear."

He hurried away and Melisa took off her glasses and looked up at me. She was crying. I sat on the deck chair next to her and took her hand.

"Did you find him?" she asked.

"Not yet," I said. "But I've got some questions for you that might help."

"Okay," she said, wiping her eyes with her palm and putting the sunglasses back on.

"First, your stepfather's name wasn't Conforti or Jacobs," I said. "It was Grazzo."

"Grazzo? My name's Grazzo? God. Isn't my name Rockford?"

"That's a little premature," I said gently. "We'll think about that later. Your stepfather was in a witness protection program, federal. I think he saw a mob leader murder a man. For some reason, your mother married Grazzo and they began almost nineteen years of hiding."

"I guess I'm not surprised," she said. "I guess . . . I don't know what I think or feel."

Her eyes were on my face, looking for answers. All I had was questions.

"Me, the police and federal marshals are looking for your stepfather," I said. "I want to prove he killed your mother. I want someone to prove he killed your mother. If he killed your mother, there's no reason for anyone to try to find you and maybe threaten Grazzo that you might get hurt if he testifies. He'll be useless as a witness against the mob boss I mentioned if he's a wife murderer."

Melisa shook her head and looked at her knees. She spotted something I didn't see and wiped it away with her fingers. I remembered a gesture like that. Rene had done that once, but I couldn't quite remember when or where. It probably wasn't even Rene and maybe it never happened.

"My stepfather won't care if anyone wants to kill me," she said. "He'd probably drink a toast to the television when they announced finding my body on the nighttime news."

"He drank?" I said.

"Lost Weekend," she said with a look of angry revulsion.

"When did you see *Lost Weekend?*" I asked.

"Television," she said. "I had a lot of time to watch television. Mom liked old movies."

"I remember," I said. "Her favorite was *Mildred Pierce.*"

Melisa smiled. It wasn't much of a smile, but it was a smile.

"He drink at home?" I asked.

"Drank at home, maybe saw bats flying around. Hit Mom," she said. "Sometimes he'd say he couldn't stand it anymore and he ran out. He kept getting different jobs, not much and he didn't keep them long. He said all his jobs involved working alone in a shipping room or mail room or something."

"He went out," I repeated. "Where?"

"In Florida, a place called Saigon," she said. "I never went there. I don't think Mom ever did either. He'd just come back and say he'd been back to Saigon and smile like a drunk, you know?"

"I know," I said.

"Once he said 'The Saigon,' " she went on, so I figured it was a place.

"And here? In Pasadena?"

She shook her head and said,

"We haven't been here long, but . . ."

"He went someplace."

"Tin's," she said. "I think that's what he called it."

"Tin's?"

"Said it once," said Melisa.

"What else can you tell me?" I asked.

"I think he loved my mother," she said. "Whatever was going on just kept driving him crazy, but he stayed with her and she stayed with him. I never understood. I hated him for what he did to my mother. I hated him for making moves on me. Being drunk is no damned excuse."

"No excuse at all," I said. "If we get to the point where you have to talk to the police, I've got a lawyer who'll tell you what to say and how. Okay?"

She nodded.

"Anything else about Grazzo's life here?"

"Grazzo? Oh, yes," she said. "Nothing. Just Tin's."

"Angel treating you well?" I asked.

"Fine," she said. "I like him in a weird kind of way. He complains and feels sorry for himself and then he does what he can to try to make me feel better. He went out and bought a whole bunch of videotapes and carry-out pizza."

"Angel's an angel," I said. "What are you reading?"

"Poetry," she said, holding up the book. It had no dust jacket. "It was on the shelf in the den downstairs. I like poetry. I don't always know what it means exactly, but I like the way it sounds."

"I know a guy who loves poetry, but you're safer if you stay away from him," I said. "Tin's?"

"Tin's," she repeated.

"I've got to go, Melisa. People are following me, looking for you, and I've got to find Grazzo fast if he's even still in town. I'll try to get back tonight sometime."

I got up and put my hand on her shoulder. She put a hand over mine.

"Angel says tonight we're having Chinese carry-out and we're watching a Thin Man movie and *Bloodsport,*" she said.

I went back into the house and she picked up the poetry book. It was back in her lap unread before I had the sliding door closed.

The office in the house had a full range of phone books. I couldn't find a Tin in Pasadena, Glendale, Burbank or anywhere else in the valley or out of it. Maybe Melisa had heard it wrong. Then it hit me. He had hung out in a Vietnamese bar or restaurant in Florida. Maybe he had started the same thing here. He was a Vietnam vet, apparently, and a Vietnam hangout might be a reasonable place to remember the bad old days and not be spotted by mob guys who liked tougher or higher-class places.

I tried Tin's again, but this time I looked under bars and restaurants. And this time I tried various ways of spelling it. Tihn's Vietnamese Restaurant was in Burbank on Alameda.

Angel headed me off at the door on my way out and put a hand on my chest, saying. "I can use your help, another character, but not Billy Bob. More subtle. I don't know how well these society people know each other and I don't want bad vibrations if they start talking about meeting a guy named Billy Bob when they purchased their genuine Angel Velasquez Martinez portrait."

"I'm in a hurry, Angel," I said, checking my watch and knowing I had to stop for gas, find an ATM machine and stay off main roads and highways as much as possible to keep from getting picked up by everyone who was trying to tail me.

"It'll take you a minute," he said. "Look, here's a tie."

He handed me a silk tie that actually went with the sport jacket I was wearing. I made a face, but I put it on and Angel grinned.

"I knew you'd do it, Jimmy," he said, patting my arm as

I put on the tie, looked in the front hall mirror and made myself presentable.

"Bloodsport?" I asked when I was ready.

"I'm a sucker for Van Damme," he whispered, leading me into his studio, where a man and a woman stood talking.

They turned when we entered. They were an odd couple, and bells should have been going off in Angel's greedy mind, but the thought of stacks of green were inclined to dull Angel's senses. The man was no more than forty, well dressed, thin, suit well tailored but a little out of style. The woman was at least a dozen years older, well built, yellow suit and a little matching hat.

"Mrs. Wertzel, Mr. Lyons," said Angel. "This is another of my fine clients, Señor Stavros."

I shook hands. Lyons didn't smile.

"Nice to meet you both," I said, not bothering to fake a Greek accent. Greek was my worst accent.

"Señor Martino said he had done a portrait of your wife," Lyons said with more suspicion than I liked. Angel didn't seem to notice.

"A beautiful portrait," I said, looking at Angel with satisfaction. "I will not be crass and give you your check in front of these nice people, but it is in an envelope on the table in the living room."

Angel bowed slightly.

"What business you say you were in, Mr. Stavros?" Lyons asked.

"Sutures," I said. "My company in Athens was started by my grandfather during World War One. The war, I am both sorry and happy to say, made him wealthy. My father took over the business after the second war and made deals with every country, hospitals, clinics, big drug chain distributors. Our company is now the top producer of sutures in the world."

"That a fact?" said Lyons. "Your company have a name?"

"Enough questions," said Angel, jumping in after finally getting the idea that Mr. Lyons was asking a lot of questions. "Mr. Stavros has a plane to catch and we wouldn't want to make him late."

I looked at my watch and said,

"I should just be able to make it. Good-bye. Good to meet you, Mrs. Wertzel, Mr. Lyons. And Señor Martino, you have my wife's and my deepest thanks. We shall treasure your work for us."

I glanced at Lyons. I had the sense that he wasn't buying the show. I knew Angel would keep them in the studio and do his best to stop them from seeing me drive away in an old Firebird, but something was going on and I didn't have time to worry about Angel right now.

I stayed away from my trailer and crossed Topanga Canyon into the valley. I knew Burbank and I knew Alameda, but it took me a while to find Tihn's. It was one of a half dozen businesses, including a hot dog stand, about four blocks from the Disney Studios. Next to Tihn's was an office supply store. It wasn't doing much business, maybe in part because it still looked like rain.

Tihn's, on the other hand, was bustling with activity, at least by comparison. The place was dark. The place was small. It was mostly a bar, but it had a few tables and smelled of Vietnamese food, which would have been better if the smell were fresher. There was a Vietnamese bartender behind the bar watching CNBC as he dried glasses. One guy was at the bar, also Vietnamese, in his fifties or older, and very close to drunk. The tables, except for one, were empty. The one table with customers had another Vietnamese man, pushing toward fat, and a beautiful Vietnamese woman who could have been any age. She was smiling at the well-dressed, overweight man, who spoke in Vietnamese, ate and drank. She had only a drink in front of her. Her clothes were decidedly American, skirt, white blouse, a little too much makeup and some very black, long hair.

I went to the bar. The bartender looked at me and then back at the television.

"You want food, something to drink?" he asked as if he didn't much care what my answer might be.

"Vietnamese beer," I said, "and something not too spicy with those soft noodles."

He nodded and reluctantly turned from the television set long enough to shout something toward the back of the dark bar. Then he served me the beer.

"You know a man, white, maybe as big as me, comes in here once in a while," I said. "Gets drunk, maybe talks about his days fighting the Cong?"

"You a police officer?" the bartender said.

I could see now that he was in front of me and giving me some attention that he was older than I had thought.

"No," I said with the Rockford grin and a shake of the head as I poured the beer. "Just a friend."

"Could be lots of people," the bartender said. "They find us. Like to think when they get a little drunk that they're back in Saigon and maybe they won the war instead of losing it."

"You Tihn?"

"Yes," he said.

I pulled out the photograph of Rene and me and showed it to Tihn.

"Recognize the woman?" I asked. "Picture's old. Take your time."

He looked and shook his head.

"No," he said.

"Guy I'm looking for probably had a little edge to him," I said. "Looking over his shoulder once in a while."

I pulled out a twenty-dollar bill and pushed it across the bar. He pushed it back.

"MP," came a voice at my side.

It was the drunk who had been leaning on the bar. He was Vietnamese and he was looking at the twenty. The bartender said something sharply to the drunk in Vietnamese but the drunk waved him off and pointed at the twenty. I pushed the twenty toward my new source, took another drink of the beer, which wasn't bad, and watched the drunk pocket the bill.

"He used to be an MP," said the drunk. "Likes to tell stories about how he broke heads, fought drugs and prostitutes. Way he tells it, he was cleaner than Bruce Wayne. Maybe he was. He has money. He buys drinks. We listen to him talk, especially Bayan."

"Bayan?" I asked, looking at the bartender, who was decidedly upset now.

The drunk nodded at the girl at the table with the nearly fat man.

"You Immigration?" Tihn asked.

"No," I said. "I told you. I'm just looking for a guy."

The drunk pushed the twenty toward Tihn, who poured him a drink.

"You know anyone in Immigration?" Tihn asked, looking at me again.

"I'm not Immigration. I'm not a cop. I'm not the FBI," I said.

"My sons have been in a camp in the Philippines for almost eight years," Tihn said. "Now they're being sent back to Vietnam because your government says they have to prove they deserve political asylum. They took a raft to the

Philippines. Spent eight years. Now they're being sent back. They could have gone back long time ago if they wanted. Just being there eight years should make them deserve political asylum."

He looked at me for agreement. I agreed. It made sense to me.

"How many people are we talking?" he said, clearly on his favorite subject. "No more than thirty-five thousand. Why can't the United States take them all in from all the camps? More than that come in illegally every month from Mexico. We were loyal. I was a colonel. You took almost a million of us and we live here, prosper, contribute."

"Tihn," said the drunk. "I'm getting sick of hearing the same thing from you every day."

Tihn answered the drunk, who had the glass to his lips, with something sharp and Vietnamese. The drunk shrugged it off.

"I told him he could go somewhere else," Tihn said, looking at the drunk. "But he won't. He's my wife's brother. He's a computer repair man, works for himself. Two, three hours a day. Sophisticated. Makes lots of money. Spends his time here drinking in the dark. Lost his wife, his daughters, his mother in the war. Doesn't know if the daughters are even alive."

"I'm sorry," I said.

Tihn looked at me, and I met his eyes. He nodded. He believed me, at least for the moment. An old woman came out with a bowl in her hands. She wore an apron over a dark dress. She handed the bowl to Tihn, who placed it in front of me with a fork and spoon.

"You going to ask for chopsticks?" he asked.

"No," I said.

"Good," said Tihn.

The drunk moved two stools back to where he had started. He'd had enough social contact for the day. I ate the noodles and said,

"Good."

"My wife is a good cook," he said with confidence.

I looked over at the woman talking to the nearly fat man.

"Bayan," Tihn said, "is my niece. My brother died. Executed by the Cong. You will be polite to her."

"I will be polite," I promised.

Tihn accepted my word but I knew he would be watching me.

"She will expect to be paid," Tihn said. "She has two children."

"She will be paid," I said between awkward forkfuls of noodles.

Tihn called out something to the man and woman at the table, and the man looked at his watch and cursed in Vietnamese. He stood up, dropped a few bills on the table from his wallet and hurried out the door.

Bayan stood, picked up the dishes and the bills and disappeared into the back of the restaurant-bar. She was back in a few seconds. She handed the bills to Tihn, who gave one back to her, and he nodded at me.

"This man has some questions," he said in English.

Up close I could see that she was not as young as she looked in the dark and at a distance, but she was still a clear-skinned beauty with an overly red mouth. I finished my noodles and followed Bayan back to the table where she had sat with the nearly fat man. I had brought my beer with me, and I asked her if she wanted a drink.

"I don't drink," she said in perfect English. "I pretend to drink. We have a profit margin to maintain, and my uncle is a good man."

"And you're telling me this because . . . ?" I prompted.

"You are not here to pay for personal pleasure," she said, looking at me. "My uncle says you want information and will pay."

I pulled out another twenty and handed it to her.

"You want twenty dollars' worth of information?" she asked.

I gave her another twenty. There wasn't much left in my wallet, and I was beginning to worry about gas money. I'd have to hit another ATM machine soon.

"Man known as the MP, when did he start coming in here?" I asked as she took the bills and put them in the pocket of her white blouse right over her left breast.

"No more than a month," she said. "He gets drunk fast. Talks GI Vietnamese, which is terrible, but he pays for the right to be obnoxious."

"You have daughters? Your uncle told me."

Bayan nodded, hands on the table. Her fingernails were long and very red.

"Got a picture?" I asked.

She looked surprised for an instant, then suspicious, and finally she reached under the table, came out with a small purse and opened it to pull out a small photo carrier. She opened it and showed me a picture of herself and two young women, one on either side of her. Bayan was smiling in the picture, a real smile.

"This one is at UCLA," she said, pointing to the girl who looked older. "And this one, the baby, is at Cal Arts. They are both A students. I had a boy too. He would have been twenty."

There was silence except for CNBC, where an older guy in a dark, rumpled suit was leaning forward on a table and talking about the stock market while a white ticker of letters and numbers ran by under him.

"What do you know about the MP?" I asked.

"Not much," she said. "But a few things. Dropped them when he wasn't careful. He tried to be careful. I got the feeling he expected someone to walk through the door and . . . who knows . . . shoot him, drag him away. Lot of GIs even now get a little crazy. It's something I understand."

"A few things?" I prompted.

"He had a wife," she said. "There was also a girl he referred to a few times, a Melisa. He was in trouble. He was frightened. He talked brave, talked about his honesty in Saigon, but he is a frightened man."

"Do you know where I could find him?" I asked.

"Yes," she said.

That wasn't the answer I had expected, but I kept a straight face, finished off my beer and asked if they had Vietnamese coffee, the really sweet kind. She said they did and ordered one for each of us from her uncle.

"You know where he is?" I repeated.

She smiled now, a sad, knowing smile.

"That, I can see, is more than a forty-dollar question," she said.

I had forty-eight more in my wallet. I gave her twenty-five more and showed her the inside of my wallet. She nodded in acceptance and took the twenty-five.

"You're not going to hurt him?" she asked. "Kill him?"

"No," I said. "I may save his life."

"He was here last night," she said as her uncle brought coffees. "He got very drunk and was very frightened. Something had happened. He wouldn't say what it was, just that it was terrible. I thought he would cry, and he was disturbing the other customers. He's good for at least eight dollars a night in drinks, but most of our customers are Vietnamese and a drinking white man talking about the war is not good for business."

"So . . . ?"

"We took him to Chi Nyugen's," she said. "I think he is there now, still sleeping. I'm not sure."

"Chi Nyugen's?"

She gave me an address. It was about a block from where we were sitting, down a side street. She didn't say so but I got the distinct impression that it was a "house of pleasure." We finished our coffees, and I pulled out my wallet to pay for the beer, noodles, and coffees.

"On the house," Bayan said. "You have any kids?"

I didn't know how to answer.

"Looks like I may," I said.

I went past the drunk, who was staring at a freshly filled glass, and nodded at Tihn, who gave me no response.

The sun was out. High in the sky. Late afternoon. Muggy and hot, and coming out of the darkness of Tihn's I was almost blind for a few seconds. I considered leaving the Firebird where it was but decided to drive to Nyugen's. I almost missed it. It was a three-flat building, pretty much like the other rectangles that surrounded it. It was about a block off of Alameda and there were no signs.

I went to the doorway and into the lobby. It looked like the lobby of any three-flat. The three bells had names next to them: Reed, Proshanski, O'Brien. I pressed O'Brien. A few seconds later a man came to the inner door and looked at me through its small glass windows. The man was Vietnamese.

"Bayan sent me," I said.

He opened the door and said,

"I know. She call. Come."

The inside of the apartment building beyond the inner door was completely Oriental, carpeting, paintings on the walls. The man was old and wearing a traditional Viet-

namese shirt and white pants. He moved quickly up a set of
stairs.

"He still asleep," the man whispered in front of a door.
"You take him away. He smells of death. I know smell. I
know fear. You take him away."

The old man opened the door and hurried away. I stepped
in, wondering if I should have brought my .38. It was too
late for wondering and there was no need.

The room was furnished somewhere between late Dragon
Lady and Fu Manchu's daughter. On the bed, sprawled out
and snoring, lay a big man, bigger than I had imagined
Grazzo might be. He lay on a black, silky-looking blanket
with red flowers sewn into the material. His head was
pressed into a pillow and he was on his stomach. Even with
the pillow, the snoring was loud.

I moved to the side of the bed and poked him. I wanted
to beat him with my fists or the nearest heavy Oriental object I could find, but I knew I wouldn't. At the moment, I
wanted information, not immediate revenge.

"Grazzo," I said.

He stirred, moaned and rolled on his side. I could see his
face now. He needed a shave. He needed a bath and he
needed fresh clothes. He was wearing blue slacks and a
badly wrinkled button-down-collar short-sleeved white
shirt, most of which wasn't tucked in.

"Grazzo," I said louder, reaching over to check for
weapons.

That got to him. He opened his eyes and sat up, his shoe-
less feet dangling over the edge of the bed, his face a cari-
cature of terror. There was almost a comic element to his
look because his thin hair was standing up and sticking out.

He threw a punch at me from where he was sitting and
barely missed my face, but he was in no position for battle.

"Hold it," I said. "I'm not here to hurt you. Not yet. Melisa sent me."

He was trying desperately to wake up and shake his hangover. His life might depend on it.

"They didn't send you?" he asked.

"If by they, you mean Barini, no," I said. "If they had, you'd be dead by now, wouldn't you?"

"Maybe," he said, running his hand through his mess of hair. "Maybe they'd ask questions first and then . . . Who are you?"

"My name's Jim Rockford," I said. "That ring any bells?"

"Jim Rockford," he repeated, closing his eyes. "Jim Rockford. Rene talked about you once or twice."

"What'd she say?" I asked.

"Good things," he said. "Help me up, will you?"

I helped him up. We stood facing each other.

"Why did you kill her?"

"Kill who?" he asked.

"Rene," I said.

"Rene's dead?" he said. "They killed Rene?"

He sat back down on the bed with a bounce and put his head in his hands, sobbing.

"I told her I could keep us safe," he said. "I promised her. We lived in something worse than fear. I knew fear in 'Nam. I was an MP. But this was worse. It went on for years. I wasn't ready for it. We fought. The last time I saw her, yesterday I think. We fought. I loved her, Rockford. I think she loved me."

"What happened, Grazzo?" I said without sympathy and thinking about what Melisa said he had tried to do to her.

"I remember we were in the car arguing," he said, looking around the room for the blurry memory. "We drove. I stopped in a parking lot. A restaurant that wasn't open till dinner. We were shouting. I got out, slammed the door, said I couldn't take it anymore. I walked away, found my-self at Tihn's."

"And Rene was alive when you left her in the car?" I asked.

"Alive, angry, looking away from me," he said through tears. "That's the last memory I have of her. What did they do to her?"

"Stabbed her," I said. "Tried to make it look as if Melisa did it."

"Melisa? She didn't even know where we were."

"I think I should make a call to a cop I know," I said. "He can bring you in, keep you safe and decide if you killed Rene."

"They killed her," he said. "They killed her."

He got up again and looked into my face. He grabbed my shirt and put his face inches from mine. I started to push his hands away and he said,

"You don't believe me."

"I don't know," I said. "I'm trying hard not to lose my temper here. Let's just call my friend Lieutenant Becker, get you someplace safe and maybe see a pair of U.S. Mar-shals."

"They didn't save Rene," he said. "They won't save me."

"Well, we don't have much choice, do we, Grazzo?"

He thought of another choice. The punch to my stomach came from nowhere. It was good. It was fast. Another punch with the other hand caught me in the gut, too. I went down in pain, wondering where the nearest toilet was because I was going to throw up. Another thought came, and I waited for the kick or punch to the face as I doubled over in pain and went to my knees.

Grazzo didn't hit me again. He went for the door and was on his way to who knows where. I couldn't follow him. I rolled on my side holding my stomach. I curled into a ball and lay there.

When I looked up, the old man who had led me to this room was kneeling next to me.

"Lie on floor," he said.

I tried, but I couldn't stop holding my stomach. With surprisingly strong hands, the old man laid me out on my back and put his hands on my stomach.

"You lie still," he said.

I didn't have much choice. His hands were working. I could feel heat. I could feel the pain going away, not completely, but going. I looked at the open doorway. A Vietnamese girl who couldn't have been more than twenty stood there in a white gown that was open to her navel. The gown was a see-through. I thought I might be dreaming or in a state of delirium. I blinked and the girl was gone. After a few minutes, the bad pain passed and the old man helped me up.

"Thanks," I said.

He nodded.

"You go now," he said. "You don't come back here, ever."

"I won't," I said.

"And the MP," he said. "You keep him away too. He is death."

"I'll do my best," I said, walking slightly doubled over and out the door.

I made my way down the stairs, through the small lobby, and outside. I was beginning to form a simple plan through my pain. Grazzo was on foot, hungover and looking like a mess. He didn't have that much of a start on me. Maybe. I'd drive around the neighborhood looking for him. He had no car. He had left Rene dead in the car he owned. My chances of finding him were good. Actually, they turned out to be better than good.

I went to the trunk to find a tire iron for the meeting I planned with Grazzo somewhere on the street. When I opened the trunk, I looked down at Grazzo's corpse stuffed into my trunk. There was something that looked like a bullet hole in his forehead, and his eyes were open, looking at me. I closed the trunk, got in behind the wheel and wondered what the hell I was going to do now.

CHAPTER FIVE

I got out, left the car sitting in front of Nyugen's pleasure house and walked to a gas station on Alameda. There was an outside phone. The walk took about ten minutes. It should have taken five. In spite of the old man's treatment, my stomach still hurt from Grazzo's punches. I needed change so I bought a package of Raisinets. I put the box of chocolate-covered raisins in my pocket instead of eating them.

Archer answered the phone eagerly and I told him my story.

"Doesn't sound too good, Rockford," he said.

I could imagine him adjusting his glasses and trying to think quickly of some way out of this to impress Beth.

"I hope you don't plan to charge me for that bit of shrewd observation," I said.

"Hey, ease up on the sarcasm," he said. "I'm here to save your sorry derriere. Call Becker. Tell him everything. Tell him you called him immediately and you're coming in with your lawyer. Where are you? I'll pick you up."

I told him and he said he'd be there in less than half an hour.

"Leave your car where it is," he said.

"That's why I'm calling from a phone booth," I said.

He hung up and I stood looking up at the Shell sign and decided to eat some Raisinets. I bought a bottle of Dr Pepper inside and the girl taking in gas money said,

"You look like you could use a doctor."

She was young. She was fat. She sounded like she came from the South. I thanked her and went back to the outside phone, where I dropped in my quarter, got down the last of the chocolate-covered raisins and called Dennis. He was on another line so I had to wait. It took me another quarter before he came on.

"Dennis, this is Jim."

"I don't like your voice," he said. "I've known you long enough to know I'm not going to like what you're going to tell me."

"Grazzo is dead," I said. "He's in the trunk of my car."

I gave him the address.

"You want to tell me how he got there?" asked Dennis.

"Someone shot him," I said. "Bullet in the head. Used a silencer or I would have heard it. I went looking for Grazzo, found him in an apartment. He used my stomach for karate practice and ran. When I got outside, he was gone. I went to my trunk to get a tire iron and go look for him. His body was in the trunk."

"Someone shot him on a street in Burbank during the day in a residential neighborhood, then opened your trunk, shoved him in and took off?"

"I guess that's about it," I said. "I think they figured it would be a while till I found the body. I'm coming in with my lawyer. You might want to get Donahue, Troy and Diehl. Diehl will want to be toastmaster at the roast."

"I'll come out and check the car with a couple of men and the Burbank police," said Dennis with a sigh. "Trunk open?"

"No," I said. "I left the keys to the ignition and the trunk under the visor on the passenger side. Always trying to make the life of our law enforcement officers a bit easier."

"Jim, Jim, Jim," Dennis said.

I didn't say anything. He hung up the phone and I waited, watching women in heels pumping their own gas and cleaning their own windows. I watched a kid in his twenties with a Ferrari fill it with super unleaded. He left his radio on full blast while he pumped, and the top of the Ferrari was down so the entire two blocks in any direction could enjoy a rapper go "Uh-uh-uh" and say it wasn't cool to kill women and most senior citizens.

Archer beat the police to the gas station. I had stepped inside so Dennis wouldn't catch a glimpse of me if he happened to come by first. I talked to the fat girl. She said she was from Oklahoma. I told her I was too. She said she was twenty-one and was going to acting school at night when she wasn't working.

"I know I won't be any kinda Demi Moore or like that," she said. "But I could be best friends or misunderstood or funny. You know? Like Rosie O'Donnell. Something like that."

"Anything is possible," I said.

A woman in heels came in and paid. A local police car drove by, siren blasting, turned the corner with a skid and headed down the street toward my parked Firebird.

When the woman in heels was gone, the cashier said,

"I could lose some weight," she said, "but an agent I talked to said I've got the face for best friend or maybe comedy. You know. One of the dumb young nuns with Whoopi Goldberg?"

"Anything is possible," I said again, looking out the window as a dark car pulled in next to the phone booth. A young black man in glasses, Archer, was driving.

"My ride," I said, heading for the door. "I'll look for you on television."

"I really want movies," she said. "But hey, I'll take what I can."

When I got into Archer's car, he pulled away slowly and looked at me. If possible, he seemed even younger than when I had last seen him, but this time he was dressed in a suit and tie and well-polished shoes.

"Look like a lawyer now?" he asked.

I nodded.

"You look like the rent collector for a slum landlord and I look like a potted palm someone forgot to water," I said.

"Got any ideas on who killed Grazzo or why?" he asked.

"None," I said. "Everyone wanted him alive unless there's some other thing going on that has nothing to do with Rene, the marshals and the mob."

"It'd be a coincidence," he said.

"It would be one hell of a coincidence," I agreed.

Fifteen minutes later we were back at the table in the interrogation room. Diehl looked madder than hell and I knew he was bursting to say "I told you so," or at least a slightly more original version of it. Troy and Donahue looked calm. Donahue had his hands folded on the table. The tape recorders came out and were turned on.

"My client found Mr. Grazzo through an informant," Archer said. "Mr. Grazzo was sleeping off a hangover in a house of prostitution. Mr. Rockford awakened him and Grazzo, a very large man who claimed to have been a former military policeman, began to punch my client in the stomach. Mr. Rockford went down and Grazzo stumbled out. My client took a minute or more to gather enough strength to follow Grazzo. Grazzo was not in sight. My client went to his trunk to get a tire iron with the plan of roaming the nearby streets in the hope of finding Grazzo.

When Mr. Rockford opened his trunk, he found Grazzo's body. He closed the trunk and, like a good citizen and a professional in the field of criminal investigation, he touched nothing, left the keys for the police and walked to the nearest phone. He immediately, as we agreed in this very room, called Lieutenant Becker. Of course he called me too. Questions?"

"Why'd you kill him, Rockford?" asked Diehl.

Archer nodded and I answered,

"I didn't kill him. I had no reason to kill him. I wanted to nail him for Rene's murder, remember. He wasn't any good to me or you dead. You lost a witness. I lost a killer who could save my client from a dumb murder charge."

"You found him," said Diehl. "Had a fight. You couldn't control yourself. You followed him outside, shot him and stuffed him in your trunk. Then you got the idea of calling it in and playing innocent. It won't work. We're going over that car and that body, and you're going to be our guest for a long time."

I looked at Donahue. He was strangely passive for a guy who had just lost his key witness in the Corlis murder case.

Diehl went on,

"The mob is even happy. No witness. You've got lots of motive, Rockford. You think Grazzo killed your old girlfriend. The mob, by your own admission, offered you money to find him."

"And prove he killed Rene," I reminded him. "I don't own a silencer and my guess is you'll find my .38 hasn't been fired. Diehl, even you can figure out that it would have been easier for me to just close the trunk, drive somewhere and dump his body."

A cop knocked at the door. Not the same one as before. This one was black, a wide end in a blue uniform. He looked at Archer and then at Diehl.

"Lieutenant Becker is on the phone," he said.

Diehl nodded and picked up the phone in front of him, looking at me the whole time.

"What've you got, Becker?" he said.

The silence was long, very long, and the look on Diehl's face changed from eager anticipation to confusion to a familiar anger. He hung up and glared at me.

"What are you pulling, Rockford?" he said.

"Would you care to make that accusation a bit more specific?" Archer said.

Donahue and Troy looked at Diehl impassively.

"There was no body in your trunk," Diehl said. "No body. No blood. There's no whorehouse at that address, and no one in the building remembers ever seeing you or Grazzo."

"Are you sure he was dead?" Archer whispered to me.

"I'm sure," I whispered back.

"Gentlemen," Archer said, "there has clearly been a misunderstanding here. There is no crime and, according to the agreement made earlier, my client would like to be back at work trying to find Mr. Grazzo."

"Who he says is dead?" said Diehl. "Let's try an arrest for filing a false report."

"Misdemeanor," said Archer. "Guilty plea. Fine. What do you get?"

"He's right," said Donahue. "Rockford, you're saying someone shot Grazzo on the street, stuffed him in your trunk, and then removed the body when you went to call the police?"

"Looks that way," I said.

"Why?" asked Donahue.

"To keep me from getting Grazzo alive and getting him to tell the truth," I said.

"Weak," said Donahue.

"But," Archer interjected, "true. I'm sure there are other

explanations, but my client is not responsible for finding them. That is the responsibility of the Los Angeles police and any other law enforcement agencies that might be involved. You have no corpse. You have no witnesses. Mr. Rockford may have had a drink or two too many."

I looked down at my hands and felt the pain in my stomach. I bit my lower lip.

"Go," said Donahue.

Diehl didn't say anything this time, but Troy added,

"We still want your client."

"When the time comes," said Archer, rising. "Gentlemen, it has, once again, been stimulating to talk to you."

The recorders went off again.

When we were back in Archer's car, he adjusted his thick glasses once again and looked at me.

"What the hell is going on, Rockford?"

"I don't know," I said. "My stomach hurts. Grazzo's gone. Melisa's still in a frame for killing Rene."

He started the car and said,

"Take heart, big man. We're going to bring Melisa out and as next of kin she's going to demand a copy of the autopsy of her mother."

"And she'll be arrested," I said.

"Nope," he replied as he drove badly at best, dangerously at his worst. "Got a contact in the medical examiner's office. Friend of a relative. Low-wage job handling bodies, but he's smart. He got a look at the autopsy finding on Mrs. Grazzo's body. Damndest thing. She'd been dead for at least three hours when someone stabbed her with that kitchen knife. No doubt. She was long dead when she got stabbed with the knife with your client's prints."

"I don't get it," I said.

"That makes two of us," said Archer.

"So we go get Melisa," I said. "Take me back to my car."

"Nope," said Archer. "We park and you do some reading."

He pulled over, reached into his briefcase and pulled out a file. For some reason, partly my aching stomach, I didn't want to look, but look I did while Archer stared ahead watching pedestrians go by.

"Simple enough," he said. "Just went to the library and made copies."

The copies were of twenty-year-old articles from New York newspapers. I stared down at them.

"You want a summary?" asked Archer.

He took my lack of response and the fact that I wasn't reading as a sign that he should speak.

"The articles are all about the Caralova, aka Corlis, murder trial. Corlis had gotten into an argument with a man named Wendkos. Wendkos had accidentally bumped into Corlis as they were leaving a restaurant. Wendkos said he was sorry and walked out. It was late. No one around. Corlis, one of his men, a Louis Aspermonte, came out of the restaurant after Wendkos and told him to get on his knees and apologize. Wendkos said no. Corlis shot him and walked away. There was a car parked at the curb two cars back. A witness sat in the car watching. Fortunately for the witness, Corlis and his men walked the other way. When they were gone, the witness got out of the car, went to Wendkos, who was dead, and screamed for help. The witness testified. Corlis went to jail. Witness disappeared, into the witness protection program. The witness was . . ."

"I know," I said. "Grazzo."

"No," said Archer. "The witness was Wendkos's wife, Adrienne. Flip a few pages."

I did. On the third or fourth page was an article with a photograph, a photograph of Rene Henley, only the caption read: Adrienne Wendkos.

"So," said Archer. "It wasn't Grazzo who was going to testify in the new trial for Corlis, if there is one. It was Adrienne Wendkos or, as you knew her, Rene Henley."

"What about Grazzo?" I asked.

"A little information," he said. "A few calls and some guesses. Grazzo was assigned to guard the witness while she was in the protection program. I guess they got close, not unusual under the circumstances, and he married her and went into the program with her. The rest is history."

"Not quite," I said. "She ran away from the program for a while and came to California. I met her. We were more than close and then she disappeared. My guess now is she was afraid Corlis's people had tracked her down. She went back to the feds, married Grazzo and disappeared."

"Sounds reasonable," he said. "But other things might sound reasonable too. Keep the file. Read it. Get your car and get your client in to ask for that autopsy report. Give me a call when you're ready. I'm having lunch with my cousin. He'll tell me O.J. tales. He's an assistant DA."

"Have a nice lunch," I said, clinging to the file and trying to ignore the dwindling but distinct pain in my stomach.

We drove back to my Firebird. If a crowd had gathered, it was gone now, as were the police. Archer waited while I found my keys under the passenger-side visor where Dennis had put them. I opened the trunk while Archer parked and waited.

Nothing. No blood. Everything looked like it was in the same place I'd left it—a small folding stool with a dirty orange canvas seat, a few old books I'd tried to sell at a used-book store and failed, maps, an ancient sweatshirt, which I used to use for working out and now used for cleaning the car's windows, and various other things. Then I noticed and called out to Archer: "Oregon."

He nodded, not having the slightest idea of what I meant. I went through the scattered maps of California cities, Washington State, Nevada. Oregon was definitely missing and I was definitely sure it had been there. I'd used it only weeks earlier. I closed the trunk and went over to Archer's car.

"Oregon is missing," I said.

"I gather this is not some sudden premonition about a state sliding into the ocean after an earthquake this morning," he said.

"My map of Oregon is missing," I said.

"They kill Grazzo, stuff his body in the trunk of your car, take the body out and notice a map of Oregon and say, 'Hey, I could use a map of Oregon.' And they pause to take it."

"No," I said, and Archer suddenly understood.

"Blood," he said.

"There must have been blood on the Oregon map," I said. "Maybe something else too I can't remember being in the trunk."

"Where does that get you, Rockford?" he asked reasonably.

"Helps convince me I'm not crazy," I said.

"Find the map of Oregon and find your killer," said Archer. "The map's gone by now, probably burned along with anything else they took from your trunk."

"Probably," I said.

"Advice from your lawyer, Rockford," Archer said. "Go see a doctor about your stomach. You look awful. And get Melisa in for that autopsy report. Take care of yourself. I talked to Beth last night. She asked if I was taking care of you."

"You're doing a good job, Fred," I said.

"See you soon, Jimmy," he said and pulled away, leaving me standing in the street.

Nobody but Angel ever called me Jimmy. Angel, my mother who died so young I barely remember her, and Rocky, my dad, who let out a Jimmy once in a while when he was about to say something he thought was particularly important. I knew it was "Jimmy" and "Fred" from that point on.

I knew a few doctors. Two of them were orthopedic surgeons who dealt with my wrecked knees. One was a retired general practitioner named Bohanan, from Nebraska. I had cleared him of a malpractice suit just before he retired. Client had claimed he had botched some office surgery on her arm and caused her a loss of use of arm and hand. Doctor had no record of treating her for her arm, just for a gynecological problem for which he recommended a gynecologist and gave her several names. The woman's lawyer claimed my client had altered the records. Anyone could see the woman's arm didn't function. Anyone could see the scars from the surgery.

Doctors could be brought in to testify that the woman had lost the use of her arm because of a poor procedure. The only problem was that when I found a surgeon to look at the victim he said he would testify that the operation had taken place at least six months earlier than the woman claimed. A little digging found that she had been botched up by her own ex-husband, the town doctor in a place called Price, Montana.

I stopped at the doctor's house. It was a small place reasonably on the way to Angel's. He answered the door himself when I knocked and urged me in. He was older than I remembered, but I was probably looking a bit older than he remembered. He reminded me of the old character actor Guy Kibbee. Looked enough and acted enough like him.

"Wife's in North Hollywood, visiting her sister," he said, ushering me in. "How's life treating you, Rockford?"

"Better than Job, worse than the President," I said.
"Stomach. Someone hit me. Someone big. Hit me hard. Hit
me deep when I wasn't ready."

Doc Bohanan nodded, and led me into his office, which
included an examining table.

"Treat a handful of old patients now and then," he said.
"But mostly I'm into tinkering with antique radios, fixing
'em up, selling 'em. Damned if I don't make as much as
when I had my full-time practice."

I pulled down my pants in pain and unbuttoned my shirt.
Doc Bohanan felt around my stomach with his fingers and
palm. It hurt.

"No vital organs seem to have collapsed," he said. "No
major bones or other vital parts seem to be broken or torn.
Doubt if you have internal bleeding or you'd be hurting a
lot more, but I could be wrong on that and you should be
in a hospital where they can check you out and be sure."

"No time now, Doc," I said, pulling up my pants, buttoning my pants and buttoning my shirt.

"Suit yourself," he said. "I'll give you something for the
pain. I suggest you eat soft and easy for a few days. And
remember, I said you should be in the hospital checking
this out."

He ambled off to his desk, opened it, put on his glasses
and read the labels on several plastic containers before he
found the one he wanted. He ambled back and handed the
container to me, saying,

"Two every four hours with water, probably not really
cold water. Don't eat anything for at least six hours and
then only soup or pureed spinach or some such."

"You think I'm crazy, don't you, Doc," I said standing,
pills in hand.

"No," he said. "Crazy is the guy who bought one of my
radios last year and claims he can get radio stations on it

from fifty years ago. He's being crazy. You're being stupid."

"I've got important reasons, Doc," I said, walking toward the the sink in the corner.

"Sure you do," he said, standing in the middle of the room while I took two capsules and got them down with a little water from a glass on the sink. "Fella who can hear Phil Harris and Alice Faye has his reasons too. Doesn't make him sane, and your having a reason doesn't make you smart."

"Thanks, Doc," I said, rinsing the glass and putting it back on the sink.

"I owe you plenty, Rockford," he said. "I know it. You know it. Take care of yourself."

We shook hands and I headed for Angel's retreat. I spotted the car following me minutes later on the highway. It was Donahue, and he wasn't trying especially hard to go unseen. In fact, I thought he actually nodded to me once when I looked at him in my rearview mirror.

It didn't matter. I was getting Melisa and we were going to get the autopsy report on her mother that would clear her. I parked under the stilted legs of the house and the U.S. Marshal parked just off of the highway and sat.

Angel greeted me in a state of frenzy.

"Jimmy," he said. "Thank God. You're here. I need you, Jimmy. I need you bad."

Angel was wearing his white suit, white shirt and black tie. He grabbed my arm and pulled me in the house, kicking the door closed.

"Remember that guy who was in here this morning? Lyons?"

"I remember," I said.

"Well, Mr. Lyons called an hour ago and said he and a friend wanted to see me."

"Sounds like new victims," I said.

"Sounds like the jig is up and maybe I should run," said Angel. "Lyons said he knows what I'm up to and the guy he's bringing is an art expert from some gallery. I'm nailed, Jimmy. I gotta run."

"Angel," I said, "My advice is to pull yourself together and face Lyons and his expert. Stand your ground. The paintings may not be great, but the clients bought them after seeing them."

"True," he said. "But I did say I was the great-great, you know what I mean, of Velasquez."

"Two choices, Angel," I said. "Stick to your story. I doubt if they can prove you're not a distant relation. Or, you can admit that you told a small lie, that you're in no position to pay anyone back, and each client has a portrait they were initially happy with. You go down, the clients get nothing and lose the value of their portraits. I'd say deal to call it square with the promise that you give up the painting scam."

"It's such a great scam, Jimmy," he said.

"Choice is yours, Angel," I said. "I've got to get Melisa."

"You're not going to be here when Lyons and his expert come?" he said, holding my sleeves and looking into my eyes.

"Your scam. Your jam. I've given you advice. I don't plan to be a party to your game. I've done that twice already. I'd like to be forgotten, not placed center stage. Count your money and your blessings and close up shop."

"Jimmy," he cried. "After what I've done for you."

"I need Melisa," I said.

Angel was sitting in a leather-and-metal chair, his head down. He motioned toward the rear of the house. Melisa wasn't in the pool. Melisa wasn't on the deck. Melisa wasn't anywhere. I went back to her bedroom, which I had already looked into. Nothing. Somewhere a phone rang. I paid no attention. I kept looking. Then Angel shouted, "It's for you."

There was a phone on the table next to the bed. I picked it up.

"Rockford?"

It was a man's voice, muffled, disguised.

"Yes."

"The girl is fine. The girl is healthy. The girl is happy. Listen."

There was a slight pause and Melisa came on.

"I'm okay," she said, not sounding frightened. "Please do what he asks."

The man came back on and said,

"Stop looking, go home. Make a living. This case is over. If you're stupid, you've got no guarantees."

He hung up. I stood for about a minute and moved toward the front door. My stomach was much better, but the rest of me was almost in the same state as Angel. Only I didn't show it. I was too mad to be afraid.

Angel was waiting for me in the hallway.

"Melisa's gone," I said.

"No," he said. "She's . . ."

"Gone," I repeated. "Someone came in here and took her while you were in your studio conning some old lady."

"Jimmy," he said. "I . . . I'm sorry."

"Good luck with Lyons and his friend," I said. "I'll come by or call later if I can."

When I got to my car, Donahue was standing at the driver's-side door. Sunglasses.

"The girl?" Donahue said.

"You don't know?" I returned.

"Know?"

"She's gone," I said. "I left her here and just came to get her. I was bringing her in. You know why I was going to bring her in? To demand the autopsy report on her mother. You know why I want the autopsy report on her mother?"

I waited for an answer and finally Donahue nodded a small yes and said, "Federal authorities have the autopsy report, all copies. Evidence in a very important case."

"Why doesn't that surprise me. Now, if you don't mind or if you do, I'm going to find Melisa," I said. "Either you have her or Barini has her or I don't know who the hell has her or why, but I'm going to find out."

Donahue moved away from my door. I got in and drove away, kicking gravel back at him in first gear.

I was angry with him. I was angry with Angel. I was angry with the dead Grazzo for not saving Rene's life. I knew I'd never think of her as Adrienne. For me she was and always would be Rene Henley. I was angry with Diehl, Troy, Donahue and, mostly, with myself. I couldn't figure out what was going on or why, and the only one I had to go after would probably have me killed or, worse, break my legs.

I had no choice. At least I couldn't think of one and didn't want to. I drove to the cove and pulled in front of my trailer. I had no visitors, at least not ones who had come by car. Mrs. Bailey was writing away. She looked up and waved. Then Travis hurried across the parking lot to catch me as I was about to step through my door. He was huffing and puffing and holding down his cowboy hat to protect it from a wind that didn't exist. He looked a little like Walter Brennan this morning and I half expected him to say something like "Consarn rustlers."

Instead, he panted and came out with,

"Some men, three," he said. "Early in the morning, six-twenty-two. Went into your trailer. Stayed about fifteen minutes. We heard noises. I called nine-one-one. By the time they finally got here, the three were back in their car and gone."

"Thanks, Travis," I said.

"Just logging your visitors, wanted and unwanted, is taxing our vitals," he said.

"Then I suggest you stop doing it," I said.

"Hell no," he said. "First you. Then maybe Mrs. Bailey. Then me and my Mrs. I can't say we'd be unhappy if you sold and moved, but we're not moving."

"Thanks for telling me about the visitors, Travis," I said.

He didn't answer. Hand on his hat, he headed back to his trailer. A few people were on the beach. No one was in the water. I was hungry and felt well enough to eat, but I was going to do what Doc Bohanan said.

The trailer was a mess. When Troy had gone through it, he had been careful to leave everything in place when he was finished. All he had taken was a pair of Melisa's underpants. Whoever had gone over it this time was not only in a hurry, they had a message to send. They had looked and not found what they were looking for, because there was nothing to find and they had torn and tossed to let me know they could make my life short and miserable.

The trailer had been tossed and torn before. I had no insurance for the contents. Even the insurance companies I sometimes did jobs for wouldn't insure me. It would take time. It would take work. It would take money to put it back together.

I checked the cookie jar. They hadn't taken my .38. I loaded it and found my holster in the rubble near my closet. I put on the holster and gun and checked the phone. It had been ripped out.

They had probably eaten the cottage cheese in the refrigerator. I didn't check. I went into the bathroom, used it, washed, looked at the angry face in the mirror and warned it to settle down, think. I knew it wouldn't listen.

I left the trailer. Donahue was sitting in his car waiting. I went to the car and he opened the window.

"We've got to stop meeting so often," I said with more than a touch of anger I couldn't hold back. "People will start to talk. You gay, Donahue?"

"No," he said calmly. "But my brother-in-law is. And he's got HIV. I don't like gay jokes."

"Neither do I. I just need someone to be angry with. My trailer's been tossed, torn up," I said. "You can look if you like. I think I know who did it. I think I know who has Melisa. I don't know why. She doesn't know anything, and the only witness against Corlis is dead. You're going to follow me and I'm going to lose you. Now it's your turn."

He looked at me and said nothing. I got into Rocky's pickup truck and hit the highway with the federal car behind me. Fifteen miles down the road I found a steep hill I remembered. I geared down and started up the hill, four-wheel drive grinding. There wasn't a chance he could follow me. There wasn't all that great a chance I could make it, but I did, got hooked for an instant on the rim of the hill, hit the gas and the front wheels pulled me over the top with a slight scratching sound of undercarriage against gravel.

Donahue would drive till he came to a road that would take him into the hills. The road, I know, was about three miles down. By the time he figured out where I had gone up the hill to the road, I'd be long gone and on my way.

I caught a branch bank just before it closed and took out a few hundred dollars, leaving not much to keep the account alive. Then I drove to Sunset Boulevard. I had an idea of how I might reach John Barini and I dearly wanted to reach John Barini.

The office building on Sunset where I had been brought

by Wright the poet to see Barini was open. I found a button and a room number for the building manager. I didn't
press the button. The office was on the fourth floor. I
walked up. It hurt, but I wanted a little pain to remind me
of how I was making a mess of the job, how I had lost
Melisa, lost Rene, lost most of the things I owned in the
trailer. When I got to the fourth floor, I stood for a few seconds, took the small jar Doc Bohanan had given me, opened
it and popped a few pills into my palm. I looked around for
a rest room or a water fountain. There wasn't any. The
building superintendent's office was clearly marked. It was
also open.

"You the building manager?" I asked the guy behind the
desk. He was reading a book.

I figured him for about sixty. He was big. He was balding and what hair he had left was still reasonably dark. He
had a mustache, a nice full one but not for show. He looked
like an executive, though he was wearing a neat yellow
pullover and, when he stood, I could see he was wearing a
pair of navy pants. He was not dressed for major repairs.

"You the building manager?"

"Yes," he said with a smile of false teeth. "You want an office?"

"Water," I said, showing him my pills.

"Help yourself," he answered, nodding at a door to his
right.

I went through the door. The room was small, a broom
closet with a sink. There were rust stains in the sink. I
turned on the cold tap, threw the pills into my mouth and
used my hands for a cup to take in some tepid water and
wash them down. I came back into the office, closed the
broom closet door and faced the big man behind the desk.

"You want to rent an office?" he asked with a smile like
a used-car salesman in a television comedy.

"I want to send a message to Barini," I said.

The smile on his face fell away.

"The police were already here," he said. "They asked about someone named Barini and one of my empty offices. I don't know anything."

I pulled out my gun and aimed it at him.

"I'm not asking you to tell me where to find him," I said. "You probably don't know. I just want him to get a message to him. I think you can do that. In fact, you better be able to do that. I'm not a patient man. Crazy bears are holding paws and dancing in a circle in my stomach. My home has been torn apart. A woman I . . . a woman's been murdered and a girl has been kidnapped. In short, I am in one bad mood. How do I reach Barini?"

"Mister," the man said, holding out his hands, "you've got me wrong."

"I've got you right. He didn't just stumble on that office."

"I've got a family," he said.

"Most people do," I answered. "If not shooting people because they had families was the rule, nobody would be shot. Where would the homicide detectives come in. What would they do?"

"Mister," he said, "you're crazy."

"Mister," I answered, "I think you're right. Now I'm seeing dancing mice on your desk and bright lights all over the place. You're dealing with a crazy man with bears inside him and mice in front of him."

I moved forward and he stepped back in fear. I checked the number on his phone. I'd write it down as soon as I left.

"Get me a number I can call," I said. "I'll call you here in an hour. Tell Barini my name is Rockford. He'll know it. If you don't have a number when I call . . ."

"Okay," he said. "Call in an hour."

I put my gun away, went into the hall and closed the door. As soon as I was alone, I dropped the crazy act. I held on to my anger, though. I didn't want to think of what would replace it. I ran down the stairs, making as much noise as I could. I went all the way down two flights feeling the pain in my stomach and wondering if I could take a few more of Doc Bohanan's pills. When I got well out of the building manager's earshot, I took off my shoes and went slowly back up the stairs. By the time I got to the manager's door and put my ear to it, he was well into his conversation and apologizing to someone.

"Rockford," the manager said. "So what do I do?"

I opened the door and said,

"You hand me the phone," I said, pointing my gun at him.

The man's false teeth clacked and he dropped the phone on the desk. I picked it up.

"This is Rockford. I want to see Barini."

The person at the other end covered the mouthpiece and there was a long pause. Then the voice of a man, a voice I didn't recognize, said,

"Go outside. Wait. Someone'll pick you up in about fifteen minutes."

"Fifteen minutes," I said and hung up the phone.

"You don't have to shoot me now," said the manager, his hands in the air.

"No one was going to shoot you," I said. "Put your hands down and go home to your family if you've really got one."

"I really do," he said.

"Well, maybe that's more than I can say," I said.

"Look," he said. "What was I supposed to do? My cousin Augie works for Barini. Augie calls, says how's the kids and wife and we need an office. I know who Augie works for. I don't say no."

I put on my shoes, left him standing and went down the stairs and out the front door to wait for a mob boss, who would not be happy with me, to have me picked up. The chances of my being alive at the end of the day were not great, but I had a plan, a weak one, but it might work.

I held on to my anger, touched my .38 and waited.

CHAPTER SIX

THE car, a big white Lincoln, pulled up in front of the entrance to the office building and the passenger-side door opened. All the windows were tinted, which is not uncommon in this part of the world. I went to the car, got in, closed the door and looked at blond Mr. Wright, who was impeccably dressed as if he were about to go out for a night of go-go dancing and challenge John Travolta to a tango solo contest.

There was soft classical music playing, an opera. The tape light was on. Wright drove and said gently,

> "I reason, earth is short
> and anguish absolute,
> and many hurt;
> But what of that?"

"Shakespeare," I said, doing all I could to stay calm.

"Emily Dickinson," he said.

"I don't know if I understand," I said. "But did you just confess to something?"

"Read *Understanding Poetry,*" he said. "An old book but a good one."

I didn't answer. He turned up the volume slightly.

"Listen," he said. "Here."

He went silent and we listened as we drove.

"Domingo," he said. "Such strength. You know, Rockford, it's another one of those ironies. I work mainly for Italians, but they don't seem to appreciate opera. They don't read."

"Television," I said.

"Maybe," he answered. "When we get where we're going, you leave your gun and your holster in the car."

"I don't think so," I said.

"Then I'll have to kill you," he answered, looking at me.

"I'll leave the gun," I said.

"Good," he said with a smile. "I like you."

"I can tell," I said.

We listened to the opera the rest of the way to a road off of Laurel Canyon. I knew most of the roads, but not this one. For one reason, it didn't go very far. It dead-ended after two houses. Three cars were parked, including Wright's red sports car. Wright parked the white Lincoln next to it and looked at me.

"What if I change my mind?" I said. "What if I feel more comfortable talking to Barini with a safety net?"

I had been watching Wright from time to time as we drove. He seemed simply to be listening to his opera, humming along occasionally and not paying too much attention to me.

I was wrong. I felt the pressure on my left side, about kidney high, and looked down. The blade in Wright's hand was long, thin and looked very sharp.

"Rockford," he said in disappointment. "I told you I like

you. Calm down and don't do anything that's going to get blood all over the white upholstery."

I opened my jacket, unstrapped my holster and dropped it and the .38 on the seat as I stepped out of the car. Wright was right with me and around the car almost before I stood up as straight as I could. The pain was still there, in my stomach, but not as sharp. Doc Bohanan's pills were kicking in.

Wright's knife was nowhere in sight. He didn't say anything, just walked to the nearest house in the cul-de-sac. It wasn't much of a house—one story, dark wood, a picture window in the living room looking out into the street and a driveway.

We went to the front door. Wright opened it and we walked in.

The living room was through an arch on our right. There were three steps down into it. It was decorated in early 1950s, not one of my favorite decades for furniture, but the Cleavers would have been happy here.

There were three men. Two, Barini and an old man with glasses and a cane leaning against his leg, sat on a sofa facing us as we came in. The third man was big, with Schwarzenegger muscles under his white short-sleeved shirt. He was standing next to the sofa.

They were definitely waiting for me. Two judges and an executioner.

"Rockford," said Barini. Wright stood several paces behind me as I entered the green-carpeted room. "You failed and now you want to irritate me. You have some reason?"

"Grazzo is dead," I said.

No one looked surprised.

"Unfortunate," said Barini. "You got some proof he murdered his wife?"

"No," I said. "I talked to him before he died. I don't think he killed her."

The old man next to Barini said something in Italian. Barini listened respectfully, straining to understand, and nodded. Then he returned to me with,

"We've still got a problem," Barini said. "It's possible a judge will allow the original witness's testimony to be read at the hearing for a new trial."

"Adrienne Wendkos from the grave," I said.

Barini shrugged and said,

"You've been doing research. That's good. My friend says they can try to introduce her testimony even if she's dead. My friend here says it's possible, but we can say the basis of Mr. Corlis's case is proving Adrienne Wendkos committed perjury, and it isn't legal to have someone testify who can't be cross-examined if that's the heart of your case."

Barini looked at the old man, who nodded.

"What do you want, Rockford?" Barini asked.

"Oregon," I said.

A look came over the face of Barini that suggested he had allowed a lunatic into the house. The old man with the cane looked at me without emotion.

"Oregon?" he asked.

"Whoever killed Grazzo took my map of Oregon," I said. "It had his blood on it. When they took the body away, they took the bloody map and who knows what else."

"So you come in here for a map of Oregon?" asked Barini.

"I'll make a deal," I said. "You keep Oregon. Give me the girl."

"The girl?"

"Don't I speak clearly enough for you? I want Melisa."

"What've you got to deal with, Rockford?" Barini asked.

"Did you kill Rene?" I asked.

"Me, personally?"

"No, Wright, or that Terminator in the corner," I said.

"You're some kind of crazy man, Rockford. You've got guts, but your brain is working part time. I could have you killed and dumped and go out for a nice dinner."

"If you didn't kill her," I said, "who did?"

"Who did?" Barini repeated.

"That's what I want to find out," I said. "I find out you didn't have her killed and you've got evidence Frank Corlis didn't kill the witness that could keep him behind bars."

"They still have her testimony from before," Barini said with interest.

"So your lawyer knows he can keep the testimony from the first trial out of a new trial. And my guess is he may be able to get the hearing board to look the other way when the state tries to enter the trial testimony, especially if I can prove you and your friends had nothing to do with killing Rene."

The old man leaned over and whispered to Barini, who nodded and said,

"You really believe we didn't kill the Wendkos woman?"

"I don't know, but I'll give you the benefit of the doubt," I said. "For a while."

"Pretty thin, Rockford, but I'll give you two days. My people think something should be done about your telling the federals and the cops about my being here."

"Some police have big ears and full wallets," I said.

Barini shrugged, adjusted his tie and said,

"You can tell your cop friend we didn't kill Adrienne Wendkos," he said.

"Grazzo?" I asked.

"We don't know anything about that," he said, making it clear that he knew a great deal about it.

"Melisa," I said.

"Yeah, the girl," he said. "Tony, show him."

The man from muscle beach stepped toward me. I wanted to step back. Anything but my stomach. I stood my ground. The big man handed me an envelope.

"The way they can develop and print those things so fast is amazing," said Barini. "Got those in a one-hour photo place."

I opened the envelope and looked at a stack of photographs. If you set them up to flip through, you'd see Melisa coming out of Angel's house with United States Marshal Troy, getting into his car and driving away. She seemed to be going willingly.

"Good pictures," Barini said, looking at the strong man, who couldn't hold back a smile of pride. "Now, what bothers me is why does it look like she's going with him without giving him a problem? If you look close, she even looks like she's smiling."

He was right. On the phone she hadn't seemed frightened either.

"What's going on, Rockford?" asked Barini.

"I'll find out," I said.

"You do that," said Barini. "And don't do any more stupid things. And don't look for me again. I told you, we'll find you. You look for me and I'm gonna have to get upset."

He looked around the room and shook his head and then said,

"Looks like a place one of my old aunts would have lived in when I was a kid," he said. "Place even smells bad. Don't try to find the real estate dealer or who owns the house, Rockford. I'm being nice to you. You be nice to yourself. Go find who killed Adrienne Wendkos and do it before the feds or the cops cover it up."

"What were you looking for in my trailer?" I asked.

Barini shook his head and said something to the old man before turning back to me.

"Maybe," I went on, "you were looking for a copy of an autopsy report."

"Maybe," Barini said, sitting up.

"There aren't any copies," I said. "The feds have them all."

"You got anything else to say?" Barini asked, a touch of impatience in his voice.

"I want three thousand dollars for everything you tore up in my home," I said.

Barini shook his head and simply said, "Tony."

The big man with the big arms was standing to my left looking at me. He took another step closer. I knew Wright was behind me. I figured one of the two had killed Grazzo. I wanted to know why, but I didn't ask. What I wanted most was to get out of there alive and look for Melisa.

"Figure yourself lucky you're walkin' out of here instead of crawling," said Barini. "That is if you turn around now and move fast."

I nodded at Barini and the old man, turned and walked past Wright, who followed me.

When we were outside, it was starting to get dark. Wright looked at the sky and said, "You handled yourself very well in there, Rockford. If I were a betting man, I would have given the odds at six to four that you'd be dead or on the way to a hospital."

I walked back to the Lincoln, put my holster back on before I got in and then sat next to Wright, who looked over his shoulder to back out and recited,

> "Truly, My Satan, thou art but a Dunce,
>   And dost not know the Garment from the Man.
>   Every Harlot was a Virgin once,
>   Nor canst thou ever change Kate into Nan."

I didn't try to guess who the poet was and I wasn't sure what, if anything, he was trying to tell me, but I was pretty sure it was something.

"William Blake," he said, "from *The Gates of Paradise.*"

"It's never too late to pick up some culture," I said with sarcasm.

"Sometimes it is," he answered.

There was only one more exchange between us as we drove back to the office on Sunset, where Rocky's pickup was parked. *The Forge of Destiny* was playing.

"Why did you kill Grazzo?" I asked.

"Why can we cryogenically freeze the petals of a rose and crack them off like crisp, cold paper?" he answered. "Let us say Grazzo came out of that Vietnamese whorehouse, bumped into me while I waited for you to come out. He hit me, went for my gun. I hit him harder, better, shot him with a silenced gun and considered what to do with him. Your car was parked at the curb. I opened it with one of my picks and deposited the body. You really want Oregon back?"

"Keep it," I said.

"I've got something better," Wright said. He handed me a brown envelope.

"I'll pass on being on the payroll," I said, dropping it in his lap.

"Open it," he said. "It's interesting."

I opened it. It was a copy of the photographs of Troy taking Melisa from Angel's house. I pocketed them.

> *"Seguir el camino que se aleja de todo,*
> *donde no este atajando la angustia, la muerte, el invierno*
> *con sus ojos abiertos entre el rocio."*

"I got the *muerte* part," I said.

He gave it to me in English:

"And, pride, what have I now with thee
An other brow may even inherit
The venom thou has poured on me—
Be still my spirit."

"A warning?" I asked.

"Poe," he said.

When I got home, the place was no longer a mess. Someone had not only cleaned it and carted away the rubble, but a new, bigger television set sat where the old, broken one had been, and new, if slightly tacky, furniture was in place. My refrigerator was stocked and my clothes were neatly hung. My laundry had even been done and my phone was working again. There were two messages. One from Angel saying,

"Good news. Call me from someplace safe."

The other message was a man's voice saying,

"You're too late, Rockford. Keep looking for surprises in your trunk. One of these days, the surprise will be you."

Night had fallen. I went down the empty beach to the phone and called Angel. I hoped he had some information, a call from Melisa. If not, my first stop in the morning was with Troy and Donahue. A woman answered,

"Yeah."

Noise, cackling, laughter, music behind her made it a little difficult to hear.

"Let me talk to Angel," I said.

"Angel?" she asked. "This a gag? You want Heaven, you better dial 911-GOD."

She thought this was very funny. Her laughter was a small choke.

"You're in Angel's house," I said. "Get him."

"The artist? The guy with the curly beard? He's pretty cute," she said.

"He's very cute," I agreed. "Now, please get him."

"Listen," she said, the sound of one mixed drink too many in her voice, "you're not very funny."

"I'm sorry," I said. "I got beaten, found a murdered man, lost a young girl and had a run-in with a mob boss. It's been a bad day."

"You're not funny," she said again. "I should know. My partner and I write for some of the top sitcoms. You need a gag and a topper every ten seconds."

"Your profession explains a lot about this conversation," I said. "Now, for the last time, please get Angel."

The next voice I heard, after about four minutes of laughter, noise and merriment, was Angel.

"Hello," he said cheerily.

"Angel, it's Jim," I said.

"Jimmy," he said brightly. "Come on over. You can't believe this party."

"Angel, did you hear from Melisa? Anything about her?"

"No, Jimmy. I'm sorry."

"And you don't remember anything about her leaving?"

"Only that she must have gone quietly," Angel said. "Come on over here. Have a little fun. Take your mind off things a few hours."

I almost considered it.

"No, thanks," I said.

"You want to know why I'm throwing a party?" he asked, his voice dancing.

"Why not?" I said, looking toward the pier. It looked like a giant abstract artwork in the moonlight instead of the daytime rusting hulk it was. Mrs. Bailey and the Travises were inside their trailers, and the lights were on in the bar down the beach.

"Remember Lyons?"

"Vividly."

"Well, like I told you," Angel went on over the noise behind him, "he came back today with a long-haired guy, maybe forty or fifty, in washed white pants and a designer silk pullover, white and blue. Lyons says the guy's name is Miranda, Peter Miranda. It sort of rings a bell. Anyway, without asking, Lyons leads this Miranda to the stack of paintings I've got leaning against the wall, you know, the ones I made when I was supposed to be doing the portraits. Just all kinds of colors all over the place. I've got their faces to the wall. Before I can stop him, Lyons is showing Miranda the paintings. They whisper. I sweat. I'm thinking of stories, decide to act it out and then run like hell if I can get them to leave or even let me go through a side window and run."

"Sounds like your usual plan, Angel," I said.

"But Jimmy, they turn to me and Miranda—he's got this deep voice, no smile, dark face, deep cheeks, scary looking—says, 'Mr. Lyons is right. You're perpetrating a fraud.' "

" 'Fraud,' I said with indignation, knowing my hair is wet with sweat. I can't stop that when I get scared."

"I know," I said.

" 'You've sold indifferent, second-rate work to your clients,' said Miranda. 'And you've kept the really creative work for yourself.' I look at the two of them like they're loony bugs, and Lyons says, 'We will keep the fraud to ourselves on one condition, Mr. Martinez. You will sell me those works against the wall at a fair price and contract with me to represent you at a thirty-percent commission for me and my gallery.' "

"I'm standing there looking at two loonies and not knowing what to say when Lyons pulls out a checkbook and starts writing while he keeps talking.

" 'I think you have little choice,' he said. I guess I nodded. I don't know. The next thing I know, I'm holding a check from the Lyons Gallery on Rodeo Drive for one hundred and fifty thousand bucks. I'm just standing there with my mouth open staring at it while Lyons and Miranda pick up the paintings in the corner.

" 'I've just bought this series outright,' says Lyons. 'Mr. Miranda and I suggest you do no more of those portraits you've been selling and concentrate on your abstract work.' Then he pulls a contract out of nowhere, holds out the pen he wrote the check with and hands the contract to me. I'm a little slow sometimes and I was scared, but I ain't Papa Martinez's idiot son. That distinction belongs to my brother Juan. I read it. I sign it. They leave. Lyons says he'll be back and let me know when he schedules a show. Says he needs maybe six more paintings. I say he'll have them in three weeks. Truth is, Jimmy, I could have knocked them off after lunch and still had time to watch *Wheel of Fortune*. They left. I ran for the bank, cashed the check, called a bunch of people and . . ."

He must have held the phone up so I could hear the noise even better and louder.

"Hear that?" he said joyfully.

"I hear it," I said.

"Get over here," he said.

"Angel, did Melisa say anything, get a phone call, make a phone call before she left?"

"I don't know," Angel said. "I don't think so. Wait. Maybe she got a call. The phone rang when I was painting Mr. Lionel Herzog, the furniture guy. There was nothing on the machine when I checked later. I figured whoever it was had dialed a wrong number or changed their mind or something."

"Or Melisa picked up the phone," I said.

"Could have happened," Angel said. "Like the new television?"

"You fixed my place?" I said.

"Stopped by on the way back from the bank," he said. "Wanted to show you the wad so big you could break an arm falling off of it. I saw the toss, went home, called a cleaning company, the phone company, and Alex Mancuso's television and appliances, and Sweeny's Furniture. Paid cash. Top dollar."

"Thanks, Angel," I said, suddenly feeling a lingering, tender ball of pain in my stomach.

"Not coming to the party?" he asked, sounding genuinely disappointed.

"Not tonight," I said. "I've got things to think about and a stomach ache."

"Melisa," he said.

"Melisa," I said.

"I'm sorry I lost her," Angel said sincerely. "I'd give all I've got left of the bundle to get her back. Believe me."

"All?"

"Well, most," he said. "And remember, Lyons is going to sell my paintings. There'll be plenty more."

"Be careful, Angel," I said.

"What could go wrong?" he said with confidence.

"That's what Nixon said."

"There's a young lady waving at me across the studio," Angel said. "I gotta go."

He hung up before I could thank him again. I called Dennis.

His wife answered. We chatted. She told me Andy was doing great and she was proud of him. I said I was too. Then Dennis came on.

"Dennis," I said, "Melisa's gone."

"I know," he said. "Troy and Donahue came in. They said you told 'em."

"Did they say Troy was the one who took her?" I asked.

Very long pause.

"No, they didn't. Can you prove it?"

"Set up one of our fun meetings for the morning, say ten. Archer and I'll be there with proof and some questions and maybe a few answers you'll like and a few you may not like as much."

Dennis sighed and said,

"I'll work on it now. If you don't hear back from me, that means it's set up. Do me a favor, Jimbo. Come up with something or I'm in even bigger trouble I don't need."

"I've got something," I said. "Good night."

My last call was to Archer. I had to pull out his crumpled card and I dialed. He answered on the second ring.

"Working late?" I said.

"Rockford? I could say I was doing an Abe Lincoln working on your case, checking to see if there was a full moon, that kind of thing. Truth is, this is my apartment. Calls go through from the number you called to my house if I'm not in the office, which, at this point, consists of an answering machine."

"When you're done with my case, you'll have enough money to rent an office, as soon as I can pay you," I said.

"You're strictly pro bono," he said. "Small payback to Beth."

"Archer . . ." I said.

"Fred'll be fine," he said. "I feel like we're already old friends. You know how to age a newcomer, Jimmy."

"How are you set for another meeting with the three godfathers of criminal investigation tomorrow at ten?"

"My calendar is clear," he said.

"Place across from the station," I said. "Diner."

"I remember."

"I'll meet you there at nine-thirty."

"Nine-thirty," he repeated.

I hung up, went back to my trailer, hid the photographs, got ready for bed and went to sleep early after taking two more of Doc Bohanan's pain pills. I slept with my gun and holster on the chair next to the bed. I had locked the trailer door and put a chair under the knob. It wouldn't stop anyone from coming in, but it would make enough noise to wake me.

I had come to the conclusion that the pain pills were a good part of why I was sleepy. I didn't care. My last thoughts were that I had a sore stomach from Grazzo's punches. I'd get over the pain. Grazzo wouldn't get over his, if he had any.

The next thing I knew it was morning and the phone was ringing.

"It's on," Dennis said.

The clothes in my closet and drawers had been cleaned and pressed by Angel's crew. I shaved, showered, dressed casually in a tan slacks and a blue pullover and headed for the diner. I was there at ten to nine. Fred Archer was already there reading the *Times* and drinking coffee. The place was reasonably crowded with cops, people who work for the cops, and people who get arrested by cops. Archer had a booth.

"Good morning, Jimmy," he said.

"Good morning, Fred," I said, sitting.

My stomach was much better now and I was hungry. I ordered the special—English muffin, two eggs over, two slices of bacon, two hot cakes and coffee. Fred Archer ordered the same, putting his newspaper aside with a shake of his head, saying,

"I thought people back East were crazy. I'm sending this paper to my brother."

We spent the next twenty minutes talking about the meeting. I handed him the envelope with the photographs, and he asked me questions after examining them carefully through thick lenses.

"You see something odd about these pictures?" he asked.

"Melisa looks as if she's being kidnapped without a struggle or a protest and with a smile on her face," I said.

"Something else," Archer said, adjusting his glasses.

I looked at the photographs again and didn't see anything else. I handed them back. He put the photos back in the envelope and put the envelope in his briefcase.

We were early so for about ten minutes we talked about family, friends, baseball and poetry. I asked him if he knew any poetry. He said,

"Not much."

"Anything you can remember?"

"I guess," he said.

He recited. I wrote in my notebook and thanked him.

I insisted on paying the bill. He didn't argue, and off we went.

We crossed the street and were led to the familiar interrogation room. It was beginning to feel like a regular work schedule. There was one difference. Donahue and Diehl were at the far end of the table. A cop stood in the corner. There was no Troy.

While the tape recorders were coming out, I said,

"Downsizing?"

"What?" asked Diehl.

Donahue understood.

"Marshal Troy is working on a lead," he said.

The tape recorders were rolling now. Archer touched my arm to keep me from saying more. I shut up.

"First," Archer said, "my client has informed you that you have a leak in the department, one who has access to our meetings and information on the investigation of the murder of Adrienne Wendkos, also known as Rene Henley, also known as Rene Conforti, Rene Grazzo, Rene Jacobs and who knows what else."

"We're aware of the leak," said Donahue. "Captain Diehl is working to plug it. That's not new news."

"My client—with your tape recorder off—is willing to solve a murder for you," said Archer.

"No," said Diehl.

Donahue, wearing the same suit he had worn the day before, turned off his tape recorder. Archer nodded to me.

"About my height, lean, strong, blond, about forty, but he could hold his age well," I said. "Uses the name Wright."

This meant nothing to Diehl, but I could see that it meant a lot to Donahue, who took a long time before carefully asking his next question.

"Who did he kill?"

"Grazzo," I said. "Possibly Rene too."

"How do you know?" asked Donahue.

"He told me."

"That he killed Grazzo?"

"He made it a what-if when he told me, but the details were there," I said.

"Never quite came out and said, 'Mr. James Rockford, I murdered Irving Grazzo,' right?" said Donahue.

"Not exactly," I said.

"So it's just your word. We don't even have evidence that Grazzo is dead, Rockford. Just your report. There's no body. Even if we find a body and you were willing to go on a stand and testify," said Donahue, "a decent mob lawyer would crucify you, with your record and no witnesses to this Wright's confession. Even if he had confessed, it would be your word against his and neither of you is a member of the church choir."

"You know who Wright is," I said.

Donahue turned on the tape recorder and didn't respond to my statement.

"My client wants to speak to his client, Melisa Wend-kos," Archer said. "If she is being held on some charge, we would like to know what it is and would still like to see her or, to put it as more than a request, we wish to see her immediately."

"We don't know where your client is," said Diehl. "It's not our problem if you lose a client. You could have turned her over to us when you still had her."

Archer removed the envelope of photographs from his briefcase and slid the envelope across the table to Donahue, who opened it with Diehl looking over his arm. Donahue put the photographs in a neat stack and returned them to Archer, who let them lie on the table.

"Would Captain Diehl like to amend his statement that he doesn't know where Mr. Rockford's client is?" Archer asked.

"Neither Captain Diehl nor I wish to amend the statement," said Donahue.

Archer shrugged.

"My client saw John Barini yesterday," Archer said. "As a good citizen, he feels it is his responsibility to so inform you."

"Bumped into him at a hot dog stand?" asked Diehl.

"No," said Archer. "Sought him out through a source the police could have found had they done the work my client did."

Diehl folded his arms and sat back in disgust, saying, "Bull."

"I don't think Barini had Rene killed," I said.

"This guy Wright told you," said Diehl. "You believed him."

"Barini could have killed me," I said. "I was less than nice to him. I thought he had killed Rene. I thought he had taken Melisa. Now I don't think he did either, and I think killing Grazzo was our Mr. Wright's mistake. Now, Barini still wants me to prove that Grazzo killed his wife."

"Gonna be hard with no Grazzo," said Donahue.

"I'm going to try, Marshal Dillon. I'm going to try," I said.

"My client has given you information and will even tell you where he met Mr. Barini, though we doubt if you will find him there or any trace of him," said Archer. "My client has once again told you that you have an informant in your ranks. My client has identified the killer of the still missing Irving Grazzo. Now, Mr. Rockford wants to see his client."

"We need time," Donahue said.

"Why?" Archer asked.

"We need time," Donahue said.

Archer rose, turned off his tape recorder, put it in his briefcase as Donahue turned off his recorder. Archer touched my arm. I stood.

"How much time?" asked Archer.

"A day, possibly two," said Donahue, who was doing a better job, but not a perfect one, of hiding his anger than Diehl.

"Two," Archer agreed. "If we haven't heard from you in two days . . ."

"I understand," said Donahue.

"By the way," Archer said, "we have copies of these photographs in a very safe place, so if you were thinking of confiscating these and then misplacing them before I can get a court order for their return, forget it."

Archer and I left. Dennis wasn't at his desk as we walked past it. I had the feeling he wanted to be very scarce this morning.

Back on the street, Archer said,

"God, Jim, this is great. I'm sorry about the girl. I'm sorry about the woman, but experience like this is more than . . . and I pulled the chair out from under a U.S. Marshal, one who looks like he's been around. And I shut up a police captain."

"You did great, Fred," I said. "But we didn't get Melisa."

"What was different about today in there?" Archer asked.

"No Troy," I said.

He pulled out the envelope with the photos and handed it to me. A three-piece suited older man in a hurry bumped into Archer and didn't pause to apologize. Archer did his best to ignore the bump.

"Look at the photographs again," he said. "What's missing?"

I looked. Troy was clearly there. Melisa was there. Then it hit me.

"Donahue," I said.

"You assumed he was in the car," said Archer. "But the photos show Troy getting into the driver's seat after Melisa gets into the front passenger seat. I don't think Donahue was in the car. I don't think Donahue knew Troy took her. Did you watch his face when he looked at the photographs? No giveaway but he actually turned color, went to near white and didn't know what to say."

"I don't get it," I said, looking at Archer for an answer as I handed the photos back to him.

"I don't either," he said. "You're the detective. I'll have copies made of these photographs right now and put the copies in that safe place I told Donahue about, as soon as I can come up with a safe place."

"What the hell is Troy up to?" I asked.

"Jim, that's your question for the day. You got my number."

THE ROCKFORD FILES: DEVIL ON MY DOORSTEP

He walked jauntily down the street past a pair of vice detectives I knew. I turned and went to the parked Firebird. Dennis was sitting in the backseat, slouched down.

"Get in and drive, Jim," he said. "Don't look back and don't talk till we're at least two blocks away and sure you're not being followed."

CHAPTER SEVEN

I drove. Dennis talked. I said I thought we were being followed, by two cars.

"The feds and Oliver and Riordon from our department,"
said Dennis.

"You think they can see me?" Dennis asked.

"No," I said, trying not to move my lips.

"Troy's missing," said Dennis. "I heard Donahue make a
call. He doesn't know where Troy is. Diehl doesn't even
know Troy is missing."

"Thanks, Dennis," I said. "Dennis, Troy has Melisa or
knows where she is."

"You sure? There are other explanations."

"Give me a few," I said.

"I don't have any at the moment," he said. "Do you ever
clean the carpet back here?"

"You saw the photographs to prove Troy took her," I said.

Dennis was slouched so low that I couldn't see his face.
He was quiet for another block and then said,

"But we don't know why or for who and we don't know
if she went willingly. I'll see what I can find out and let you
know. In the middle of the next block there's an alley on the

right. Make a quick turn into it and stop. I'll get out. There's a restaurant there with an open back door."

I did what Dennis told me to do, and just as he leaped out he said, "Find the girl, Jim. Whatever's going on, I have a cop's feeling she hasn't got a lot of time left."

With that comforting premonition, he was gone, safe before the first of the two cars following me entered the alley. I drove slowly and so did they. When we got to the end of the alley almost to the next street, I gently turned my Firebird to block the exit. I got out, moved around the car and stood with my arms folded, shaking my head at the cops and the bad guys who either had to wait me out or back all the way out.

I was prepared to put in an hour or two in the alley with the odor of garbage, rotting fruit and really awful Chinese food. The cops were in the closer car. Barini's people were in the farther car. The bad guys gave up first and backed down the alley. One of the cops, Oliver, in the driver's seat of the closer car, gave me the finger and then their car pulled back. When they were both out of sight and probably racing around the block to find me, I got in my car and followed them down the alley. I crept out slowly, didn't see them and drove back down the street past the police station.

Where should I look for Troy and Melisa and where was Grazzo's body?

There were two messages on my machine when I got home about forty minutes later. I was happy to see that Grazzo's body hadn't been dumped on my new brown imitation-leather couch. One of the messages was from Angel. I had no time for Angel. The other was from the Acme Insurance Company, a Mr. Clyde, who said he'd like to talk to me about insurance and that I could call him back at the number he gave me if I did it within fifteen minutes. After that, he'd have to call me back. I recognized the voice.

It wasn't Mr. Clyde. It was Davis Davis, one of Dennis's street snitches. Dennis, Davis Davis, Rocky and I had once had an evening of telling lies to top each other's lies over beers and nachos at Friendly Morelli's on Fairfax. Davis Davis was almost eighty. He had shown us his World War II medals and liked to tell the story about how he earned each one of them. I thought he bought them at a pawn shop. Dennis wasn't sure. Rocky, who'd been in the same war, said Davis Davis was a stand-up guy.

By now I was fairly sure that the phone down the beach was bugged. I got in the pickup, looked around for the cops and robbers who were following me. They weren't there yet. I drove to a bar I didn't usually go in, but it was close and I was within the fifteen minutes. The beer wasn't quite cold there and the sandwiches were always raw. The music at night wasn't bad, blues, usually by old guys and old women, usually black old guys and women. The crowds came to listen, drink warm beer and eat raw hamburgers that stood a three-to-one chance of poisoning them.

The bar was dark and almost empty. A Blind Lemon Blake CD was playing. I ordered a beer from the barkeep as I headed for the phone in the back. He nodded.

I called the number Davis Davis had given me, and he answered after the first ring. From the sounds behind him, I figured he was at a phone on the street.

"We make it fast, sweet, Rockford," he said. "Guy you're looking for, the fed. He's got a room at the Golden Sun Motel on Melrose. Friend at the desk says the cleaning lady, who speaks no English, saw a girl in the room in the morning. Nothing unusual, but something looked off. Girl didn't look like a hooker. Guy didn't look like a John, and they slept in separate beds."

"How good is this information?"

"Guy registered as Carl Kolchak," said Davis. "Remember the Night Stalker on television?"

"I remember," I said.

"Fits the description of your guy," said Davis Davis. "Look, I can't stay on this phone long. What's this worth to you?"

"If it comes up gold, let's say fifty bucks."

"I wanted you to say a hundred. A certain source told me what this is about," said Davis Davis. "I just wanted to know what it was worth. No charge, Rockford, but you owe me."

"Thanks, Davis Davis," I said.

"Good luck to you, Rocky's son."

He hung up before I could ask him the room number at the Golden Sun Motel. There was no point in calling him back. He wouldn't be there or he wouldn't answer.

I called Dennis at his office and said I was an insurance salesman named Sandy Boone. I used my prissy voice. Dennis knew it. He said he was calling a police officer on duty and would report this call to Sandy Boone's company.

"I could care less," I said. "I work for myself and broker policies all over the place."

I hung up. Dennis knew the Sandy Boone Bar and Grill. We'd had a warm beer or two here over the years and had even come one night, me alone and him with his wife, to listen to some good blues by a woman who must have been well over eighty.

I nursed my beer at the bar, listened to Blind Lemon tell about his woes and tried to think. The phone behind the bar rang after ten minutes and the bartender answered and then said, "You Rockford?"

"Yeah," I said.

The bartender was beefy with thick black hair and a pink

face. He wasn't Sandy Boone. There wasn't any Sandy Boone. The owner was a man named Joseph Goldmacher. He made up the name.

"Dennis?" I asked.

"Yeah," he whispered.

"Thanks for the Davis Davis lead. You want to go pick up Melisa if she's still there?"

"Feds would take her from us. Jim, I don't know why I'm doing this. I could lose my job, my pension."

"For Melisa," I reminded him. "For Rene."

"Okay," he said. "I've got something else for you. Louis Aspermonte."

I had heard the name before but I couldn't place it.

"John Corlis's driver," Dennis said. "He was with Corlis the night Wendkos was murdered. Adrienne Wendkos was not the only witness to her husband's murder. But she was the only one who told the truth. Lou Aspermonte, who was on Corlis's payroll, said he saw nothing, heard nothing. When Adrienne Wendkos went to the stand, she said another man was with Corlis at the time of the shooting. She was seated in her car, but there wasn't much doubt it was Aspermonte. When Aspermonte was called to the stand, he said he heard and saw nothing. He had come out of the restaurant with Corlis, got into their parked car and drove away without talking to anyone. He added that he couldn't believe that Mr. Corlis would ever hurt anyone. Corlis, according to Aspermonte was a kind, generous man. The jury believed Adrienne Wendkos. The DA's office went after Aspermonte with a vengeance, got him on perjury for some things he said at the trial. He already had counts against him. Aspermonte did his time. The judge made it hard time, probably because of the Wendkos case.

"So how does this help me, Dennis?" I asked.

"Aspermonte's out," said Dennis. "He'll be called if

there's a new Corlis trial. He'll probably lie again this time, even with pressure from the half a dozen law enforcement agencies. He's not under witness protection and I understand he's living in Los Angeles. That's all I could get. No address. I'll keep looking for more. Get Melisa back, Jim. Oh, and Jim, Troy showed up. He and Donahue huddled in Diehl's office. They kicked Diehl out and he went like a kitten. I just kept my head down and pretended I was on the phone. Troy and Donahue kept their voices down but I could tell they were arguing, couldn't hear anything they were saying."

"Thanks, Dennis," I said.

"Find the girl, Jim."

He hung up. I already had an idea of how I could use Aspermonte if I could find him, but first I had to find him. I threw some quarters in the phone and called Angel. An answering machine came on, saying,

"You have reached the temporary residence of Angel Martinez. Please leave a message and *Señor* Martinez or his secretary will call you back as soon as possible."

"Answer the phone, Angel," I shouted after the beep. "This is Jim. It's important. Angel, it's about Melisa."

The machine was about to beep off when Angel picked up the phone and said, "Jim?"

His voice reeked of hangover and confusion.

"Yes."

"It's morning?" he asked.

"It's well into the day, Angel," I said.

"You know what that party cost me last night?" he said.

"No," I said.

"Really good parties are expensive, Jim. Take my word."

"I'll take it," I said. "I need your help."

"Can you call back later? My head's starting to hurt."

"No," I said. "This is about Melisa."

"Okay," he said miserably.

"Louis Aspermonte," I said.

"Doesn't ring any ding-dongs," said Angel thickly.

"Testified in the Corlis trial, one of Corlis's lackeys, probably just a driver. See no evil. Hear no evil. Speak no evil. Do seven hard ones for perjury in a murder case."

"Sorry, Jimmy, still no bells."

"He's in Los Angeles," I said. "I want to find him fast, very fast. You've got money, connections with ex-cons; use them now. Call me at this number with whatever you've got in a half hour or sooner. I think I know where Melisa is or was and I can't wait."

"Jimmy, I'm gonna need some time on this," he whined.

"Sorry, Angel, Melisa just doesn't have the time."

I hung up, nursed another beer and talked to the bartender about modern jazz. We remembered Charlie Parker, Chet Baker, the Lighthouse at Laguna, the Australian Jazz Quartet, the Modern Jazz Quartet, Dizzy Gillespie, Lou Levy, Gerry Mulligan, Dave Brubeck, Lester Young, Cannonball and a few dozen others. I had a bunch of LPs from the fifties once, but a pair of goons had smashed them years ago turning over the trailer in search of something I didn't have. History, as Roger Mudd or somebody once said, keeps repeating itself.

After about twenty minutes, Angel called back.

"Nothing yet, Jimmy, but I'm working on it and a very painful head. Can I call you in an hour?"

"I'll call you, Angel," I said. "Find Aspermonte."

"I've got a guy who knows a guy who was on the same cell block with Aspermonte," he said. "He's gonna try to get me closer. Jimmy, this is going to cost me bucks."

"You lost her, Angel," I said.

"That's not exactly fair," he said. "I really care about her."

"That's why you partied all night," I said.

"It was too late to call off the party," he said. "And I wanted to try to forget how I'd screwed up. I deserved a little celebration too."

"Find Aspermonte," I said. "I'll call later."

I hung up, paid the bartender, who said that they had tried a little modern jazz a few times but the crowd wasn't into it.

"This is a blues bar," he said.

"That's not bad," I said.

"Not bad at all," he said. "Think of what it could be."

I tried not to as I went out into the light, got into the pickup and headed for downtown Los Angeles. I parked in a twenty-four-hour lot, which would cost me more than fifty bucks a day, took a tackle box and old Giants cap from the space behind the seat and went to a car rental place down the street, and rented a dark Taurus with tinted windows. I put the tackle box and cap in the trunk. Then I bought a coffee, kept the lid on and circled police headquarters looking for Donahue and Troy's car. It was parked in the small lot. I parked where I could watch it, drank my coffee and waited.

I could have headed straight for the Golden Sun Motel and tried to con my way to the room where Melisa was being kept, but something bothered me, bothered me a lot. If Troy wasn't in the room, why didn't Melisa just call me or leave? What had he offered, promised, threatened her with? And what if they'd already moved her? It was a fifty-fifty decision. I decided to follow the marshals.

They came out about ten minutes later. I had almost missed them. Maybe luck was turning my way on this.

The marshals came out together, but they weren't talking to each other. Donahue drove. I followed. I was sure they didn't spot me. Why should they even think anyone was following them? They parked in front of the midpriced

Golden Sun on Melrose. Troy got out and Donahue pulled away. I didn't worry about Donahue. I watched Troy, looking less than happy, walk to a stairway, disappear for a few seconds, and then show up again on the second floor. He walked along to a room and opened the door. I couldn't see the room number from where I was sitting, but I could tell which room it was.

I parked, got out, threw my empty coffee cup into an almost overflowing garbage can and opened my trunk. I picked up Rocky's small fishing tackle box and put on the beat-up Giants baseball cap. I took off my jacket after looking around, and removed my holster. I put my .38 in the pocket of my windbreaker. Then I went up the stairs, my jacket open. There didn't seem to be anyone around and Troy had placed the DO NOT DISTURB sign on the door.

I took out my .38 and knocked.

"What?" called Troy.

"Plumber," I said, moving into my Swedish accent, which was just this side of John Wayne in *The Long Voyage Home*. "Got a leak. Got to check. Flooding downstairs."

"All right," said Troy with a sigh.

I turned my back on the draped window, knowing he would check me out before opening the door. I hoped that what he saw was a big man slouched over, carrying what might have been a toolbox and wearing a windbreaker and a battered baseball cap.

The door unlatched and started to open. Before it got very far, I pushed hard. I had almost forgotten my sore stomach. The push set it off again. I had my gun in his chest before he could pull his own.

"Rockford," he said. "You're crazy."

I kicked the door closed and looked around. No one else was there, but I could see that both beds had been used and there were two tri-folds hanging on the rack near the bathroom. Donahue and Troy didn't travel in style, but they did travel for speed. Both bags were carry-ons.

Troy had taken off his jacket and loosened his tie.

"What do you want, Rockford?" he said wearily.

He should have sounded angry, but he wasn't up to the act.

"First," I said, "a glass of water."

Troy cocked his head, closed his eyes for a second and backed up slowly. I followed him to the sink in the little alcove next to the bathroom and he said,

"You're lucky. There's one clean one left."

He filled it and turned with it toward me.

"From now on we stay at least ten feet apart," I said. "Just put down the glass and come back and sit on the bed away from the door."

He shrugged and I backed away to let him pass. With my gun trained on him as he sat, I fished out a pair of Doc Bohanan's pain pills and gulped them down with the water. Then I came back into the bedroom, where Troy looked at me. He wasn't afraid.

He was as big as I am. He was younger than I am. I'm sure he was in better shape than I am and even more sure that he would do better in any encounter between us in which I wasn't holding a gun.

"Rockford, you know and I know you won't shoot me," he said. "I've read your file—about the size of *War and Peace*—and you're not fool enough to shoot a federal officer and probably not anyone else unless someone's life was on the line. Put the gun away. We'll talk."

He was right, but I kept the gun in my hand, pulled a chair away from the small table near the window and sat facing him.

"What do you want?" he asked.

"You know."

"The girl."

"Melisa."

"She's safe."

"Prove it," I said.

"Hell," said Troy. "I wanted to be in the FBI. Father was FBI. My brother is FBI. Dad said I could get farther as a federal marshal. Things were going to be breaking all over the country. Federal hate crimes, militias, terrorists. The marshal's office was the place for promotion."

"What's the point?" I asked. "Why did you start working for the mob?"

"The mob?" he said, looking at me.

"Did Donahue tell you about the pictures of you taking Melisa?" I asked. "I've got a set if you really want to see."

He waved me away. He was tired. Clean shaven, neatly clothed, hair trimmed, but tired.

"Melisa was a decoy," he said. "The goat. We knew where you took her from the start. We played with you in case Corlis's friends were watching. We were watching too. My bet is you got those pictures from Barini's people. They're trying to set me up. When I got Melisa, I had a little trouble losing them. Now they don't know where she is and neither does my partner. I didn't like taking a chance with her life to keep an old man in jail. Donahue and the people in the Washington office thought it was worth the chance. I've been doing this long enough to know that it's easier to throw a human being to the dogs to get a solid arrest if you don't know the human being."

"So you took Melisa to save her?" I asked with more than a touch of disbelief.

"And I'll probably lose my job," he said. "I think my dad will understand. Maybe not. I'll probably wind up on a small-town police force doing night patrol and hauling in drunks."

"Married?"

"Yes," he said.

"Kids?"

"Two," he said. "Melisa reminds me of my youngest, but Dotty is only six. I wouldn't want Dotty set up for target practice."

He was either telling the truth or was a great liar. He didn't look like a great liar.

"Where is she?" I asked.

"Safe," he said. "I'm not telling you. I had her here last night, moved her this morning. I told Donahue because he had the same idea that I might be on the take from the mob. Rockford, with my family history, why would I . . . forget it."

"What if I can come up with another stakeout goat?" I said. "You get the credit, maybe save your job. I get Melisa."

"What've you got in mind?" he asked.

I got the phone on the table and dialed Angel, who answered on the second ring with, *"Señor* Martinez' residence."

"It's me, Jim," I said.

"Got something," he answered eagerly but softly. "Found Aspermonte's cell mate. He got out three years ago. Tracked him down in East L.A. Two grand it's gonna cost me, but I've got an address for Aspermonte. Only he's not Aspermonte anymore. He's William Johnson."

"Not much of an imagination," I said.

"Long-washed-up hired gun, if he was ever even that," said Angel. "Story I got was he was a driver and runner who was in the wrong place, wrong time. He was scared of Corlis. He was loyal to Corlis. He wanted to stay alive so he lied on the stand. Now he's sitting low and waiting for Corlis to die, unless Aspermonte dies first. Word is the mob was supposed to take care of him when he finished his time. Word is he was given a few thousand and told to disappear and keep his mouth shut."

Angel gave me the address. Still holding the gun, I wrote it on the motel notepad with one of those little yellow pencils they leave next to the pad. I checked to see that I hadn't written hard enough to go through on the next sheet. Just to be sure, I tore off the sheet below, crumpled it and put it in my pocket. The sheet with Aspermonte's address on it I put carefully in my pocket.

"Mind my asking what you've got?" asked Troy.

"Aspermonte, Louis Aspermonte," I said.

Troy laughed, a laugh with no mirth, and said,

"Aspermonte did hard time to keep Corlis and his friends from shutting him up," Troy said. "We've tracked him down every once in a while and tried to turn him, but it was useless. He's still more afraid of them than he is of us. He's been missing for a few years now, since the day he finished having to check in with a parole officer."

"He's in Los Angeles," I said.

"He's from Los Angeles," said Troy. "Doesn't surprise me."

"I'll find him and we trade. Melisa for Aspermonte, who agrees to testify against Corlis if there's another trial."

"Good luck," he said, "but I don't have the power to turn the girl over to you, Rockford."

"You didn't worry about that when you saved her," I said. "Melisa was supposed to lead Barini to Grazzo, but Grazzo's dead. Melisa doesn't know anything and there's no one alive who could testify against Corlis, except Aspermonte. The mob doesn't need Melisa."

"Theory in Washington is," said Troy, "that they want to make an example of the girl. Kill her and let the word out that testifying against the mob means losing your family."

"You buy that?" I asked.

"Maybe," he said. "Maybe."

I got up.

"We have a deal?" I asked.

"I have anything to lose?" he answered, lying back on the bed after kicking off his shoes. "Give us a willing Louis Aspermonte and I'll do what I can to stop my partner from using her as bait. She's committed no crime. If she wants to go with you then, I think you've got a smart lawyer."

I left, closing the door behind me and backing away from it, .38 in my hand under my Giants cap. He didn't come flying out of the door. By the time I got to the trunk of my rental car, I was sure Troy wasn't even looking out the window. I put my tackle box in the trunk and headed for the address Angel had given me.

THE street where Louis Aspermonte, aka William Johnson, lived was just off of the old downtown area that was already headed to hell when I was a kid. Now the street was the closest thing to the lawless towns of the old West that you saw in movies, only those cowboys had six-shooters and rifles. These cowboys had automatic weapons and sharp knives. All the signs were in Spanish, and the street was alive.

I drove slowly, looking for the address. There were young men on the street talking. There were a few old men doing the same. There were no young women and only a huddled, hurrying old woman. I found the address. One of the numbers was almost rubbed off. The place was on a corner in a building that looked as if it had once been a respectable hotel, back when the Doughboys came home from France.

My problem now was parking. The rental car people would be a little unhappy if I called them and told them the car had been stripped or stolen. I found a parking lot a block down and pulled in. The attendant was a tough-looking heavy little man with a big belly. He was wearing a green-and-yellow-striped short-sleeved shirt, a pair of black jeans and a very wary look.

"What'll it cost to park here for maybe an hour?" I asked, hoping he could speak English. I could probably get by on my Spanish, but life was easier when I didn't have to.

"Ten bucks," he said.

"Ten bucks?" I said.

"And Miguel Ramirez guarantees the car will be just like you left it," he said without any trace of accent.

"You're sure?"

"Me and the shotgun in that shack are sure," he said. "I've got a reputation and my lot is neutral ground, at least for now."

"You've got a deal, Mr. Ramirez," I said, getting out and handing him the keys. He gave me a ticket in return, a small yellow movie theater–style ticket with a four-digit number.

"Your car will be safe," he reassured me. "This is my business. I've got four other lots. My sons and a nephew run them. My sons and my nephew all go to college part time. I went to college. Got a degree in social work. Parking lots make you more money and are safer than case work in this neighborhood. Your car is safe. However, I'm not responsible for you, and that little gun under your jacket won't do you much good around here. How's your Spanish?"

"Fair," I said.

"*Bueno suerte,*" he said, climbing into my rented Taurus and closing the door.

I walked back to the address of Louis Aspermonte. I got suspicious looks and picked up a few words in Spanish that made it clear that this was not a place I was expected. There were music shops, groceries, clothing stores, restaurants and something called El Gato Blanco y Azul, which I figured for

a nightclub. It looked closed. There was a neon cat under
the sign. I guessed it lit up white and blue at night. I went
into the hotel and found myself in a lobby that wasn't quite
falling apart, but close to it. The chairs looked rickety, the
carpet ancient, and plant urns empty. There was a woman
behind the desk. She didn't look pleased to see me.

"You wan' a room?" she asked with a slight accent.

"No," I said.

"Din think so," she said.

She was about fifty, dark hair short, dress dark with no
pattern.

"I'm looking for William Johnson," I said with a smile.
"I'm a friend of an old friend. I have some money the old
friend owes Mr. Johnson."

"Take my advice," she said softly, though the dusty lobby
was empty. "Don't talk about money around here and don't
show it. That little pistol won't do you much good."

She was the second person in five minutes who had spotted the gun and holster under my windbreaker.

I took out a twenty and slid it to her across the desk. She
took it and put it in her pocket.

"We don't keep no cash in the drawer," she said. "Johnson owed me for two weeks. I would have told you his room
just so he could get his money. You're no a hit man?"

"I'm not a hit man," I said with a winning smile.

She shrugged and said,

"Two-oh-two."

I nodded and headed for the stairway while she picked up
a Spanish magazine. I doubted if there were phones in the
rooms so I didn't expect her to warn Aspermonte that anyone was coming up. The hallway on the second floor fit in
perfectly with the decor of the lobby. This wasn't a flophouse, but it wasn't more than a level or two higher than
one. The bulbs in the hall were missing and I didn't think

they'd be replaced. The once-white walls were now gray and dusty, but there was no graffiti and there were no holes in need of repair.

Two zero two was at the end of the hall. I knocked.

"*¿Quien es?*" came a careful answer.

"Mr. Johnson," I said, "I have a Social Security check for you."

"Social Security?"

"Hard to track you down," I said with a positive note. "But we did it."

"Mistake," he said with a touch of fear. "Go away. Slip it under the door."

"You're going to have to sign for it," I said. "Mr. Aspermonte, we know it's you. You've got a check coming. I want to get out of this neighborhood as fast as I can. So open the door, sign, take the check and I move out. If you don't open the door and sign, I'm counting five and getting back to my car and my office."

I started to count aloud. By the time I got to four, the door opened enough for whoever was behind it to point a rifle at my chest.

"Give it to me," he said. "I'll sign."

"Use your real name," I said, starting to reach into my pocket and making a sudden lunge at the door.

I hit it hard and I heard Aspermonte fly back, losing his rifle, which hit the old wooden floor with a loud clap. I went in, gun in hand, and closed the door.

A very old man was sitting on the floor. He was thin, with sagging skin, white hair. The room was like a cell, a cot in the corner, a small wooden table with a wooden chair in front of it. A noisy little refrigerator hummed in one corner on the floor. It looked like the kind college kids kept in their rooms, only this was a very old one with a chipped surface. There was a picture of Jesus over the cot. Jesus was looking to his right toward the sun. There was a night table and lamp near the cot. The table was covered with paperbacks and an old black-and-white television set with a small screen.

"They sent you to kill me," he said. "Do it. Fast. Then go. I'm tired of hiding."

"They?" I asked.

He didn't answer, just closed his eyes, waiting for the bullets.

"I'm not here to kill you," I said. "I may be here to save you. I'm a private detective."

I put my gun back in the holster and helped the old man to his feet. I felt guilty about what I had done to him, but I was about to feel even more guilty because I needed this man. He coughed, a prison smoker's cough, as I sat him on the cot, whose springs twanged even with his thin body.

He didn't look at me but at an old small carpet on the floor and at the rifle he had lost that lay across the room.

"I used to be a con," I said to break the ice. "I did about as much time as you, but what I did was enough to convince me that I didn't want to go back. You want to go back, Louis?"

"For what?" he said.

"Corlis is asking for a new trial," I said. "He'll probably get it. You'll have to testify again. You'll have to either lie and face going back to prison for perjury or tell the truth and hope the government will put you in witness protection."

"Great choice," he said, still not looking at me. "They can find you in witness protection. I'll bet you're here because they found that woman, Angela, no Adrienne Wendkos. I thought I'd never forget that name. I'm getting old fast. You're here 'cause they found her and shut her up and the feds need me to nail Corlis."

"Something like that," I said.

"Then why didn't the feds come instead of sending a private detective who's an ex-con?" he asked reasonably.

"You know, Louis, that's a damned good question," I said.

He cocked his head and looked at me. His rocky mess of a face looked puzzled, and he held back on a cough that came anyway.

"I thought about this a lot," he said, his voice rasping now. "Waiting for someone like you to come through that door, blow my brains out. No gratitude. I put myself on the line, go to prison for Corlis, and do they take care of me? Hell, no. They want me dead."

"Louis," I said, "if I found you, they'll find you. Why don't you pack up and I'll move you somewhere else, somewhere safe where you can think about this a little while, a very little while."

"I could be packed and have everything I own in my hands in ten minutes. The rifle'd be a problem. I'd trade it for a hand gun, not that it would do much good. My hands shake."

He started to cough now and couldn't control it. His face grew red, and I considered patting him on the back. He pointed to the refrigerator. I hurried to it, opened it, found some bottled water and poured a drink into a reasonably clean though chipped white coffee cup with a picture of a cute kitten on the side.

Aspermonte drank the water in little sips, gradually controlling the coughing. He finished the water and handed me the cup.

"Emphysema," he said. "I also got a bum ticker—bypass operation two years back—a liver that's going fast and one of the hepatitis things. Not to mention dandruff."

He started to laugh now. The laughter turned into coughing and more water.

"Thanks," he said. "You know what I'd like to do?"

"What?"

"Outlive Corlis," he said. "Read in the paper one day that he's dead. Maybe go to his funeral and smile at Barini. Then maybe I could die happy."

"I'll bet the feds can arrange the funeral trip," I said. "Just keep yourself alive and tell the truth this time. There's no double jeopardy. You've already been convicted and served time for perjury on your testimony."

"Yeah, but like you said, in case you forgot, they can get me on other counts of perjury. New ones. Smart lawyer can lay me out. My mind's not as sharp as it used to was, you know?"

"They'll be on your side this time," I said.

"Not if I testify the same way, and if I don't, Corlis's big-time lawyers'll tear me to pieces."

"I don't think you have much choice, Louis," I said.

"I don't know," he said, shaking his head. "You read *The Bridges of Madison County*?"

"No," I said.

"Book stinks," he said, "but I hear the movie's good."

I didn't know what I had here or if Aspermonte, if he lived long enough, would be a credible witness. He was right. A million-dollar lawyer could probably tear him apart, but then again . . .

"Well?" I asked gently, taking the pussycat cup from his hands.

"Got nothing to lose," he said with a shrug. "Feds might get me good doctoring to keep me alive."

"And you'd be safe," I said.

"Safer," he amended.

"Safer," I agreed.

"You got yourself a witness," he said, standing on wobbly legs. "Beats sitting here and waiting for one of Barini's

goons or some neighborhood crack head to beat me to death
for that crap of a television and my rifle."

It took Aspermonte about five minutes to pack all his
worldly goods and tuck his television under his arm. I carried the rifle at my side. When we got to the desk, the
woman looked at us over the top of her magazine and
glanced at the rifle, saying,

"That's better than the cap gun, but you're still way un-
derarmed. I guess our treasured tenant *Señor* Johnson is
moving out?"

"Right," I said.

"Thirty-two bucks, he owes."

Aspermonte shifted the weight of the television. I took
out four tens and handed them to her, saying, "Keep the
change."

"Hide the gun," she said, putting three of the tens in a
metal box she took from the drawer under the counter and
stuffing the fourth in the pocket of her dress. "Someone out
there might think you're lookin' for troubles."

I thanked her, considered where I might hide a rifle, and
decided to walk the block with the gun at my side and my
arm covering most of it. I didn't think I'd fool much of anyone, but I wanted to try to show that I wasn't looking for
trouble. Aspermonte shuffled with his load. I wanted to get
moving fast, but it wasn't in him.

"Between you and me," he panted, "and I deny it if you
say anything, I done a lot of things in my life I shouldn't. I
even killed a couple guys back in the old days. Self-defense.
But I was always loyal to Frankie Corlis. We grew up together. He was the smart one."

We caught a few looks on the way to the parking lot, but
nobody stopped us till we were at the cross street with the
parking lot just ahead past the traffic. The fat man with the

kids in school was sitting on a chair near his booth reading a newspaper. I didn't figure him for much help anyway.

There were two of them, both no more than fifteen or sixteen. They were dressed in identical black slacks and red shirts. I was sure there was something written in Spanish on the back of the shirts, but I wasn't sure I wanted to know what it was. They were both dark. One was good-looking enough to be on television. The other was bad-looking enough to be on television.

They barred our way.

"Listen, fellas," I said. "We don't want any trouble. Just let us . . ."

"*Viejo,*" said the good-looking one, "*mira alla, a la tienda en rincón.*"

Aspermonte looked across the street to our left without turning his head.

"*Queremos—*" the good-looking one began, but I stopped him with,

"English."

"There are three guys across the street," he said. "We got the word that they think the old man has a stack of cash he's been keeping under his pillow or something. They plan to come and take it when you cross the street."

"Why are you telling us?" I said. "They friends of yours?"

The ugly one smiled.

"We're gonna save your lives," said the handsome kid. "Diego and me are with the Brazos. We ain't saints, but we don't want to see some dumb gringo with an old rifle and an old man who never done anything to anyone get blown apart. We'll walk you to your car. They see us, 'specially Diego, they ain't gonna cross the street."

"Lead on," I said.

Diego got on my left. The other kid got on Aspermonte's

right and took the television. Aspermonte tried to hold on, but he gave up after one tug. The two bodyguards knew my car was in the lot. The guy with the gut who ran the lot nodded at the four of us. Diego and his friend stopped at the gate and turned to face the street. I paid for the car and got Aspermonte into it as quickly as I could. He dumped his bag, television and a few books on the backseat and I put his rifle on the floor.

We drove past the two Brazos at the gate and waved at them. The ugly one turned his head and grinned at us. I could have turned left and gone past the three guys in front of the store who were glaring at our bodyguards, but I turned right instead and hit the gas.

I thought the question now was where to hide Aspermonte till I could deal him for Melisa. I didn't trust Troy. I couldn't take him to my place or Angel's.

When we were safely out of the neighborhood I pulled off onto a residential street. I wanted the rifle, for which I doubted Aspermonte had a permit, in the trunk. I planned to put his television and books in the trunk of the Taurus too.

I worked fast and opened the trunk when I was fairly sure no one was watching. Lying on his back, knees folded, Irving Grazzo, eyes wide open, face white, looked up at me. He was still dead.

CHAPTER EIGHT

I drove slowly, trying to think, checking to be sure I wasn't being followed. Only now I knew they could probably follow me even when I didn't see them. They—the feds or Barini's people—had probably put a stinger somewhere on the Taurus, something that would send out a signal and let them know where I was.

Aspermonte sat clutching his television like a teddy bear. I had to give the old man credit for a few things. He had been hiding for years in cheap rooms waiting to be killed, but he was now, and probably always had been, clean shaven, clean and wearing clean though old clothes. Aspermonte still had a sense of dignity about some things. A good sign. The bad sign was Grazzo's body in my trunk.

When it had been put there was a puzzle. It wasn't there when I left Troy. I had put the tackle box in the trunk. The only way it could have been put there was when I was parked in Ramirez's lot. I had liked Ramirez and figured him for honest, but how much does it take to bribe an honest man?

More likely they had followed me and . . . I pulled over to an outdoor telephone on Santa Monica, told Aspermonte

to sit low. He sat numbed as I went to the phone. I looked
in the phone book. There was no Ramirez's parking lot. I
didn't remember any name on the little shack or the wire
fence. I asked information for the number of the parking lot
and gave what I thought must be the address. The opera-
tor said there was a parking lot listed at that address and the
robot gave me the number. I dialed and checked my money.
I was running low. This case was costing me, and my only
client had given me one buck, which was still in my wallet.

"*Sí,*" came the voice of the man who picked up the phone.

"Mr. Ramirez?" I asked, holding one hand over my open
ear to keep out the sounds of passing traffic.

"Yes," he said warily.

"This is Rockford, the Taurus. I just left your lot with an
old man carrying a television."

"Yes," he repeated.

"Did anyone else who looked like he didn't belong in
that neighborhood park in the lot after me?"

Ramirez hesitated. Something was wrong. He didn't
want to get involved, but . . .

"Yes, two men in a new white Lincoln," he said.
"Wouldn't let me park the car. Wanted to do it themselves.
Gave me a ten-dollar tip up front. I told them they had to
leave the key with me when they parked."

"You see them park?"

"Didn't pay much attention," he said.

"They park near my car?"

"I think so. Maybe. They took a few minutes so I looked
up, but they were coming back in the Lincoln.

" 'Changed our mind,' the Lincoln's driver said with a
smile and handed me another ten. You people are crazy.
They're crazy in Mexico too, but it's a crazy you can understand. I've been in this country more than twenty-five
years and I can't understand gringo crazy."

"I can't either," I said. "What did the two guys in the car look like?"

"We almost done?" he asked.

"That was my last question," I said, looking back at the Taurus and Aspermonte, who was hunched down over the television in his lap.

"One guy," said Ramirez. "Big. Passenger. Looked real strong. Liked to show his muscles. Muscles don't mean much against a round of bullets or a shotgun, but you don't give advice to gringos. The driver. He was good looking, good shape, nice suit, blond hair. He smiled a lot and thanked me. He was the one who handed me the money. He was the one who looked crazy."

"Thanks," I said.

"You want my address?" he asked.

"Why?"

"Send me maybe ten bucks for telling you," said Ramirez. "Remember . . ."

". . . you've got kids in college. Okay, give it to me."

I wrote the address in my notebook. It was nowhere near the garage. It was in Culver City in an area, if I remembered right, which was residential and pretty nice.

"*Muchas gracias,*" I said.

"*De nada.* What did blondie and the other guy do?" he asked and then immediately added, "Forget it. I don't want to know. Take care of yourself and the old man."

He hung up and I got back in. None of my problems had gone away. What should I do with Aspermonte? What should I do with Grazzo's body in my trunk? Why had Barini decided to set me up?

I came up with an idea. It was crazy, but it would do two things. I looked up the nearest car rental, gave them my credit card number and said I'd be in to pick up the car in about five minutes. The new car wouldn't be bugged or recognized, at least not for a while. I got back in the Taurus and headed toward the car rental place I had called. I took some side streets, ones with body shops, small factories, stained-glass-window studios. I wanted Wright to wonder where I was going. It seemed like a good idea at the time. It was daytime. It had started to look like rain, but there had to be people around, not many maybe, but some. I went to Florida a couple of times. I got the impression that only Hispanics in Miami went outdoors. The rest of the population of the entire state went from car to garage to wherever and never walked anywhere.

It was after my third turn around the same block that I saw the Lincoln. It wasn't in my rearview mirror. It was heading right for my rented Taurus.

"Get down low," I told Aspermonte. "Real low."

He crawled down into the foot space in a ball with his television.

The shot came through the window, making a neat hole with just a little bit of sunburst cracking. The window wasn't bulletproof, but it was safety glass. That first shot came through right where Aspermonte had been sitting.

Now we were playing my least favorite game, chicken. Even if I wanted to shoot, I couldn't drive and fire through the open window with any hope of hitting the Lincoln. Wright had the luxury of a passenger who could concentrate on trying to shoot Aspermonte and probably me.

The second shot came through the window right in front of me. I don't know how much it missed me by. At first I thought it hadn't missed. I figured the Lincoln was no more than forty feet in front of me now, but it was hard to tell. I could see Wright driving, a small smile on his face. I could see Tony, the big guy who covered Barini's back, leaning out the window ready to take a third shot. I wasn't sure whether

Wright meant to go past me and get his pal a good shot or to hit me head-on. There wasn't much I could do.

Without thinking, I pulled into the driveway of a used-tire shop with an open garage door. The Lincoln shot past on the street. I heard its tires skid as Wright tried to stop. I didn't look back. I got a glimpse of a couple of grease-covered men working on a jacked-up car in the garage and drove over their curb and down the street away from the Lincoln, which was just starting to turn. I could try to find a policeman, but I knew and Wright knew that it would be hard to explain Grazzo's body in the trunk. Then again, I didn't plan on spending the rest of the day being shot at until I got hit. My best chance was a busy street—maybe. These guys might find it easier to trap me in traffic and shoot me and Aspermonte with a crowd watching. It happens every day in L.A. I lost Wright with a few more turns, but I knew it would only be a matter of minutes before he picked up the beep from his bug. Hell, he might even have a computer or radar.

I took a chance, parked in the employees' lot of American Plywood Products and got out to look for the bug. I tried crawling under the car. I didn't see anything. I was getting a feeling of panic and was looking for the Lincoln when I got the idea. I looked around, opened the trunk and searched Grazzo's body. It made sense. They had put the bug on the corpse. Maybe it had just been in the trunk before, but Wright had outsmarted himself and put it on the body. It was a small box with a blinking light. It did have a magnet. A quartet of plant employees came off shift and got into a car four cars down. I took the bug, moved behind their car and stuck the magnetized beeper on their bumper. Since I knew they had seen me but hadn't seen me plant the bug, I moved to the driver's window, looking for the Lincoln all the time, and asked the driver if they were hiring at the plywood plant.

He was a tired-looking guy in his late fifties.

"What do you do?" he asked.

"Sell," I said.

"Try the office, inside," he said. "Tell Rosalie, Tillio sent you."

"And Jerry," said one of the passengers.

"And pinch her bottom or top for me," came another voice.

I said thanks and watched the car pull out. I hurried back to the Taurus, got in and drove. No Lincoln. I didn't know how long it would take Wright to find the four plywood-factory workers and describe me to them.

He might need his gun and they might not cooperate.

Aspermonte was still curled in the foot space on the passenger side.

"You'll be all right," I said.

"I'll be all dead," he said. "What the hell."

I parked the Taurus two blocks from the car rental agency and told Aspermonte to get out of the car. He felt better curled up. I told him the guys who shot at us, Barini's guys, might find the car. That convinced him. He got out with my help and I took the television and his bag from him and left them on the seat. I locked the doors. Louis was not happy, but he trudged at my side up the street. I kept expecting the Lincoln even though I knew we had a good start, but I didn't want to push our luck any further than I had to.

When I got the car, I apologized for being a few minutes late, gave them my credit card and waited while the big black woman in a neat company blazer looked at the cowering Aspermonte.

"My father," I whispered to her. "Alzheimer's. Have to watch him all the time, but . . . hey, he's my father."

"I know," she whispered back. "Grandmother's over ninety. Can't remember her own name. Thinks she's Myrna Loy half the time. Got to the point where we don't even correct her. When she asks for William Powell, we tell her that good old Bill is dead."

The new car was a Buick with a big trunk. It was a light blue. I didn't care. Aspermonte and I got in and drove off. I circled the block, parked half a block behind the bullet-holed Taurus, made sure no one was watching and then pulled next to the Taurus. I got Aspermonte's worldly belongings, and opened the trunks of both cars.

Strength born of adrenaline and blind fear helped me get Grazzo's body out of the Taurus trunk and into the Buick. I could feel the pain in my stomach from the effort, a pain caused by the man I was carrying. I don't know how long it took me, probably fifteen seconds. I closed the trunks and got in the Buick.

"What was that?" asked Aspermonte, clutching his television again.

"What?" I asked, heading for the busiest street I could find.

"You moved something from the trunk of the other car to this car. I seen in the mirror."

"Evidence," I said. "I can't say any more. It would be safer for you if you didn't know."

"Safe?" he said, slouched. "I can't be no more unsafe unless you just call Barini and tell him where to pick me up so he can grind me in a wood chipper or something."

"I've got a stop to make. Then I'll take you someplace safe."

"There ain't someplace safe," he said.

He was probably right.

I stopped at a hardware store and bought a pair of cheap work gloves. Then I drove to the all-too-familiar police sta-

tion where Dennis, Diehl and possibly Donahue were trying to figure out what to do next. The street was reasonably
busy for late afternoon.

"I'm hungry," said Aspermonte.

"I'll feed you when I finish this," I said.

I'd known Captain Diehl for more than two decades. I
knew his car. I knew where he parked it and it wasn't in the
small lot next to the station where a cop who wasn't as fond
of the captain as I was might clip a fender on the way out—
which had happened at least once that I knew of.

Diehl parked in an indoor lot around the corner, which
was where I headed, got my ticket from the machine and
drove through the lot, looking for his Saturn with the van-
ity plate: DIEHL. I found it on the first level. I would have
preferred it higher, but I didn't have much choice. There
was a handicap space next to the Saturn. I pulled in, got
out, put on my gloves, and went through the keys in my
pocket till I found one that fit Diehl's trunk and opened it.
The trunk was as neat as if the car was new, and there was
nothing in it but a spare tire. Somewhere upstairs someone
was gunning the engine of what sounded like a sports car.
I waited. No car came past. I opened my trunk and lugged
Grazzo's body into Diehl's trunk as fast as I could. He
seemed to be getting heavier. I wiped Aspermonte's old
rifle clean with my gloves and threw that in after Grazzo,
who was beginning to take on a definite unpleasant odor. I
needed clean clothes and a long shower. Then I slammed
Diehl's trunk closed, got back in the Buick and pulled out
fast, taking off the gloves.

"A body," Aspermonte said. "You dumped a body in
somebody's trunk. That's what you've been schleppin'
around."

"The less you know, Louis, the better," I said.

"I coulda helped you," he said. "I know how to put bodies in trunks, boxcars, shipping boxes. That was the old days, but the old ways still work."

"I'll remember that," I said.

I checked out of the lot, paying the minimum to the young guy, who didn't even bother to look at us and wasn't bothered by the fact that we had been inside for only about five minutes.

One or two problems were taken care of, at least for a while. Now I had Aspermonte. I didn't call. I just drove across Canoga to North Hollywood and to the small house where Eddie lived. Eddie was one of Rocky's friends. Back a half century, Eddie had been a real contender for the lightweight title. He was black, still wiry, but he didn't walk any too fast. I figured he was about Aspermonte's age.

I knocked at the door with Aspermonte sitting in the car. Eddie didn't get out much. Once in a while when I was in the neighborhood, I'd stop by and see him, and he stayed in touch with me. Rocky, he said, had told him to look out for me. Eddie was home. He opened the door and gave me a grin. He was wearing clean jeans and a gray short-sleeved shirt that looked new.

"Jimmy," he said, taking my hand. "Come on in."

"I will," I said, "but first I have to ask you a favor. See the guy in the front seat of that Buick?"

Eddie looked. There was nothing wrong with his sight.

"I see him," I said.

"Think you could put him up for a few days, keep him out of sight?" I asked.

"You need it. You got it. No questions."

I almost offered Eddie money but I stopped myself in time. He would have been offended. I went back to the car and helped Aspermonte out. He carried the television and I carried his bag.

Eddie backed into the house so Aspermonte could get

in. The living room was dark, comfortable and small. Pictures of Eddie in his fighting days were on the wall in the built-in bookcases. Some of them were pictures of Eddie with people like Henry Armstrong, Sandy Saddler, Kid Gavilan, Jack Dempsey and the mayor of New York. Aspermonte paused, looked around the room, saw the photographs and turned to Eddie with the return of something like life in his eyes.

"You're Eddie 'Lightning' Thibidou," Aspermonte said.

"I'm Eddie Thibidou," Eddie answered, "but the 'Lightning' is long gone.

"Saw you fight Charlie Rogers. Saw you fight lots of times in New York," said Aspermonte.

Eddie took the television out of his guest's hand and took the suitcase from me.

"You were fast," Aspermonte said. "When I was in the money, you made me more than a few bucks on bets. But the Rogers fight. Best twelve rounds I ever saw."

"I won a split decision," Eddie said. "Lucky to come away with that."

"You deserved a unanimous," said Aspermonte.

"Come on. I'll show you your room. We can leave your television in the closet. I got cable and color right over there and in my bedroom."

"Can I use your phone?" I asked as Eddie moved toward the small guest room/den/trophy room.

"Whatever you want, Jimmy," Eddie said.

I called the car rental company where I'd gotten the Taurus. I put fear in my voice and said I'd accidentally driven through what must have been a bad neighborhood and had outrun a car full of dopeheads who had shot at me. I told them where the car was parked and said I'd locked the key inside. I told them I had taken a cab to a hospital where I could get something for my nerves. The man on the other end said he hoped I was all right. I didn't tell him about the bullet holes. My story would cover that.

Eddie and Aspermonte came out of the bedroom with Louis saying,

"It was your left. Setting up with body shots. Boom. Boom. Bang. Jabbing with that lightning left. Following through with the right when it was right. Switching to southpaw to confuse the other guy."   ·

"But I didn't have the power to take me to the championship," said Eddie with maybe a touch of regret. "No real knockout punch. Sixty-three fights, fifty-nine wins, four losses. Only five of the wins were knockouts and they were in the last rounds when I wore the other guy down."

"But you could fight," said Aspermonte. "The people who knew boxing came to see you. People in my business, we saw enough blood and KOs outside of stadiums. We came to fights to see speed and boxing."

"Wish there had been more of you," said Eddie.

I stood watching them as Eddie offered his guest a seat and a cold drink. Louis accepted both.

"Can I ask you something?" asked Aspermonte. "Personal. If I'm out of line, don't be offended, you know what I mean?"

"I know," said Eddie, who looked as if he knew what was going to be asked.

"You lost to Jorgenson," said Louis. "I was there. Second row. You woulda had a championship bout if you beat him. Instead, he won, got the fight and went down in the third round. Jorgenson disappeared back to Sweden or wherever. You threw the Jorgenson fight, didn't you?"

"Yes," said Eddie. "I was getting too old for fighting. I wasn't sure I could beat the champ and I knew without a knockout punch that even if I won the championship, I wouldn't be a popular champ. I didn't draw blood and I didn't put people down on the mat."

"What'd it get you?" said Louis sadly.

"You're inside it," Eddie said, looking around the room and toward the back of the house. "I got enough to retire on for the rest of my life if I lived simple and invested careful. I did and for a while I picked up money doing a little sparring with the heavier fighters. Most of them were slow. A few could have stayed in there with most of the big names and even the champs by jabbing, dancing and staying away, but . . ."

"Lightning," Aspermonte said.

"I walked away with my common sense and an unscarred face," he said.

"I see what you mean," said Aspermonte. "I wish I could do that."

"I'll be back for Louis as soon as I can," I said.

"Don't hurry, Jimmy," Eddie said, walking me to the door. "I could do with a little company, especially company that pumps my ego, knows the fight game and remembers the old days. I put the gloves away a lot of years ago and picked up a fishing rod with Rocky, but I still watch on the television and it doesn't hurt to remember."

"Doesn't hurt at all," I said. "Thanks, Eddie."

"Anytime, Jimmy. You know that."

I looked at Aspermonte, who seemed at home, and went to the Buick. I had a deal to make and I had the feeling I might have to make it fast. I found a Radio Shack, parked, went in and bought the smallest tape recorder they had, complete with tapes. I paid for it on my credit card, which was very close to the maximum. Then, with the salesman watching, I took the recorder out of the box and tested it. It seemed fine. I told the salesman to throw the box away, and I put the loaded recorder in one pocket and the package of two extra tapes in the other. Then I drove to the motel where Troy and Donahue were staying. I had what I had gone for and was ready to deal for Melisa.

I got to the parking lot, looked up at Troy's window and started to get out of the car.

I didn't see where he came from, but Wright was standing there, tall, hands folded, back straight, blond hair in place. I got out, looked around for Big Tony and the Lincoln and saw neither. I did see Wright's red Porsche.

"You are a clever man with a sense of humor," Wright said as I closed the Buick door and stood in front of him. "Whose car was that you dropped Grazzo's body in?"

"A cop named Diehl," I said. "A captain."

"Someone you're not fond of," said Wright with a smile, white teeth closed as if the sun hurt them, the way Rod Serling used to talk on *Twilight Zone.*

"Someone I'm not fond of," I said.

Wright shook his head, smiled and then said,

"Grazzo's getting as much travel as when he was alive, and he's certainly causing more fun."

I was sure he was about to quote some poet in the parking lot, but I beat him to it with part of the poem I had learned from Archer.

"Lo! Death has reared himself a throne
 In a strange city lying alone
 Far down within the dimming West,
 Where the good and the bad and the worst and the best
 Have gone to their eternal rest."

"Poe," Wright said with a big grin. "Did you learn that knowing you'd be running into me again?"

"I'm a poetry lover," I said, putting my hand into my

pocket to turn on the tiny tape recorder. "Did you kill Troy?"

"Kill . . ." he looked offended as my hand came out of my pocket with a celophane-wrapped mint. "We don't kill the FBI, the CIA, the Secret Service, the ATF or federal marshals. No, the reason you're alive right now is that you got away from us and hid Aspermonte somewhere. We want him."

"You came alone," I said.

"Let's say I'm freelancing on this one to get back in the good graces of Mr. Barini, who thinks I'm not making a professional effort to take care of the problem."

"I'm sorry," I said sarcastically.

"I think we should get in my car and go somewhere where we can talk, don't you?" Wright said.

"I can't think of anything else I'd rather do, given the circumstances," I said.

He walked at my side, about two paces away. We got into the red sports car. He started the engine, which purred in perfect tune, and said,

> "Oh! Who in such a night will dare
>   To tempt the wilderness?
>   And who 'mid thunder peals can hear
>   Our signals of distress?"

I could see that this was not going to be a really fun ride.

"Lord Byron," Wright said. "If you live through all this, I strongly recommend Byron to you. I think you may have a lot in common."

We left the parking lot and headed wherever Wright had in mind.

CHAPTER NINE

IT was called Cafe La Luna. It was in Westwood, not far from the UCLA campus. The evening crowd—college kids, people who had heard of the place—were just starting to come in when we sat at a table near the window. Wright picked the place and the table so he could see out the window and his back would be against the wall.

The place wasn't big, but it wasn't tiny either, about a dozen tables, a small platform stage and a coffee bar.

"Try the coffee de la luna," Wright said when the waiter, a thin kid with a white shirt and black pants and curly hair that didn't want to cooperate, came to the table. "Specialty of the house."

I nodded.

"Two coffee de la luna, large, not decaf, and two biscotti with almonds," he said.

The waiter nodded and went away. I had turned off the recorder during our ride and now, out of sight covered by the table, I took out the tiny recorder, placed it between my legs, and hoped I had enough tape and Wright didn't get suspicious. My plan had been to tape my conversation with Troy. This was turning out to be something better.

"We'll be out of here when the show starts unless you want to stay," said Wright. "It's open-comedy-mike night. College kids come because they've been told they're funny. They bring their friends who laugh. The amateurs are usually not very funny, but every once in a while . . ."

"I think I'd like to skip the comedy," I said. "You killed Conforti."

"His real name was Grazzo. I told you," said Wright, seriously looking with interest at the people coming in. "I shot him in the head. I could say it was like the old West, him or me, but you wouldn't believe me and it wouldn't be true. Barini wanted him gone. He was a loose end. Putting him in your trunk was my idea. I didn't have much time to plan. I like the challenge of improvisation."

Gotcha, I thought. Mr. Wright, you're not quite as sharp as you think you are. Wright's weak spot was his ego. He had to have someone to quote poetry to, and he had to have someone to tell how smart he was. I was that person for now and he was in a bragging mood.

Don't run out of tape, I ordered the tiny machine in my lap, hoping that it was picking up the conversation between us.

"So the police would nail me for killing him?" I said.

"Arrest you, maybe," Wright said, smiling at a pair of young girls a few tables down. "You called the police. They didn't have enough evidence to hold you. My idea was to slow you down. But when I called Barini on my car phone, he told me to get the body out of there. So it was gone before the cops showed up. You have to talk to Barini carefully. He's got a temper. He doesn't want to go to jail. Grazzo's body was in the trunk of my car, a situation which I would have preferred not to exist. Barini told me to get rid of it. I took a chance and told him we should give it back to you. By then he was convinced that he didn't need you anymore.

The business about finding Adrienne Wendkos's murderer was a large, neat pile of . . . You were on a wild grouse hunt."

"Then?" I asked as the large cups of coffee and the two plates of biscotti were placed before us.

Wright handed the kid a twenty-dollar bill and said, "No change."

"Thanks," the kid said and hurried away.

It was getting crowded at the Cafe La La. The smells of coffee filled the smoke-free air.

"Then," said Wright, "things started to go crazy and you were in the middle of it. First, a federal marshal decides on his own to take the girl. You've got the pictures we took. Barini doesn't know what the marshal is up to or why he took the girl. If he's trying to turn her into cash, he hasn't tried to contact us. So we get curious. You get on the job. Barini's not about to turn me or anyone else loose on a federal marshal. We play wait-and-see. Then, pop, you bring Aspermonte back into the picture."

"Coffee's good," I said. "Is it safe to dunk the biscotti or will everyone stand up, point at me and give me the biggest laugh of the night?"

"Dunk," he said. "The Italians do."

I dunked.

"Renting the car was a good idea, but we were watching," he said, drinking his coffee a sip at a time. "We planted the bug on Grazzo's body, followed you. Barini almost went berserk when we told him you'd found Aspermonte. We've been looking for him for two or three years. Since he'd been convicted of perjury and had a record, Barini didn't feel his testimony would be particularly believed when Frank Corlis's lawyers tried to get him out. The lawyers figured it balanced out. No Adrienne Wendkos. No Louis Aspermonte. Canceled out."

"Did you personally cancel Adrienne Wendkos?"

"No," he said. "And I don't think Barini ordered it. His plan, I think, was to scare her into not testifying at a new trial. Find her, take her kid, kill her husband. Killing her would be bad for Frankie Corlis. It would probably keep her testimony out of a hearing or a trial. The lawyers would claim they had no opportunity to cross-examine the witness and their case was based on showing that she had lied about seeing Frankie kill her husband, but the prosecutors would get in the information that Adrienne Wendkos had been murdered and Corlis would not get a sympathetic hearing."

"So who killed her?" I asked.

The biscotti were good. I considered ordering another one. Wright anticipated and waved at the kid waiter and then pointed at our empty plates and held up two fingers. The kid nodded. Seconds later we had two more biscotti, the kid had another tip, and the place was jammed.

"Barini figures the feds killed her," Wright said.

"Why?"

"Who knows? Maybe they didn't want to take a chance on her changing her story about the murder. They're better off with a dead martyr than a live witness who changes her testimony."

"You're telling me the federal government had someone in its own witness protection program murdered?" I asked, finishing off my second biscotti. He hadn't started his.

"You don't think it happens?" he asked.

"I don't think so, but I'm a kind of Goody Two-Shoes," I said. "How about a renegade agent acting on his own against policy? He's supposed to protect her and kills her instead."

"Possible," said Wright with a shrug, looking around at the two girls. "But you found Aspermonte and it looks like you turned him. Barini's cheap. He could have spent fifty or sixty thousand and sent Aspermonte to live in Honduras. But Barini didn't want to take any chances. Barini wanted Aspermonte found. He wanted Aspermonte to have an accident. Frankie Corlis said no, Aspermonte was a stand-up guy, went to jail for Frankie. You've got good sources, Rockford. You found him before we did."

"I've got good sources," I said.

"Want to tell me the easy way where you put him?"

"No," I said. "I want a deal. And not from you. I'm trading Aspermonte to the police and his testimony against Corlis in exchange for the girl. You and I have no business. Even if you had Melisa, I wouldn't give you Aspermonte. I know you don't have one, but I've got a conscience. Lots of people do. Gets in the way sometimes, but we have to live with it. I wouldn't turn Aspermonte over to you to be killed."

"Even if it meant getting the girl back?" he asked, looking at me with interest.

"I couldn't do it, Wright, but I could get awfully mad at anyone who hurt the girl."

"Me? The feds?"

"Anyone," I repeated.

Wright grinned and said,

"We shall lie to each other but be the truth.
Whenever you lie to me I shall know it.
Whenever I lie to you, you will feel it.
Let us lie often, for lies between us two
Are secret stories of truth."

"John Lennon," I guessed.

"Elizabeth Sargent," he said. "Now the truth or a lie. How old would you say I am, Rockford?"

"How . . . forty."

"Closer to fifty," he said. "I like my work. I like the money. But I have a fatal flaw right out of Shakespeare. I'm ambitious. I've collected enough on Barini to put him away even longer than Frankie Corlis. I've got it safe and I keep getting more. Barini talks about his old friend and mentor Frank Corlis, but I think he'd be happy if Frank stayed in jail. Barini's been King of Clubs for almost twenty years. He doesn't want to become number two."

"Then why does he want to find Aspermonte?" I asked. "Why was he looking for Adrienne Wendkos?"

"Did he find Aspermonte?" asked Wright.

"No," I said.

"Would it look a little strange if he didn't look for the only witness against his own pal and boss?" he asked next.

"He had almost fifteen years to find her or have her found," Wright said, finishing his coffee. "Grazzo had her running from ghosts that weren't there. Now . . . it's a mess and I'm supposed to clean it up. So Grazzo goes back in your trunk and I'm supposed to get rid of you, the girl, Aspermonte and even Dan Rather or John Travolta if they get in the way."

"But you're not going to do it?" I asked.

He was looking up at the small platform. The lights had gone down. It was still early in the evening, but I got the impression that they started early and finished late. The early acts would probably be the weakest, but you never knew.

"I've got nothing on Frankie Corlis," he explained. "I don't want Corlis out any more than Barini does or the feds do. Nobody wants Corlis out but Corlis. What I've got can only be used against Barini and only when I'm sure Corlis isn't coming out. My immediate problem's going to be explaining why I didn't kill you. I could have shot you and Aspermonte while I was driving today, but I let Tony do the shooting. He can't hit anything even standing still. He's a thumper, not a shooter."

"You're not going to kill me?" I said.

"Here," he said, reaching into his jacket pocket and coming up with a gun that looked awfully familiar. It was my .38.

"Under the table," he said.

I reached under the table and took the gun. I looked down carefully. It was loaded. The tape recorder was still running.

"Make your deal with the feds if you can," he said. "Give 'em Aspermonte. Hide the girl till Corlis loses his trial or hearing, if they even give him one. I'm going to have to put my tarot cards on the table for Barini sooner than I thought. I don't want Barini's job. That he wouldn't give. I want him to help me get a piece of territory where I'm giving the orders."

"He might take a chance and have you killed," I said.

"It would be his mistake," said Wright. "I plan to show him some of the evidence. He and I aren't going to be friends anymore, but he's going to want me alive."

"Amazing where a good education can get you," I said.

Wright shrugged and looked first at the girls, who were looking at him, and then at the guy on the lighted stage. There was a high stool with a glass of water on it and a microphone. The guy on the stage wasn't a kid. He was wearing worn jeans, a flannel shirt and an Exxon cap. He was at least fifty-five and round.

"Some smart-ass kid told me this was Dotty's Diner," he said. "I'm on my way up the coast with my rig. I'm carrying eighty-two thousand tonsil clamps, whatever the hell they are. I never know what I'm carryin'. That's why I keep getting work. I think this used to be Dotty's. Now the corned beef and beer's gone and all they got is coffee that doesn't taste like coffee and desserts it takes ten of to equal a slab of cherry pie. Guy who owns this place talks to me, says I'm funny, says go up there, just tell them what's what. So I figure, what the hell. If there's eight-two thousand people in Fresno needing their tonsils out, it must be catchy and I ain't in no hurry to catch it. You know what I mean?"

"Yeah," came a few voices.

The truck driver took a drink of water, grimaced and said, "Water. You know what's in that stuff? Bugs, chemicals. Beer is healthier. Guy who owns this place now says Dotty went back to school, got all sorts of degrees, teaches philosophy at UCLA. Maybe that's what I should do. Hell, I taught Dotty half of what she knows, some of which can be considered philosophy."

"Let's go," said Wright, putting his napkin on the table. "They like him but they don't think he's funny. Someone should tell him to keep the act short and tell the audience that he'd better get back on the road, but he won't do it. He'll run it into the ground till they stop laughing. You can only laugh for so long at something that's not really funny."

I agreed with him and carefully pocketed the tiny tape recorder when he looked over at the two college girls. We quietly left the Cafe La La after Wright made a brief stop at the table where the two girls were sitting. He pulled out a leather-covered pocket pad while they gave him their phone numbers. He rejoined me at the door. The truck driver on-stage looked at us with a touch of fear. Was he losing his audience? Not yet, I could have told him, but there's trouble right down this lonesome highway.

"Those two girls are going to meet a famous producer and have walk-ons in a movie," Wright said as we stepped into the street.

"Original," I said.

"No," he answered. "They really will meet a famous producer and he really will get them walk-ons and maybe even a few lines. The producer is a good friend of a good friend who Barini once did a big favor for."

"The girls will be grateful," I said as we walked.

"I'm counting on it," he said. "I could have picked them up without the line, but I didn't want to take the time."

"Walk-ons in a movie, a little poetry, a big smile and blond hair," I said. "You can't miss."

"No, Rockford, you know what the clincher always is?"

"No," I said.

"I let them know what I do for a living. I convince them."

"We're not pals, Wright," I said.

"Hell no," he agreed. "I like you, but there's about a fifty-fifty chance I'm going to have to kill you. I need you alive and working now. You get the job done and you walk. You foul up and . . .

"In vain, quoth she, 'I live, and seek in vain
    Some happy mean to end a hapless life.' "

"Bruce Springsteen," I said.

"Shakespeare," Wright answered.

He dropped me off next to the rental car in Troy's motel parking lot. It was getting late and I still wasn't exactly sure how I was going to handle this or with who. I sat waiting for Wright to be safely gone before I pulled out the tape recorder, which was out of tape. I rewound a little and pressed Play. I had everything. I hit the rewind till I got to the conversation at the Cafe La La. There was background noise. Other voices, but the conversation between me and Wright was there and clear enough to make out what we

were both saying. I returned the car, paid the one-day rate
and got a courtesy ride to my Firebird parked less than two
blocks away. I didn't have to walk past the police station,
which was fine with me since I wasn't ready to talk to the
police or anyone else. I wanted to talk to Archer before I did
something that might not be quite legal.

There were a few people on the street, but the stores were
closed or closing and there wasn't much to do in this neighborhood unless you were a cop or a suspect or a bored-
looking guy in a wilted tan sports jacket and blue slacks
leaning against my car and smoking a cigarette. I thought
I recognized the guy so I started to cross the street. The guy
leaning against my car called,

"Rockford."

I came back and stepped in front of him.

"You mind stepping out of the way, Riordon, so I can get
in?" I asked.

"I don't like this job," he said. "I don't mean being a cop.
That I like. At least it's okay, decent pension and you get
used to the long waits. You know, stakeouts, waiting for
possible witnesses or suspects to come home or go to work.
Lots of time to think. Captain Diehl wants to see you."

"I don't want to see him," I said. "Now, if you'll get—"

"Rockford, you're going to see the captain now," said Riordon. "He is in a very bad mood. I have no intention of
going back to him now and telling him I just let you go.
You want me to arrest you? Okay, I'm arresting you for not
crossing at an intersection."

"Riordon," I said, trying to let him know how absurd he
was being.

"Rockford," he said, "you're under arrest."

"Just issue me a citation," I said.

"In addressing a misdemeanor," he said. "I noted that

the offender, you, was carrying a concealed weapon and be-
having suspiciously."

"I want my lawyer," I said.

Riordon pushed away from the car, threw his cigarette
away and said, "That's Captain Diehl's department."

I could probably have forced my way past Riordon, who
was a stringy, pale, almost bald man with a bad cough and
probably only a year or two to retirement. But there was no
percentage in adding a charge of resisting arrest and fleeing
the scene of the crime, the crime being jaywalking.

"Let's go," I said with a sigh.

Riordon nodded and we crossed the street, not at the corner. I considered pointing out this inconsistency and even
had the fleeting idea of making a citizen's arrest on Riordon
for jaywalking, but I didn't have anything to gain and he
was just doing his job.

Diehl was sitting behind the desk in his office, his glasses
on his nose, pretending to read a report.

"Here he is," said Riordon.

Diehl looked up and nodded. Riordon asked,

"Am I off now?"

"Go home," said Diehl.

Riordon left. I wished I had put a new tape in the
recorder. I prayed that Diehl would not have me searched.

Diehl continued to pretend to read the report, and I
moved toward one of the chairs in front of his desk.

"Don't sit," he said, still not looking up.

I didn't sit.

Diehl was tall, rangy, his hair showing gray and his face
showing years of frustration, failure, success at a price, and
a naturally dyspeptic disposition. While standing there
waiting, I wondered if Diehl had a family. There weren't any
pictures on his desk.

Finally, after about three minutes, he put down the report and took off his glasses.

"Sit," he said.

I sat and said,

"You have a family, Diehl?"

"We're not here to talk about my family," he said. "We're here to talk about the late Irving Grazzo."

"You found him?" I asked innocently.

"I was off two hours ago," he said. "I went to the parking lot, opened my trunk to drop my gym bag in and found your present."

"My present?" I said, innocently again.

"Grazzo," he said.

"Dead? Bullet hole where I said it was?"

Diehl was silent, trying to hold his anger in, playing with his glasses.

"I left the trunk open and called for a search of the immediate neighborhood and a questioning of anyone who might have seen who put Grazzo's body in my trunk."

"And?" I asked.

"And we found your car a block away and no you," he said. "You don't like me. I don't like you, but I know my job. I had someone call every car rental agency in the neighborhood in addition to doing other things that cost the city of Los Angeles a lot of unnecessary money and time."

I sat mute.

"You rented a car," Diehl said. "A Taurus."

"No law against it," I said. "My credit card's weak but it's not dead."

"It gets more interesting, Rockford," Diehl said. "I personally checked the car you rented. There were two bullet holes in it. They hadn't cleaned it yet. I checked the trunk. I had two guys from Forensics check the trunk."

"For DNA?" I asked.

"I got the evidence I needed, Rockford," he said.

"I don't think so, Captain," I answered, shaking my head. "But you can prove me wrong by arresting me for whatever the charge might be—moving a dead body, obstructing justice . . ."

"Murder . . ." Diehl added.

"That's a big one," I agreed. "Are you arresting me for any of those? If you are, I want my lawyer."

"We've got time," he said. "First, we talk."

"Fine," I said. "I'll call my lawyer."

"Informal," he said. "No tape. No witnesses. Just you and me."

"Let's say we limit it to ten minutes," I said.

"Let's say no limit," he answered, looking as if he were going to break his glasses.

"Let's just talk," I said. "When I want to stop, I stop and my lawyer comes or I walk."

"I'm not going to forget your little joke, Rockford," he said.

"Captain," I answered with a sigh, "there's no point in threatening me. You said you don't like me and I don't like you. You've tried over the past two decades to nail me on charges ranging from murder to illegal double parking. You've even managed to have me locked up overnight three or four times. But you've never gotten me convicted of anything."

"Maybe that's why I don't like you," he said.

"Maybe it's because you've been feeling Lieutenant Becker breathing down your neck every day."

"Rockford, let's say that Becker might be sitting in this office as a captain if it weren't for you," he said. "His record shows a long-term relationship to a private investigator who's been arrested enough times to have a file as thick as *The Celestine Prophecy.*"

"That's not too thick," I said.

"Thick enough to make it a best-seller for the promotion review board," Diehl said.

"I'm listening," I said.

"Aspermonte," he said. "I want him. I want to turn him over to the feds. You've got him."

"You have an arrest order for him?" I asked.

"No."

"Louis Aspermonte is a private citizen," I said. "He did time and isn't even on probation. If I knew where Aspermonte was, there wouldn't be a legal reason I had to tell you. By the way, how did you know I might know where this Aspermonte might be?"

"A tip," he said.

Wright, I thought.

"You've got him to agree to testify against Corlis," Diehl went on.

"Is that a question?"

"A statement."

"I was going to deal straight with Donahue and Troy," I said, "but it makes no difference to me. My deal is simple. I get the girl, Melisa, and the feds get Louis Aspermonte, who might very well be willing to testify against Corlis in exchange for witness protection."

Diehl looked down at the table, thinking.

"I'll work on it," he said.

"If it happens," I said, standing, "I turn Aspermonte over to you and Lieutenant Becker at the same time. If not, he goes right to the feds."

Diehl nodded. He'd find a way to get all the credit. His problem now was that he had to help me find Melisa.

"I've got two men on overtime going over the trunk of that rented car of yours," he said, standing. "They're going to find a strand of hair, a piece of cloth, a thread of carpet, a spot of blood the size of a needle point. They're going to find it and prove Grazzo's body was in there. We've got a deal on Aspermonte, but I'm going to get you for dumping that body in my trunk. When I prove that, I'm coming for you on a suspicion of murder charge. I'm going to get the last laugh."

I went to the door without looking back and he added,

"I'll call you when I set things up to turn the girl over to you."

I didn't answer. I went out and closed his door. I heard his fist hit the desk and I wondered if he had smashed his glasses. There were cops all over, but Dennis wasn't at his desk and Riordon was probably halfway home.

If I had it figured right, it was reasonably safe to go home. The police weren't looking for me. Barini, according to the poetic Mr. Wright, wanted me to succeed, and if Donahue and Troy showed up, they were just the people I was looking for.

THINGS looked quiet and dark on the Cove. There was a light on in the Travis trailer. I could hear a few voices and the faint sound of music from the bar down the beach. The waves were high. I stood next to my car, listening to the waves. I'd miss them if I ever decided to or had to move. Mrs. Bailey was in for the night. There was a light on in her trailer.

My trailer was dark, but I thought I heard a sound inside. I took out my .38 and turned my key slowly in the lock. Lying on my couch, munching Doritos out of a bag in the light of the television set, was Angel Martin.

"Angel," I said. "What the hell are you doing here?"

He sat up and said,

"Jimmy, don't turn on the lights. And try to show a little gratitude. Remember I had this place cleaned up and

furnished and got you the new television when I was in the
money."

I put my gun back in the holster and sat next to him to
hear his story. A cop show was on television. I didn't recognize the actors. I turned off the sound.

"Life is not a yellow brick road we walk down to take us
home," he said, still watching the silent image.

"Angel, what happened?"

"It was goin' so great, Jimmy, wasn't it?"

"It looked good, Angel," I said. "We are talking about
your artist scam?"

"Jimmy," he said, almost in tears. "That vampire of an art
critic Lyons brought, the one who said my work was brilliant . . . ?"

"I remember," I said.

"He and Lyons set up a preview showing, testing a few
canvases, for local critics and a few dealers. Did it this morning. Didn't tell me," Angel went on.

"But you got paid, Angel," I reminded him.

"After the critics looked at the paintings, Lyons tried to
stop payment on the check. I had already cashed it. He
called me and told me he was sending back the paintings
and was letting my clients know I was a fraud. Can they
come after me? I mean the ones who got the portraits
done?"

"What happened?"

"Every critic said Lyons must be trying to pull a fast one,"
sighed Angel. "They called my paintings dabs of paint even
an idiot could produce. Lyons's critic, it turns out, is a lush
looking for a comeback. There's going to be an article about
me in the papers tomorrow. They're gonna dig and find out
who I really am. People are going to be looking for me to
get their money back. But a deal's a deal, right, Jimmy?"

"I don't know, Angel," I said. "You misrepresented yourself and you didn't paint the portraits you sold. Sounds like fraud."

"Oh," moaned Angel, putting his head in his hands. "I've got to clear out."

He suddenly stood up.

"I'll go to Miami, stay with my Uncle Roberto, you know, the tile cutter," he said, starting to pace and looking at the silent image on the television screen. He paused and said, "That guy, the one with the glasses, he's the killer. You can see it coming a football field away."

"You have any money left?" I asked.

He pulled a wad of bills out of his jacket pocket.

"About thirty thousand," he said. "But I could have run it into a fortune. Now I've got to spend some of this on a car that'll get me to Miami and I'll have to sleep here tonight."

It wasn't a request and I didn't feel up to arguing with Angel.

"Make yourself comfortable, Angel," I said. "But I think you should know I might be getting a visit from a couple of U.S. Marshals about Melisa."

"U.S. Marshals?" he said, looking up from the television. "Is there some federal law about what I did?"

"I don't think so," I said.

"I don't suppose you'd let me borrow the pickup or the Firebird for a few months till things blow over and I can come back to L.A.?"

I shook my head no in the low light of the television and said,

"Not a chance, Angel."

"How about for just tonight? I'll go sleep at my cousin's and bring it back in the morning after I pick up a car."

"Nope," I said. "I've got a feeling you'd just keep driving to Florida and send me a postcard."

"Would I do that?" he asked, sounding hurt.

"You've done it before," I said. "You take the pickup or the bird when I'm asleep and I report it stolen and on the way to Miami."

"After all I've done for you," he said, sitting again and almost weeping.

"And I appreciate it, Angel, but I'm not crazy. Don't touch one of my vehicles. I'll drive you to a used-car lot in the morning."

"Burt's on Fairfax," he said.

"Burt's on Fairfax," I agreed.

"I'm hungry," he said.

"Help yourself."

"I already looked. You don't have much, Jimmy. I mean you've got food but I need a pizza or something."

"Order one," I said, moving to the phone to check my messages. "You can afford it. Or walk down to the bar. It's still open. They serve burgers and steak sandwiches."

"I'll call a pizza place," he said.

There were four calls. Three were from people I was overdue in paying and one was from a Mr. and Mrs. Roy Palmer, who said they might be able to use my services, that I was highly recommended, and they needed to hear from me soon. The Palmers left a number. I wrote it on my pad and said to Angel,

"You can turn on the lights now. I'm allowed to do that in my own house."

Angel turned on the lights, glanced at the television and said,

"See, he did it. What are you doing?"

"I'm making a call," I said.

"Let me call the pizza place first," he said, reaching for the phone book. "I need it, Jimmy."

I stepped away from the desk and pointed to the phone.

Angel checked the Santa Monica yellow pages, found a number and made his call. I took off my shoes, put my .38 back in the cookie jar and moved to my closet, where I put my shoes and hung my holster. I was starting to get undressed as Angel was saying to whoever was taking his pizza order,

"Double anchovy. No, triple. Now you've got it. Triple anchovy, pepperoni, double cheese, onion and mushroom. A large pizza. Your ad says forty-five minutes or I don't have to pay. I just checked my watch. You've got the address."

He hung up as Troy and Donahue came through the door.

Angel backed against the wall and said softly, "No."

I came back into the room and said,

"Warrant?"

"No," said Donahue. "You want us to go?"

"No," I said.

"I didn't think so," said Donahue.

Troy closed the door. Both marshals were wearing their suits. I was wearing my underwear. Troy looked as if he was having a bad migraine.

"Who are these guys, Jimmy?" Angel asked.

"U.S. Marshals Donahue and Troy," I said.

I didn't introduce Angel.

"Tell your friend to go for a walk for about ten minutes," Donahue said.

"I'm goin'," Angel said. "If my pizza comes, pay the man and I'll pay you back."

Angel slipped on his loafers, eased past the marshals with a sick grin and went out for a walk.

I went behind my desk and sat down. They stood.

"My partner got a little carried away," Donahue said. "Got a little premature in picking up the girl. But he had reasons. We had information that Barini's people knew where she was. So did we. You did a lousy job of hiding the girl, Rockford."

"Right," I said. "I did a lousy job. Now we play Let's Make a Deal."

Donahue was shaking his head. Then he spoke.

"You want to trade the girl for Aspermonte."

"Right."

"Is Aspermonte ready to testify against Corlis, to change his testimony?"

"You'd have to ask him that," I said. "My guess is that he might. But I don't know."

"Meaning you don't want to say anything that would incriminate you for hiding a government witness."

I shrugged. Troy looked heavy-lidded and beaten down. Donahue looked as if he were just warming up.

"We know about Grazzo's body," he said.

"Captain Diehl told me," I said. "I told you he was dead."

"What if the girl doesn't want to go with you?" he asked.

"She will," I said.

"She doesn't," he said.

"I want her to tell me that in person," I said.

"If we persuade her to go with you, you turn in Aspermonte, who's willing to testify?"

"I think he might be willing to testify for immunity from perjury charges and if he's put into a witness protection program," I said, wishing I had my shoes on. "I'm working with Captain Diehl on that. You should coordinate all this with him."

"What if we don't need Aspermonte?" Troy said.

Donahue gave him a "Shut up" look.

"You need him," I said. "If you want Corlis to stay in prison. If we make a deal, I turn Aspermonte over to the L.A. police and they turn him over to you."

"Barini's got a man, maybe more, in the L.A. police department," said Donahue. "Remember?"

"Maybe a woman," I said. "Let's not be sexist."

"Rockford, Barini probably knows about all this. You're the one who needs protection."

"What if Barini doesn't want Corlis out of prison?" I said. This interested Donahue.

"Interesting idea," he said. "You have any reason for supposing he might not want Corlis out besides wanting to remain in charge?"

"A source," I said.

"If you're right," said Donahue, "what would happen if Corlis found out? If we gave him some evidence that Barini wasn't really working to get him out? I'm just speculating."

"Corlis would be upset with his protégé," I said. "He might even be willing to have someone turn in evidence against Barini. You'd keep Corlis in jail and get Barini."

"You've got someone who could convince Corlis?" Donahue asked.

"Maybe," I said, thinking that Wright might be convinced to have a very private talk with Corlis or come up with someone who would. I had no idea of how Wright might react when he found out about the tape, but he was a man who looked out for himself. It was dangerous, but I thought I could deal with him. My first order of business when Donahue and Troy left would be to make a copy of the tape on the recorder in my desk drawer. Then I'd get the original to Archer in an envelope and tell him to keep it somewhere safe.

"More than maybe, I think," I said. "Now, I talk to Melisa in person before I turn Aspermonte over. We have a deal?"

"I have to check with Washington," Donahue said. "But

I think I can safely say I can convince them to make the deal if they need convincing. Stay healthy, Rockford."

Donahue and Troy left. Angel was back inside the second their car drove off.

"Jimmy," he said. "I think the younger one recognized me."

"They don't want you, Angel," I said.

"You sure?" he said, looking back at the door.

"I'm sure," I said, dialing the Palmer number. There was no answer, but there was a machine. I left my name and said I'd be happy to discuss their problem with them and that they should call me back.

Angel turned on the television. He watched Jay Leno and waited for pizza. I realized I was hungry too.

I took my tape recorder from my desk drawer, went into my bedroom, closed the door and made the copy. I heard a knock on the door and Angel arguing with someone. I kept the original in my pocket, hid the copy under a loose board in the floor, and came out as Angel slammed the door. He was holding a large pizza box in his hand.

"She was two minutes late, Jimmy," he said. "I checked on my watch and your clock. She wouldn't give me the pizza unless I paid. I should have got it free."

"Life's like that," I said, moving to my desk and taking out one of the two small brown envelopes I had left. I put the tape in it as Angel put the box on my small table and opened it. "You've got thirty thousand in cash. Forget about the free pizza and getting the delivery girl in trouble."

I was hit by the smell of pepperoni and anchovies.

"It better be hot," Angel said, "or there's gonna be trouble."

"You've already got trouble, Angel," I said. "Don't push it."

I called Archer and asked him to meet me at a coffee

shop on Melrose at nine the next morning. He agreed and I hung up.

Angel and I ate pizza and watched the end of the Jay Leno show. Angel changed the channel, found a dubbed Italian horror movie and waved over his shoulder at me when I told him I was going to sleep.

I spent an hour in bed thinking about how I was going to handle this and hearing the sound of overwrought emotion from the voices on the television.

Eventually, I got up and went out, to find Angel asleep. I turned off the television and went back to bed. I set the alarm for seven-thirty. I was asleep a few seconds later.

I woke up in the morning with an awful aching head. That was a line from the blues song Blind Lemon Blake was singing at the Sandy Boone Bar and Grill a few centuries ago. I found the tape where I'd left it, showered, shaved, shampooed, dressed in tan chinos, a white short-sleeved shirt with a button-down collar, my holster and my white windbreaker. I pocketed the envelope and went to get my .38. Angel was asleep and snoring. The room smelled like pizza.

I took a chance and called Archer's number.

"Fred Archer, Attorney," he said.

"I'm leaving now," I said. "New Hollywood Coffee Shop on Melrose," I said softly.

"Right," he said. "I'm on my way."

There was a chance I might be talking to the L.A. police, the U.S. Marshal's office and Barini when I talked to Archer, but they knew Archer was my lawyer and would assume we were meeting simply to discuss my problems with the law. If they came, they could hold a crime convention and try to hear what I said to Archer, but I doubted if they'd bother.

I folded the pizza box, threw it in the garbage, put my gun in the holster and touched Angel on the shoulder. He leaped up looking for vampires or someone from the bunco squad.

"Jimmy," he said, "I had a nightmare."

"You can tell me about it on the way to Burt's car lot, where I'm dropping you. We've got to move. I've got an appointment."

"What about breakfast?" Angel asked, putting on his shoes and buttoning his shirt.

"You can drive your nice new car to the nearest coffee shop," I said. "And then you can head for Uncle Roberto in Miami. Maybe he'll teach you the tile cutting business."

"Jimmy," he said, patting down his hair and beard and rubbing his finger across his teeth, "you can be a hard man sometimes."

"I hope you're right, Angel. Let's go."

CHAPTER TEN

ANGEL complained all the way to Burt's Deluxe Automobiles on Fairfax. Life was unfair. He was born under an unlucky star and his mother had forgotten to spit three times through her fingers. Just before he was born when his mother went out to get water, she was followed by a dark man with a strange smell who tried to engage her in suggestive conversation. The family was convinced the dark man was the devil and the encounter had marked the coming baby. It sounded reasonable to me. Angel was surrounded by enemies. Nothing ever went right.

"Am I a decent human being, Jimmy? I ask you."

I kept driving and turned on the radio. I pushed a button for the fifties and sixties oldies station. There's also a station that plays thirties and forties records but I can never find it.

"Do I take it from your silence that you don't think I'm a decent human being?"

Angel had turned in the passenger seat to face me and put a pained expression on his face and his right hand on the approximate location of his heart.

"As human beings go, Angel, you're decent," I said.

"Okay," he said. "Then why does everything happen to me? What has God got against me?"

"Angel, you make a living by convincing people to give you money in exchange for land you don't own, expertise you don't have, gadgets that don't work, religious fraud, and . . . Do you want me to go on or do we listen to the Who?"

"A man has to make a living," he said sullenly, folding his arms and sitting back. "This is what I do. I just wish I did it better. Is it fair the scams Marvin Yakamoto gets away with? Or old Sol Katz?"

"Sol Katz?" I asked before I could stop myself.

"Little, bald guy," said Angel. "Dark three-piece rumpled suits. Wears a pocket watch. Been playing a fake estate lawyer for about thirty years. Contacts people with good jobs, owners of car dealerships, managers of research laboratories, that kind of thing."

"I remember," I said. "He makes an appointment and comes in with a briefcase full of papers for them to sign so they can get the hotel in Florida their great-aunt left them."

"Gets a hefty check for 'inheritance coverage payments' and hands them a phony document saying they own a place that doesn't exist. Leaves a paper trail a Boy Scout could follow. Now, why doesn't he ever get caught?"

"He's smart," I said.

"And I'm not? Is that what you're saying? I'm not smart?"

"Let's say you tend to get a little too greedy and you hang your shingle out on the edge."

"It's not fair," he said.

"If life were fair, Angel, you wouldn't have any work at all. You've got more than thirty thousand in your pocket. I'd call that a good score."

"Could have been maybe millions, Jimmy," he said. "Jerry the shrink, the one who looks like Freud and never got past sixth grade, says I sabotage my own scams. I feel guilty or something."

"I don't think you feel guilty," I said.

"No," he agreed. "But things do always screw up just when I'm about to make it really big. I shouldn't have thrown those parties, Jimmy. Three parties, seventy thousand. You know what a decent band costs? Thought a good front would pay off. I could have had close to a hundred thousand if I hadn't thrown those parties. They were great parties, but . . ."

"You'll come up with something, Angel," I said. "You always do."

"Yeah, Jimmy, but what if I'm losing my touch? I'm not getting any younger."

"How old is Sol Katz, or Whitey Speed or Roberto Cruz or Abdul . . . ?"

"The old pros, Jimmy. Dyin' off," Angel said with what sounded like sincere nostalgia. "Portable Harris is gone. And Lou Farmerant, remember him?"

"That wasn't my point, Angel."

Angel wasn't listening. He was shaking his head when I stopped in front of Burt's. Burt's Deluxe had luxury used cars up front in the front lot and he had what Angel was looking for in the back lot. Word was around that not all of Burt's cars, luxury and otherwise, came equipped with authentic papers, but they did have papers, and the buyer could always claim he was taken and Burt could always reopen in Anaheim and call himself Mort.

Angel started to get out. He reached into the backseat for the suitcase he had packed.

"Angel," I said, "take my advice. Don't buy a hot car.

Pay the extra dollars and go in something the cops can't trace to an owner who's already collected insurance on a stolen vehicle."

Angel nodded, stood there for a few seconds trying to look forlorn.

"Have a good time in Miami," I said and reached over to close the door.

I could see him standing there on the sidewalk in front of Burt's, suitcase in hand, watching me drive away. It almost got to me. Almost.

The place where I was meeting Archer wasn't far from Burt's. I had figured it that way. At nine, the coffee shop was relatively empty. Breakfast was over for most people, and they were at work. A few older retirees lingered, talking to each other or their regular waitress. One pair of old men were arguing loudly about the Chicago Cubs, not today's team but the Cubs in the 1930s.

"Bill Nicholson," said one of the old men emphatically. He wore glasses, weighed no more than one hundred and ten pounds and gripped a cane in his lap ready for serious battle against his potbellied and bald opponent across the table, who said calmly,

"Hank Sauer."

"No comparison. Different era," said the stick of a man with the stick of a cane.

Archer was in a booth near the window. He was reading a newspaper, holding it close so he could see through his thick glasses. Archer was casual today. Slacks, a white polo shirt. When I got closer, I could see a white zipper jacket on the seat next to him. I sat directly across from my lawyer.

"What's up?" he asked eagerly.

I ordered the special, which was good till ten o'clock, two eggs over easy, hash browns, and English muffin and coffee, and when the waitress was gone, I said,

"Reach under the table. I'm going to hand you an enve-lope. Put it in your jacket pocket."

"I love this stuff," Archer said with a smile, taking the en-velope from me under the table.

"There's a tape inside it. Get it somewhere safe and see to it that Lieutenant Becker gets it if something happens to me."

"Like?"

"Like death or disappearance."

Archer nodded with understanding and I proceeded to bring him up to date. He looked puzzled.

"Why would Melisa not want to go back to you?" he asked.

"Implication is they've convinced her that Corlis's people will get her to complete their revenge and as a warning to other parents who might want to testify against mob bosses. That is, of course, unless she stays in the witness protection program."

"But she's not a witness to anything," said Archer. "There's no program like that, I don't think."

"Maybe it's something new," I said.

"There's no program like that," he said again, sipping his coffee.

The morning sun shined through the window, highlight-ing his right cheek. His face was ebony black and deep in thought.

"Okay, there's no program like that," I agreed as the waitress brought my order and I started with the coffee.

"And," he said, "from what you say, I get the impression that the marshals weren't all that hot to make a deal to get Aspermonte. They didn't put enough pressure on you. They didn't—"

"I know," I said, as puzzled as he was. "Something's going on."

"You want me there when, and if, they let you talk to Melisa?"

"I want to talk to her alone if they let me," I said. "If they don't let me see her, I'll threaten to go to the newspapers and television stations claiming my daughter has been kidnapped by the U.S. Marshal's office."

"My grandmother, who raised me from the time I was six, said, 'Don't threaten something unless you plan to do it. Once the other side knows your word's no good, they got you.' "

"Wise grandmother," I said. "But there are times in my business when you have to try a bluff or two."

"Are you bluffing about going to the press?" he asked, chewing on the remains of a piece of overdone rye toast.

"I'm not bluffing," I said.

"Interesting. Well, I'll get to work trying to get a court order for you to see her if they refuse. I don't know if I can get one since we have no proof that she's your daughter, but there are things I can do. You're forcing me to learn California law very fast."

"Sorry," I said, working on my eggs.

"Don't be," Archer said, adjusting his glasses. "I need to know and I know how to cram. Want to know a secret of law, Jim?"

I nodded. Secrets were my trade.

"Well," he said, "I learned it from one of my law professors. Not in class. At a bar at night. He said the trick wasn't knowing the law. The trick was knowing enough of the law to convince the bench and the other side that you knew it all. You have to act. You have to be confident and you have to know how much ammunition you need. Study the law first, but study your opposition—including the judge and jury if necessary—even harder."

"Sounds like good advice," I said. I was about to finish off my hash browns when Archer looked up, squinted past me and I felt someone slipping into the booth next to me.

"Angel," I said.

"Heard you on the phone yesterday when you mentioned meeting here," he said.

Angel was wearing a big white cowboy hat that was definitely not new.

"Angel, go away," I said.

"Relax, Jimmy," he said. "No one'll recognize me under this hat. Burt threw it in with the 'ninety Toyota Corolla. Got a good deal. Burt says the old engine and radiator blew and he put in an engine from a new GEO with only four hundred miles on it. Radiator's brand new. Got the car for two thousand."

Angel reached over the table, his right hand out to the wary Archer.

"Name's Jensen, Jackie Jensen," Angel said, taking Archer's extended hand. "But you can call me Angel, nickname. I'm hungry. I wonder if I can still catch the morning special."

"I'm Fred Archer," he said. "Mr. Rockford's attorney."

"Beth Davenport is Jimmy's attorney," Angel said with a you-can't-put-one-over-on-me smile.

"She's busy," he said. "It was her idea."

Angel nodded and waved at the waitress, who walked over to our booth and let Angel order the special. When she was gone, he rubbed his hands together and said, "What's goin' on?"

"Angel," I said. "Go to Florida now. And I'll give you some advice. That hat makes you stand out enough for any cop to be suspicious."

"Jimmy, I'm wearing Levi's and a checked shirt. I'm a

cowboy or a Oklahoma oil mogul. You do it all the time. Mind if I have half of that English muffin while we wait for my breakfast?"

"Take it," I said. "Eat and go. Angel, I can play a cowboy or an Oklahoma oil man. I look the part. Your casting is all wrong. Go look in a mirror."

"Jimmy, I've been thinking," he said, nibbling at the English muffin. "I don't think I want to go as far as Miami. I've been thinking San Diego and staying in touch to see when the search is over."

"I suggest Miami," I said.

"Got lots of relatives in San Diego," he countered.

"Jackie Jensen," Archer said, looking at Angel, whose face was partially hidden by the stupid hat. "There was a baseball player, good one my uncle says, named Jackie Jensen. Wouldn't get into airplanes. Drove himself and was always on time. Of course that was back in the days before Major League ball was west of Saint Louis and north of the border."

"His name is Evelyn Angelo Martinez, aka Angel Martin, aka about two hundred other things," I said.

"Jimmy," Angel whispered, giving me a nudge.

"Mr. Archer is my attorney," I said. "Whatever I tell him is in confidence."

"In confidence," Fred Archer repeated. "You need an attorney, Mr. Martin?"

Angel sat up as his plate of food came.

"Not a bad idea," he said. "Never thought of it. You expensive?"

"No," said Archer. "I'm new."

"He's good, Angel, but I think you should go to San Diego, Miami or Vancouver."

"Can we talk about my little problem for just a minute here, Jimmy?"

I looked at Archer, trying to suggest with a look of dis-

taste that representing Angel might be a very bad idea.
Angel had exhausted dozens of lawyers and still owed some
of them money. Most had given up trying to collect.

"I had a new card made up yesterday," Archer said,
pulling out his wallet. He handed one card to me and one
to Angel. "I'm concentrating most of my energy now on
Mr. Rockford's legal situation, but I'll be happy to talk to
you this afternoon. Three?"

Angel and I took the cards. Angel looked at it and up at
Archer.

"I'll be there," he said.

"I've got to go," Archer said, reaching into his wallet for
money.

"It's on Angel," I said. "He has about thirty thousand
dollars in his pocket."

"Jimmy," Angel hissed between his teeth.

Archer smiled, said he'd take care of what I had given
him and would be available if I needed him. He told Angel
he looked forward to seeing him later. He seemed to think
Angel was an interesting character. Then Archer left.

"Angel," I said, "pay the bill and I don't want to see you
again until you're clear. I can't afford right now to be ac-
cused of consorting with a wanted fraud artist."

Angel's mouth, the only part of him I could see clearly,
smiled.

"Artist," he said. "See, even you called me an artist."

"I'm leaving now, Angel," I said. "Move out of the way so
I can slide out and get on with my life."

"One question, Jimmy," he whispered, looking around
to be sure no one could hear him. "How did you get
Christopher Darden to represent you and why is he using
that phony name and hiding behind those fake glasses?"

"Fred Archer doesn't look anything like Christopher Darden," I said. "Now move, Angel, or you'll fly."

Angel got up and said,

"You don't have to get huffy."

"Yes, I do," I said. "I really have to."

Across the restaurant, the two old men were now arguing about football. Both their faces were red and they were leaning across the table.

"Bronko Nagurski," said the thin one, tapping his cane on the floor.

"Sid Luckman," said the other.

"Johnny Unitas."

"Red Grange."

"Joe Montana."

"Joe Montana? He's still playing I think."

"So, Sam Huff."

"Gonna play that way, Jerry Rice."

"That's it," said the skinny old man. "I can't carry on a civilized conversation with an idiot."

I left Angel with his food and the check. The waitress had walked over to the table where the two men were arguing and she said gently but firmly,

"Walter, Cookie, calm down."

Through the window, I could see Angel stuffing his face with food under the brim of his cowboy hat.

I hadn't parked far from the coffee shop. I still had a few minutes left on the meter. Good old Riordon was sitting back against the fender of my Firebird smoking a cigarette and squinting at me. He was wearing the same suit he had the day before.

"Déjà vu," I said.

"For both of us," he answered. "Feds want to see you. Diehl said they could use me to bring you in, that you wouldn't put up an argument."

"No argument," I said. "You have breakfast?"

"At home," he said. "Coffee, raisin bran. Let's go."

I didn't bother to ask how he found me. My guess was that I was right about my phone being tapped. I asked him if it was all right to drive my car and he could follow me. I could feed the meter, but it would run out and the chances were more than good that I'd pick up a ticket if I parked on the street near the station.

"I don't think that would trouble the captain," he said. "But we're not going to the station."

The reasons could be many, but one was that the station might be watched by Barini's people, who supposedly wanted Melisa.

I followed Riordon, who drove a two-year-old dark Mazda. He kept checking the rearview mirror to be sure I was there and no one was following us. I checked too. No one was following us. Then I had a sinking feeling. Wright or one of Barini's other people could have put a detector back on my car during the night or while I was having breakfast. There was nothing I could do about it now. I followed Riordon to Venice, where we went to the police station and parked on the street. There was no room in the lot and we had no passes.

We walked in together.

"A Captain Morris, Jack Morris, in back," Riordon said. "I'm heading back to the station to listen to Diehl tell me what he's going to do to you and Dennis. You know what, Rockford? Diehl and I have something in common. We talk too much and to the wrong people. Good luck."

"Thanks," I said and went past a trio of young cops in uniform. One was a woman.

I had no trouble finding Captain Morris's office. I knocked, and a familiar voice said, "Come in, Rockford."

I went in and Troy closed the door.

Melisa was sitting in a wooden chair. Donahue was standing at her side. She stood up, a very worried look on her face, glanced at Donahue, who nodded to her, and she took a few steps toward me. I took a few steps too and she came into my arms. She was wearing a blue-and-white-checked sundress. Her hair was brushed and smelled gently sweet. When she stepped back I could see her eyes were moist. She wasn't wearing any makeup and she looked fresh, clean and very sad.

"Tell him," said Donahue gently.

Melisa hesitated and said,

"I want to thank you for your concern and help," she said. "But I want to go with them. I'll be safer with them."

I wanted to say, 'Don't count on it,' but I didn't. Instead I said,

"Melisa, I don't think anyone is out to get you. I think you'll be safe with me. We'll figure out what to do. That's my job. You're my client, remember?"

She smiled but it passed quickly. She shook her head and said,

"No. I really thank you, but for now I want to go with them."

"Have you been threatened?" I asked.

She shook her head no.

"Did they promise you the full moon?"

Again she shook her head no.

"Well, Rockford," said Donahue. "Do we get Aspermonte?"

"I don't know," I said. "Something's wrong with this picture."

"We talked to Washington," Donahue said. "Aspermonte will be given complete immunity from all charges that might stem from his testimony. That includes perjury and anything else. Our department will stick by that promise."

I had turned on the tape recorder in my pocket before I stepped into the office, and the discussion had a definite odor I didn't like but hoped I'd never have to use. Taking on the federal government was more than I wanted to do, and I didn't plan to do it unless I had to and Archer agreed. I didn't want to take on Wright or Barini, either, but I might have to, even if Melisa didn't come with me.

"Witness protection," I said.

Donahue shook his head no.

"Washington said no. I tried to convince them," he said without conviction. "Washington thinks his testimony isn't worth anything if he's given witness protection. He's an old man who's been living in a rat hole and hasn't got the money to pay for it. We give him witness protection and Corlis's attorneys will tear him apart, say he's changed his mind again to get a free ride from the government for the rest of his life."

What I wanted to say was "Come on, Donahue. You know a review board, a grand jury, a trial judge or a jury will believe Aspermonte if they want to keep Corlis in prison. A good government lawyer can argue that Aspermonte needs witness protection or he runs more than just a risk of having more than an accident."

That's what I wanted to say, but the tape was running, so I said, "I don't think Mr. Aspermonte will be interested, but I'll ask him. Donahue, you promised him witness protection."

"I promised to ask my boss to get him in the program," Donahue said. "I didn't promise beyond that."

Melisa wasn't paying attention. She was back in the chair, looking up at me forlornly. I looked at Troy. He had nothing to say. He was a beaten man who was worrying about holding on to his job and possibly facing a criminal charge for trying to keep Melisa from Barini.

"One more reason you might want to ask Aspermonte to turn himself in to testify," said Donahue. "We understand that the car you rented and the body in Captain Diehl's trunk have a definite fiber match."

"I don't see how," I said, hoping he was bluffing and about to say it was time to call my lawyer.

"Suit yourself," said Donahue. "But it will help you if Aspermonte comes in and testifies."

"What if he testifies again that Corlis didn't do it?" I said. "What if he's too frightened to tell the truth without protection?"

Donahue stood at ease, hands behind his back, legs apart. The man had a military past.

"That's our problem," he said. "But if you bring him in, we can overlook the fiber evidence and charges of obstructing justice, among other things."

"Discussion is over," I said. "Melisa, call me tonight, collect will be just fine. Any objections, Donahue?"

"No," he said. "If the young lady wants to."

"I want to," she said, looking at me as if she had something to say but couldn't.

"Good-bye," I said, turning to face Troy, who stood in front of the door. He stepped out of the way and I had my hand on the doorknob. I looked back at Melisa with a keep-your-chin-up smile I didn't feel. She smiled back.

"One last thing, Rockford," Donahue said. "You rented two cars yesterday. The first one was turned in with two bullet holes in the window."

"I made a mistake and drove through a bad neighborhood," I said.

"Where are the good neighborhoods?" Donahue said. "Both cars you rented had evidence of Grazzo's body having been in the trunk. Think hard about our offer. Good-bye, Mr. Rockford."

I went through the door and closed it. I wanted to slam it, but I didn't. As soon as I was alone, I turned off the tape recorder. It didn't make sense. It was out of my way to go all the way back to the Cove, and I wanted to get to Aspermonte fast. I went to a drugstore, bought a cheap tape recorder and a couple of brown paper envelopes. I got back to the car and made a rough copy of my conversation with Donahue and Melisa. Then I got out and checked my car for a bug. Nothing. I even pulled into a garage half a block away and paid ten dollars to hoist the Firebird on the rack.

"What's the problem?" the little man in a greasy striped uniform asked.

"Nothing," I said after checking. "Thought I heard something."

"Want a pro to check?" he asked.

"No thanks," I said.

He shrugged, said, "Suit yourself," and let my car down.

Tarzana is in the valley, not close to North Hollywood, but not all that far, either. I didn't know when I would be back this way and I could use the time to think and be as sure as I could be that I wasn't being followed. I pulled out my notebook when I came to a stop light and found the address I was looking for. I took the San Diego Freeway to the Ventura Freeway, got off in Encino and found the address I was looking for on a street just off of Ventura Boulevard. It was a storefront. Venetian blinds blocked out the sun and eyes of the curious. In the lower left-hand corner of the door to the storefront printed in gold letters was PEMBERTON ENTERPRISES.

I tried the door. It wasn't open. There was no bell. I knocked. A few seconds later, the door opened and a young man who couldn't have been more than twenty-five stood before me with a smile. He was wearing a suit and tie. His hair was dark, neatly cut. He was short, of average weight and had pink cheeks.

"Yes sir?" he said.

"Mr. Pemberton?" I said with my own smile.

"There is no Mr. Pemberton," he said, still standing in the doorway. "I'm Jeffrey Sullivan."

"You're in charge?" I asked.

"I'm in charge," he admitted, his smile growing broader.

"May I come in for a minute or two?" I said.

"Well," he answered looking me over, "I'm expecting a client. I thought it was she when you knocked, but . . ."

"It's important," I said holding my own smile and taking a step forward into the doorway.

"It will have to be fast, Mr. . . ."

"Archer," I said, handing him the card Fred Archer had given me a few hours earlier.

He looked at the card and handed the card back to me.

"What can I do for you, Mr. Archer?" he asked, a touch of caution creeping into his voice.

I stepped past him and looked around. The store was small. There was a desk to the left with no one behind it and another desk toward the back with a computer on top of it. The floor was covered with cheap blue carpet and the walls were covered with framed photographs of famous people, a few of whom—Joe Louis, Janis Joplin, Ulysses S. Grant— I recognized.

Sullivan closed the door.

"We can talk at my desk," he said, moving back to the desk with the computer. "But I'm afraid it will have to be brief."

I followed him to the desk, where he sat behind the computer. I didn't sit.

"Mrs. Gwen Bailey," I said.

He shook his head, bit his lower lip in thought and said, "Name doesn't ring a bell."

"Check your computer," I said. "She was a client."

The computer was already on. He found the client file and quickly turned up Mrs. Bailey's name.

"Here it is," he said. "Gwen Bailey. She plans to write a book about Marcus Garvey."

"And you gave her permission to do that," I said.

"We did," he said. "That's our business."

"Marcus Garvey's life is public domain," I said in my most lawyerly tone. "So is the life of every famous person living or dead. No one requires your permission. Mrs. Bailey didn't require your permission."

"Mr. Archer," the kid said calmly, checking his watch. "I sold Mrs. Bailey our permission to write her book."

"It's a script," I said.

"Then script," he amended. "Pemberton Enterprises has the right to sell our permission if someone seeks it. You could sell your permission if you wanted to do so and someone wanted to buy it."

"Fraud, Jeffrey," I said. "Straight-out fraud."

"I don't think so," he said with confidence. "We never promised anything but our permission."

"Implying that you had the right to sell that permission," I said.

"We do," he countered.

"Sullivan," I said calmly, "I've got another appointment and I'm not going to waste time with you. I know more about con games than you'll ever know. Yours is full of holes. Mrs. Bailey is over eighty. She's black. She's a good Christian, and a judge or jury would take you to pieces without much help from me. My guess is they'd give her a lot more than I'm going to ask you to give me. My guess is after a civil trial, the police might be interested in a criminal trial. Better yet, I could subpoena your list of clients and represent them in a class-action suit."

"I'll give you a check for Mrs. Bailey for her five hundred," he said. "Even if I have no legal reason to have to do so."

"You'll give me cash, Jeffrey. Seven hundred and fifty dollars. The extra two-fifty is for mental anguish."

"Five hundred," he repeated.

"I've got a full caseload, but this one will be fun in court," I said. "I'll pick up thirty percent of what a jury gets out of you. Jerry, I was half hoping you'd turn down my offer."

"Check," he said.

"Cash, now," I said.

"I get a receipt," he said.

"A receipt and a note saying you have my permission to write a book about the life of Mickey Mantle."

Sullivan pulled a dark metal box out of a bottom drawer of his desk, opened it, came up with a pile of bills and counted out the seven hundred and fifty.

I wrote a receipt and signed it *Fred Carver.* I did my best to scrawl it so the signature was illegible. He took the receipt and I took the cash. Someone knocked gently at the door.

"My appointment," Sullivan said, getting up.

"Does this scam actually pay you enough to make it worth the risk?" I asked, pocketing the money.

"You'd be surprised," he said, heading for the door and waving for me to follow him.

He opened the door and let in a couple in their fifties. The man was wearing slacks, a white shirt and a frown. The woman was filled with eager anticipation.

"Who are you going to write about?" I asked.

"Louisa May Alcott," the woman said.

"Thanks for stopping by, Mr. Archer," he said. "And I appreciate the Mickey Mantle release."

The kid wasn't bad, but my guess was he was going to

milk this scam till it was too late. I caught him. Others would too. If he had the experience, he'd take the money, pack his computer and take the next flight to Chicago or St. Louis. I considered advising the incoming couple but even if I saved them, I couldn't protect everyone in Los Angeles, let alone whoever he was bilking on the Internet. It was Sullivan who needed the advice, but I knew he wouldn't take it. He would have to learn the hard way.

I started to step out of the door, stopped and put my arm on the shoulder of the frowning man who had just come in. His wife was following Sullivan across the room and chattering about Louisa May Alcott.

"Fella," I whispered, "this is a fraud. Your wife doesn't need his permission and you don't need to give him a penny. Call a lawyer or the library and ask."

The man didn't speak, but he nodded, and the look on his face turned from a frown to anger. He moved forward to catch up with his wife and Sullivan. I left, closing the door quietly behind me.

Twenty minutes later, when I was sure I wasn't being followed, I made my way to North Hollywood and Eddie's house. I knocked at the door, and Eddie asked who it was. I told him and he said I should come in. Eddie and Louis Aspermonte were sitting in the living room watching a videotape of *Somebody Up There Likes Me*. Eddie put the tape on pause.

"Well?" asked Aspermonte, who had shaved, washed and was wearing some clothes that had to be Eddie's.

"Immunity but no witness protection," I said.

Aspermonte looked at Eddie and then back at me.

"They'll kill me," he said. "Nothing's changed."

"They'll probably try to kill you anyway," I said.

We were all sitting. Aspermonte stopped, looked at the television screen, where Paul Newman was single-framed in the middle of a right cross. Aspermonte sat silently for about a minute.

"I'm not going in," he said.

"He can stay with me," Eddie said. "Indefinitely. Louis is fine company."

"No," he said. "They'll find me and you'll get hurt too."

I didn't say anything. Aspermonte was right.

"Bring me in," Aspermonte said with a deep sigh, "but I ain't promising what I'll say. I need me a lawyer."

"I've got you a lawyer," I said.

When Aspermonte went to pack, I called Fred Archer and asked him if he wanted another client. This one couldn't pay either. Archer asked for a broad outline of the problem.

"Rockford, I've got three clients. You, Mr. Aspermonte and Mr. Martin. My fee to Mr. Martin will cover all three of you."

I thanked him and he said that when I turned him in, Aspermonte should say nothing except that he wanted to talk to his lawyer. Archer said he was on his way to the station to meet us.

Eddie offered me a ham and tomato sandwich on white and a Diet Dr Pepper. I called Dennis to be sure he'd be in his office and said I was bringing Aspermonte in. He said he'd be there. I ate, looked at Paul Newman on the television set and tried to think. My ideas and the face of Newman started to flicker while we waited for Aspermonte, who came back to the living room about five minutes later with his bag and said,

"I'll leave the television here if that's okay."

"I'll take care of it," said Eddie. "And you come back any-time you want."

The ride to headquarters was not a happy one. Aspermonte began talking to himself. I couldn't make out most of what he said, but I did catch "I knew it" two or three times.

I parked the Firebird in the same lot where I had placed Irv Grazzo's body in Diehl's trunk. Then Aspermonte and I walked to headquarters. Louis dragged and mumbled, but he shuffled along, not giving me any problems. I wasn't sure I was doing the right thing, but at this point, Aspermonte was right. It didn't matter how he testified, Barini would have to get rid of him to be sure he wouldn't change his mind again. Without witness protection, they would find him.

Dennis and Diehl were in the captain's office waiting, according to a uniformed cop doing paperwork on a computer who didn't look up at us.

We went into Diehl's office after I knocked but didn't wait for an invitation. With our arrival, there was a good crowd that required a couple of extra chairs. In addition to Dennis and Diehl, Fred Archer sat with his briefcase on his lap, and a woman named Sarah Bright from the state attorney's office sat in another chair next to Archer. She too had her briefcase on her lap. Hers was newer than Fred's and fine leather. It was rumored that Sarah Bright, a bit overweight, fair of skin and face, with natural golden hair tied in a bun, came from big money and had a future as bright as her name. She also had a reputation for being by-the-book and tough to make deals with.

Aspermonte looked around, and I pointed him to one of the two remaining chairs. He sat dutifully and placed his suitcase close to him on the floor.

"Mr. Aspermonte is officially turning himself in to Lieutenant Becker and Captain Diehl," I said to Sarah and Fred. "We understand he is being sought for questioning."

Diehl actually smiled at both Dennis and Bright. We were even.

I was just a little surprised that Donahue and Troy
weren't there, but I guessed that Diehl thought sharing the
credit with Dennis was enough.

"My client wants to know the charges against him," said
Fred Archer, "before he answers any questions."

"We have reason to believe he may be an important witness in a possible federal murder case," said Diehl. "We also
believe that there are those who might be a threat to his life
to keep him from testifying and that he should be in protective custody."

Diehl looked at Sarah Bright, who blinked her eyes in ap-
proval of the rehearsed speech.

I looked at Dennis, who avoided my eyes.

"Would Mr. Aspermonte object to answering a few questions now?" Sarah Bright asked solemnly.

"Depends on the questions," said Archer, taking off his
glasses and cleaning them with a handkerchief. He squinted
around when the glasses were off. We waited and he put
them back on.

"Does your client object to our taping this interview ses-
sion?" she asked.

"If it doesn't turn into an interrogation," said Archer,
who looked back at Aspermonte, seeing his client clearly for
the first time. "Mr. Aspermonte, you go ahead and answer
the questions. I want you to pause and look at me when the
question is asked. I'll either nod for you to answer or I'll say
something. Got it?"

Aspermonte nodded his head glumly.

"Did you witness the murder of a Mr. Wendkos seven
years ago in New York City?"

Aspermonte looked at Archer, who said,

"My client testified in court that he witnessed no
murder."

"And," said Sarah brightly now, "your client was convicted and sentenced to jail for perjury related to that case."

"Not on the issue of the murder," said Archer. "The perjury charges stemmed from statements made by my client about his own past."

"Including several earlier arrests and one conviction for assault with a deadly weapon," she said.

"Correct," said Archer. "But you know and I know that if my client had testified against Mr. Corlis, he would not have been pursued on the perjury charge."

"I don't know anything of the kind," she said. "He committed perjury."

"I didn't see no murder," he said. "Like I said at the trial, I was with Frank Corlis when the murder happened. We heard the noise. We went to see. This guy Wendkos was laying dead on the street and this woman was screaming."

Diehl looked at me and started to stand.

"Rockford," he said, "you told me Aspermonte was going to agree to testify against Corlis."

"If he got witness protection," I said. "I've just been informed by a United States Marshal that Mr. Aspermonte will not be offered witness protection."

I took a brown paper envelope out of my pocket. Inside it was the copy of the conversation with Donahue. I had hidden the other one in the car. I handed the envelope to Archer.

"That's a copy of my conversation with U.S. Marshal Donahue, a few hours ago," I said. "Mr. Archer hasn't heard it yet, but when he does, he'll confirm that Donahue did not offer witness protection to Mr. Archer's client, Louis Aspermonte."

Archer put the envelope in his briefcase.

"After I listen to the tape," said Archer, "I'll turn it over to you, Ms. Bright, assuming nothing on it incriminates either of my two clients in this room."

"Nothing does," I said.

Archer smiled at everyone.

"Protective custody," Sarah Bright said, closing her brief-case.

"Forty-eight hours unless my client is offered a longer term and agrees to it," Archer said and turned to Asper-monte. "Mr. Aspermonte, we'll talk immediately after this meeting. On the record, though, I tell you to answer no more questions regardless of what you are promised or threatened with unless I am present. You understand?"

"I ain't no Neandertall," Louis said sullenly.

"Now," said Archer, "where can I talk to my client in private?"

Diehl didn't look quite so happy anymore. He looked at Dennis as if he were going to take it out on him. I wanted to say something about that. Diehl picked up the phone on his desk, hit a couple of buttons hard and said, "Get in here."

Seconds later, the door opened and Riordon came in. He brought the smell of breath mints with him.

"Take Mr. Aspermonte and his lawyer to Judson's office," said Diehl. "And then prepare papers for Mr. Aspermonte to be booked as a material witness in protective custody."

Riordon nodded and let Archer and Aspermonte out. Louis, suitcase in hand, looked like Willy Loman coming back from a bad month on the road. Archer was smiling and had a comforting hand on his new client's shoulder.

"Mr. Rockford," Sarah Bright said, standing, "I intend to try to persuade Mr. Aspermonte to give his full and accurate testimony if it should be called for."

"The case is federal," I said.

"I'll discuss this with Mr. Aspermonte's attorney," she said, leaving the room without looking at Diehl or Dennis.

"That's a very ambitious lady," I said, looking back at Diehl with a smile.

"You told me he'd testify," Diehl said.

"Tell it to the feds," I said. "I had him ready. I'll keep trying to get him to make a statement about seeing Corlis kill Wendkos. I've got a hunch I may succeed."

"You're going to need more than a hunch," Diehl said, leaning toward me, both hands flat on the desk.

"I delivered Aspermonte," I said, getting up, "and you both get the credit for turning him over to Donahue. I suggest you call the U.S. Marshal's office in Washington first and tell them you've got Aspermonte. I suggest you push them to give him witness protection if he has to testify."

"Thanks for the advice," Diehl said with a bite in his voice, but I was pretty sure he would call Washington or try to convince the commissioner to make the call.

I left. Behind me I heard Diehl say something to Dennis. I couldn't make out the words except for my name. Diehl was angry. He was angry about ninety-five percent of the time. What surprised me, though, was Dennis's voice. He was loud. He was even angrier, and the word I caught was "Bullshit."

I started to walk away, but Dennis came out and slammed Diehl's door behind him.

"I want to talk to you, Jim," he called.

I didn't like the sound of that. To Dennis, I was usually Jimbo. Jim was more serious stuff.

Dennis moved to his desk, and I followed and stood in front of him. He picked up some papers and put them down.

"Diehl might hear us," I said, looking at the captain's door.

"I don't give a—" Dennis stopped himself. He was the

rare cop, he rarely cursed. He had a theory. Once you start something you think you shouldn't do, it keeps getting easier to do it. So Dennis didn't beat suspects even if he knew they were guilty. Dennis didn't plant evidence, even if he knew someone was guilty. Dennis didn't curse unless he wanted to make a point. Dennis carried a backup weapon, but it was fully registered and within department regulation. In short, Dennis Becker was an honest cop. Now Dennis Becker was an honest cop who was angry, angry at Diehl and probably angry at me.

"Jim," he said, looking up and trying to keep his voice steady, "what you did with Grazzo's body was stupid. If Forensics gets enough evidence that you obstructed justice, I'm going to ask Diehl to be the arresting officer. You behaved like a twelve-year-old. And I get reamed because you're my friend. You should have thought about that."

"I should have, Dennis," I said. "If I had put Grazzo's body in Diehl's trunk, which I'm not saying I did, I'm sorry."

Dennis snorted and looked at Diehl's door. He was even angrier at the captain than he was at me.

"Dignity, Jim," he said. "If you don't have your dignity, you don't have anything, at least not if you're a cop. I don't care about threats about review boards, demotions, losing my pension. I'm gonna be treated with dignity."

He said the last loud enough and intentionally enough so that Diehl would hear him even through the closed door. Dennis just glared at the door, waiting for the battle to continue, but Diehl didn't come out.

"Go," he said, looking down at his papers. "I'm glad the girl is okay."

"Dennis . . ."

"Go now, Jim," he said, pointing toward the exit without looking up from his papers.

I went.

I realized I was hungry some time before I reached the highway. I didn't feel like cooking so I stopped for an Italian sub sandwich at a bar where I'd had been once before and remembered it was great. I didn't eat it at the bar, but took my foot-long sub home in a bag, which turned out to be a mistake.

There was a Toyota parked next to Rocky's pickup. It wasn't new but it looked clean on the outside. Angel was here.

Mrs. Bailey was sitting under the aluminum awning of her trailer listening to the radio and writing her script about Marcus Garvey in her three-ring binder notebook. I walked over to her, and she looked up with a smile and turned down the radio, which was playing Louis Prima and Keely Smith singing "That Old Black Magic."

"Nice day, Mr. Rockford," she said.

"Nice day," I said. "How's the script coming?"

"Just fine," she said. "Should be done soon."

I took the seven hundred and fifty dollars out of my jacket pocket and handed it to her. She took it and looked at me for an explanation.

"Pemburton Enterprises doesn't own the rights to anyone's life," I said. "You can write a movie script about Marcus Garvey without anyone's permission. You could even do it if Marcus Garvey were still alive."

"But . . ." she said, looking at the money.

"I made a stop at the Pemburton offices," I said. "A Mr. Sullivan admitted his error and gave me your money back plus two hundred and fifty for pain and suffering."

"I didn't have no pain or sufferin'," she said, looking at the bills.

"I did," I said.

"You should get the two hundred and fifty dollars," she said, counting bills.

"Keep it, please," I said.

"Mr. Rockford, I got my pride," she said. "I'm paying your detective fee."

"Fifty dollars," I said.

"Should be two fifty. But you got your pride too."

She counted off two twenties and a ten. I took them and put them in my pocket.

"Thanks," I said.

"No, I'm thanking you. Seven hundred dollars means something to me on my budget. I'd invite you for lunch, but I see you're carrying yours. Maybe I'll make you a dinner real soon."

"I accept," I said. "I'm in the middle of a case right now, but the end of next week is open."

"Saturday?"

"You've got a date, Gwen Bailey."

"Ain't had one in almost sixty years," she said, putting the money into the pocket of her dress. "I'm lookin' forward. I'm a good cook."

"I'm looking forward too," I said and headed home as she turned up the volume and Louis Prima croaked.

"Those icy fingers up and down my spine."

I went into the trailer with my sandwich bag and found Angel on the couch, one arm behind his head, a smile on his face and watching *Wheel of Fortune.*

"Hi, Jimmy," he said to me. "Winston Churchill, anybody can see the name is Winston Churchill, and he wastes his time buying a vowel."

"Why aren't you in San Diego?" I asked.

"Don't have to go." He beamed. "See, it's Winston Churchill. If I could get on that show, I'd make fifty thousand at least with a little luck."

"I'm glad it was Winston Churchill," I said, sitting down

in the chair next to my desk and taking out my sandwich.

"That African-American kid is one hell of a lawyer," Angel said, sitting up. "One hell of a lawyer. Worth every penny of the eight hundred bucks."

"I agree," I said.

"You planning to eat that whole sandwich?"

"I wasn't expecting company, Angel," I said. "By now I should be surprised when there's nobody here when I come home. Here, take half."

The twelve-inch sub sandwich was neatly cut in two when I bought it.

"Thanks, Jimmy," he said, dropping a piece of lettuce on the floor.

I pointed to it and he picked it up.

"It's so simple," Angel said, eating with his mouth open. "I just keep insisting I believed and still believe I'm a direct descendant of Velasquez. I may have embellished my background a bit. I may have some dark places in my past, but I insist I am an artist and that I painted the portraits I sold and the ones Lyons bought, which I did paint."

"Fred Archer told you to say that?" I asked, finishing a bite of sandwich.

"You got anything to drink?" Angel asked.

"You know where to look."

Angel got a beer and offered me one. I had a can of Diet Coke.

"No," he said. "I tried some stuff out on him, said it was all true. He wrote it down and read what I'd said back to me, pretty much the way I just told you. Archer says the worst I did was commit a misdemeanor by saying I had lived in Spain to some of my clients. That's a plea bargain with a little fine. I could probably even go back in the portrait business, but that would be pushing my luck, don't you think?"

"It would be pushing your luck," I said. "What if one of your former clients—"

"Patrons," Angel corrected, wiping mustard from his beard with his sleeve.

"What if one of them sues and they demand to see you paint a picture?"

"That's the beauty part of this," Angel said. "Archer says I just refuse. The whole thing has been too traumatic for me. I can't paint anymore, not even more like the ones Lyons bought."

"Go home, Angel," I said.

"Ain't got no home," he said. "Like the Frog Man. I can't go back to the house. Who knows who might be waiting for me? I'm supposed to stay out of sight for a day or so till Archer makes a deal. Life's grand, Jimmy," he said, finishing his last bite of sandwich, looking at the television screen and saying, "Don't spin, you moron. Just solve it. Jimmy, people can be pretty stupid."

"I know," I said. "I'm one of them. You can sleep here. We call Archer in the morning. Pretty soon, Angel, I'm going to decide that I've paid you back in full."

"Consider your debt to me paid," he said. "Remember, I said you didn't have to pay me back for fixing this place up after it was tossed."

I finished my sandwich and decided to go back in the bedroom and listen to the tapes again to hear if I missed something.

"I'll see you in a while," I said, but Angel was already absorbed in the end of the show and the contestant's final attempt to win a new Ford Escort.

I closed my door and played my tape of Wright and me and then the tape of Donahue, me and Melisa. I thought I heard Melisa say something when I gave her that first hug, but her cheek had covered my ear and I had assumed she had said something like, "I'm sorry" or "I'm all right."

I heard it again on the tape, but it was a low whisper I couldn't make out. She had thought she was whispering into my ear. I rewound a little and turned up the volume as loud as I could. I had to listen to Melisa's voice four times before I was sure of what she said:

"Union Station. Tomorrow. Three o'clock."

CHAPTER ELEVEN

"EL Greco for two thousand dollars," Angel muttered when I shook him in the morning.

He rolled over, burying his head in the pillows of the sofa.

"Get up, Angel," I said. "I need your help."

This time I shook him harder with my left hand, holding the cup of hot coffee away so he wouldn't leap up from a nightmare and scald us both.

"What?" he said dreamily.

"I need your help," I said as Angel turned around, blinked at me as if I had just stepped out of a UFO, rubbed his eyes and gradually realized where he was.

He sat up. His clothes were on a chair and he was wearing his boxer undershorts and a white T-shirt. I handed him the coffee and he took a sip and then drank the rest down as quickly as he could given the heat of the liquid. I waited while life returned to my previously unwelcome guest.

"Had a terrible dream, Jimmy, terrible," he said. "I was a famous artist and I was on *Jeopardy*. Alex Trebeck asks me what category I want. The board is full of names of artists. I don't know about any artists except Velasquez and I don't know all that much about him. And his name isn't on the board. There's, let me see, Rembrandt, Al Capp, Red Skelton and El Greco. I pick El Greco. You wake me up. You got more coffee?"

"And I made some eggs," I said. "With toast."

Angel ran his hands through his hair and beard and was ready to eat. I was dressed in jeans and a button-down white shirt.

"You said something about needing my help?" he reminded me.

I had already eaten but I sat drinking my coffee.

"Something's happening at Union Station at three o'clock this afternoon," I said. "Melisa told me yesterday. I called the station this morning. There's a three o'clock train for Chicago and three-fifteen for Dallas–Fort Worth. I'm gonna be there and I may need help."

"What kind of help?" he asked suspiciously.

"Maybe getting Melisa away from the U.S. Marshals who'll probably be taking her back to Washington."

"On a train?" he asked.

"If Barini's people are watching the airports, it's either the train, a private plane or driving across the country," I said. "The train's not a bad idea."

"Not a good one either," Angel said with a cheek full of buttered toast. "I don't think it's a good idea for me to be out where I might be spotted before Archer gets everything set up."

"I need your help today, Angel," I said. "Not the day after tomorrow."

"You figure we'll have to pull a snatch?" Angel said, looking at me now with fear.

"I think so," I answered, finishing my coffee.

"So," he said, "with people all over the place trying to say I pulled an art con, you want me to risk getting picked up in a train station for kidnapping someone from the United States government?"

"That's about it, Angel," I said. "For Melisa."

His face turned sour.

"I don't need a guilt trip from you, Jimmy. I'm not responsible for them taking her from the house."

Angel scratched his stomach and looked at me for an argument. I didn't give him one. Finally, he sat up and said, "Okay, I'm in. What time is it?"

"Nine," I said. "I want to get there early, look at the station and decide what we need."

"Check," he said, yawning. "I'll get dressed."

We were out the door about fifteen minutes later. I didn't bring my .38. When I stepped out of my door, I decided it had been a bad decision. Standing at the bottom of the steps of the trailer was Tony, Barini's giant, the one who had been with Wright and had shot at me and Louis Aspermonte the day before. He was wearing white slacks, a black T-shirt and a white sports jacket. His shoes were white, and he looked pretty good.

"Mr. Barini wants to see you," he said.

I looked around for a car and Wright, but the only car I didn't recognize was a new, black Lincoln with no tinted glass and no one inside it.

Angel looked around for a place to run. I knew in a second Angel would sprint along the narrow deck and go off the far end heading for the beach. I grabbed Angel's arm to keep him from running.

"I'm kind of busy today," I said, stepping down to stand in front of Tony on the bottom step. I'm big, but he was much bigger, and even standing on the step I was barely eye to eye. I didn't see either intelligence or stupidity in the eyes, just determination.

"You're going to see Mr. Barini," he said. "Now. Mr. Barini don't like to wait and he don't like to hear no."

"He sent you alone?" I asked.

"I don't need help," he answered, grabbing my shoulder and squeezing. It hurt. It really hurt.

"I think I'll go do that shopping we were talking about, Jimmy," Angel said, trying to pull away from me. But I held him through the pain.

"You come too," the giant said. "Mr. Barini said I should bring anyone who was with Rockford."

"I'm not going," I said with a groan as he dug his fingers deeper into my shoulder. "If he wants to see me, he should send Wright."

"Why?" asked the giant, puzzled.

"We're fellow poetry lovers," I said.

"Barini," Angel muttered to himself in fear. "Barini."

"You two come with me," the giant repeated.

It looked like we were coming with him when a voice came from behind the big guy.

"Let him go."

The big body blocked the view, but I recognized old man Travis's rasp. Still holding my shoulder, the giant turned and faced Travis, who I could now see standing about thirty feet away, legs spread, cowboy hat tilted forward, old jeans, an ugly Hawaiian shirt, and a shotgun in his hands, the barrel pointed at the large target. If the thing was loaded and Travis pulled the trigger, he'd hit all three of us.

"Go mind your business, old man," the big guy said.

"Shoot him," Angel said.

The big guy looked at Angel with a look that said I'm-going-to-get-you-later. Angel shrank behind me.

"I said let him go," Travis repeated. "It is my business. I'm responsible, the Mrs. and I, for security in the community. I'm the Cove homeowners president, or am I vice-president this year and she's the president? Doesn't matter."

The big guy seemed confused. He looked around and saw three trailers, including mine, and what looked like and was a small bar down the beach.

"I'm taking him, old man," the giant said. "You shoot, you hit all three of us with that thing. I ain't a thinker, but I know guns."

"We don't tolerate hooligans," Travis said. "I'll shoot your damn car."

The giant glanced at the Lincoln as Travis turned his shotgun on the car. I don't know why I did it. Maybe it was the urgency of getting to the train station and maybe saving Melisa. Maybe I was just angry. Maybe I didn't want Travis to do something crazy and get his chicken neck broken.

As the big man turned back to look at me, trying to decide what to do, I threw a punch as hard as I could at his Adam's apple. He made a strange gurgling sound, looked at me as if I were his best friend and had betrayed him, and he let go of my shoulder. Both of his hands went to his throat and he sat down in the sand, still gurgling. His face was turning red and he was gasping for air.

"Wife's calling the police," Travis said. "You and your friend best step away so you don't get caught if I have to shoot."

I don't know where Travis got the western accent. It probably came with the hat. He was a retired salesman from Ohio.

My left shoulder was numb. I massaged it with my right hand and ducked back into the trailer to get my .38 out of the cookie jar. I checked fast to be sure it was loaded. No time for a holster. I stuck it in my pocket and hurried back out. The big guy was still sitting there.

Over to our left Mrs. Bailey sat watching over the top of her glasses.

"Jimmy," Angel whispered, "Barini. Barini's the mob. Barini's a killer. Barini'll have us cut up into little pieces of human sushi."

"Let's go," I said. "We'll take the pickup."

"Hold it, Rockford," said Travis. "Need you for a witness when the police come."

"I'm late for a job," I said, heading for the pickup with Angel. "You tell the police I'll be back this afternoon. Mrs. Bailey'll be your witness."

Travis shook his head in disbelief. We all glanced at the big guy, who sat like a kid in the sand, gagging. In the pickup, Angel closed his door and said,

"You think he'll die, Jimmy?"

"No, Angel," I said, looking back over my shoulder to be sure I wouldn't hit Travis.

"We might be better off if he was dead, Jimmy," he said as I headed for the highway. "He lives and he'll come for you. He'll come for me. Barini. Jimmy, what've you gotten me into?"

I didn't answer. I didn't have an answer.

It was still early and we had a lot to do at the station and I had calls to make.

Angel went silent, his cheek against the window, arms crossed, feeling sorry for himself again.

"Just when it looks like I'm gettin' out of a corner," he finally said, "something worse and bigger comes along. Archer's good, but he can't cut deals with the mob."

"I'll take care of that," I said, trying not to grimace with pain. I knew I had finger bruises on my shoulder. I tried to shake away the numbness. First my stomach, now my shoulder. Pain sometimes came with the job, but I wasn't one of those guys who likes it. Some guy kicks me in the face, I can't taste my blood and smile, like Bruce Lee.

"How you gonna take care of it, Jimmy? How?"

Angel was still leaning glumly against the window.

"I've got the Ace of Spades in a safe place," I said. "I just have to find a way to play it."

I don't think Angel believed me. He closed his eyes.

WE went down Alameda. I had already made a decision about where to park. I could go into the lot, but if we had to get out fast, I might get caught in the line going out or have to spend a precious extra few seconds paying a parking-ticket taker who would be in no hurry. The street was a good possibility, if I could find a space. I cruised past Union Station, which was renovated a few years ago but didn't look much different to me from the first time I saw it when Rocky took me back to Oklahoma to visit distant relatives.

The station had opened in 1939 to handle traffic for the Union Pacific, the Southern Pacific and the Atchison, Topeka and Sante Fe Railroads. It wasn't as big as most big-city railroad stations like the ones in Philadelphia, New York and Chicago, but it had character and had been used many times for movies. It looked inside and out like a railroad station should look. I knew about the area and nearby Olvera Street because I had made it a point of reading about it to impress dates with my knowledge of history and my passable Spanish. I didn't spot a legal space and had decided to go back to the parking lot and take my chances when Angel, eyes still closed, said,

"Turn left at the next corner."

"I'm looking for a place to park," I said.

"Turn left, Jimmy, trust me."

I made a left, my injured shoulder taking the shock of turning the steering wheel.

"Another left, on the dirt, behind the first clump of shrubs," he said. "It comes up fast."

It did. It wasn't really a parking space but a dirt area behind the buildings of Olvera Street. The space was big enough for two or three cars. I could see Union Station. It was a block or so away.

Angel sighed and got out of the car.

"Wait here, Jimmy," he said, holding the door open, contemplating his dismemberment by Barini.

"Don't run, Angel," I said.

"No place to run now," he said, closing the door and walking toward Olvera.

Olvera Street, El Paseo de los Angeles, the Walk of the Angels, is a brick-paved lane running from Marchessault Street north to Macy Street. Named for Don Augustin Olvera, who fought against Freemont. The narrow street was brick-paved and restored as a Mexican tourist attraction in 1929 using prison labor. The street had changed over the decades, but not that much. Once I came with a girl to the Blessing of the Animals on Olvera, the Saturday before Ash Wednesday. Cats, dogs, bulls, cows, goats, sheep, even a llama were led down Olvera and blessed by a priest.

Angel came back while I was rubbing my shoulder and thinking about how far the station was from where I was sitting.

"All set," he said, opening his door. "We can leave the pickup here. I talked to my cousin Miguel who owns a taco stand on Olvera. He knows the guy who owns this space. The guy told Miguel it was all right to park here."

I locked the doors and got out. Angel's success in negotiating a parking spot didn't seem to cheer him. He walked

silently at my side as we headed for the train station. He
looked like he was in more pain than I was. First my stomach, now my shoulder. I was beginning to dislike Barini
and his friends very much.

We entered the main terminal—the large waiting room
with seats lined up in aisles, shops, rest rooms and a lobby
with a passenger tunnel with ramps leading to eight plat-
forms and sixteen tracks.

The overhead board showed the departing and arriving
trains for the day. The three o'clock to Chicago was up
there.

"We're going to have to improvise," I said, looking at a
little girl clutching a Buzz Lightyear doll against her chest
as she slept with her head on the lap of a woman reading a
copy of *Mother Jones.* There was a train arriving in about
half an hour, another departing half an hour after that. The
waiting room wasn't crowded yet, but it would be for the
Chicago and Dallas–Fort Worth trains later.

I bought us coffee in plastic cups and we sat as far from
the entrance as possible.

"I need you, Angel," I said.

He nodded, drank his coffee and said,

"I'm going for a Danish."

Five minutes later he was back, Danish and coffee in hand
and a copy of the *L.A. Times* under his arm.

People came and went. We read the paper, drank coffee,
had tuna sandwiches and Doritos around noon, took turns
napping. With fifteen minutes to go before the train Melisa
had whispered to me, they came in.

There were six of them. First came Donahue and Troy.
Then came Melisa, her arm being held by a woman in a
black-brimmed hat and sunglasses. Behind them, trying to
look separate from the party, were two more men, probably
marshals. Melisa looked trapped.

"Move, Angel," I said.

The four marshals were scanning the room when they came in. Angel and I moved back toward the rest rooms, and I didn't turn till I was fairly sure we couldn't be seen. The sextet was still moving forward down the center aisle. A train arrival was announced. Some people moved toward the tunnel. Melisa and the woman guarding her sat in almost the same seats where Angel and I had sat. The men moved to different places in the terminal. Donahue sat directly across from Melisa and the woman. Troy moved to a corner about twenty feet away and pretended to read a newspaper. The other two sat where they could see the girl and the woman.

I tried to think of a plan short of paging Donahue and leaving a message for him to call Diehl. I'd be at the phone when he picked it up and put my gun in his back. It was a bad idea and it probably wouldn't work. Besides, it would put me in a federal penitentiary for the rest of my life.

"Angel," I said, "you know the mariachi band that works Olvera?"

"Which one?"

"I don't care," I said. "Get them in here. Have them serenade Melisa and the woman. Have them stand right in front of them and tell them to keep singing and playing no matter what happens. Pay them whatever it takes."

"With my money?" he said.

"I'm down to a few bucks," I said.

He sighed and I handed him the keys to the pickup.

"Be in front of the terminal entrance as soon as the mariachi band comes in the station," I said.

He nodded to show he understood and headed toward the back of the terminal, where we had found a fire exit door earlier. The fire door didn't have an alarm.

My plan was still not very good, but it was the best I

could think of. Troy would be the only one of the quartet of feds who could see us had he stayed in the corner, but he had moved down the aisle about fifteen feet and he might not be able to see when the mariachi band surrounded the woman and Melisa.

While I was waiting, the woman at Melisa's side got up and said something to Donahue. He nodded and raised his hand to his head. One of the marshals I didn't recognize and who wouldn't recognize me followed the woman. The only logical place she could be heading was the women's rest room. I got there first, took a breath and stepped in, expecting to be seen by a screaming female. I would have just enough time to apologize and say I had walked into the wrong rest room. If I was fast I could get out before the woman came in and the guard was at the door.

The rest room was empty for the moment.

The woman who had been with Melisa stepped in and moved to a sink and mirror. She took off her hat and glasses and placed them on the sink next to her. She washed her face and dried it with a paper towel. She was about to put her disguise back on when I stepped out of the stall I was hiding in and said,

"You still look beautiful, Rene, or should I call you Adrienne?"

She looked at me in the mirror and said,

"You look a little older, Jim, and if you step closer you'll see I do too."

She turned. We were about six feet apart. I didn't see the aging.

A woman came in and saw me. She was about fifty, black and in a hurry.

"Sorry," I said. "Sanitation inspection. You'll have to use the men's room. There's a gentlemen standing right outside who'll see to it that no one comes in while you're there."

She was in too much of a hurry to argue. She scooted out, black handbag dangling from her hand.

"Same old Jim," Rene said with a sad smile.

"Not quite," I said. "The way I figure it we've got maybe a minute or two before that marshal gets curious, especially if more women come out and providing the lady who left doesn't complain to him. Was there really a woman stabbed in your car?"

"It was all a cover story that went wrong," she said, taking a step toward me. "Irv and I faked the fight. We couldn't tell Melisa. She had to be convincing, for her own good and mine. We parked a few blocks away the way we planned, covered by some trees. Donahue, you know Donahue?"

"I know him," I said.

"Donahue and his partner were there just the way we planned, but Irv panicked, told me he'd find me and ran. Donahue's partner went after him, but Irv had been a policeman. He had essentially been my bodyguard. The pressure got to him after a while and we fought and made up and fought and made up. Then, that day, he ran. I went with Donahue and the other man, Troy, and they put me in an apartment with a twenty-four-hour guard. They promised to get to Melisa, to tell her what was happening, to get her back to me. I don't know if there was a woman's body in the car. I do know that Corlis is asking for a new trial because he thinks I'm dead."

"Which," I said, "explains why Donahue wasn't that interested in getting Louis Aspermonte to testify against Corlis. He had you."

"Aspermonte is still alive?"

"Probably not for long," I said. "So they spring you as a surprise on Corlis either at a hearing or a trial?"

"Yes," she said. "They really didn't give me much choice.

Corlis's people found me when I was with you, when we . . . and then in Florida and then here. I'm tired of running. I'm tired of hiding. I just want to be somewhere safe with Melisa, to know she's safe. But even if they didn't have me in witness protection, I'd testify against Corlis. He murdered my husband for nothing, a mistaken insult. I loved my husband, Jim. I ran away from the program after a few months, came out here, fell in love with you. You were just what I needed, wanted. I think you kept me from suicide. I was considering suicide when you met me in the Burbank library. And then, a few weeks later, I found out I was going to have a baby."

She put her head down so she wouldn't have to look in my eyes.

Outside a mariachi band was playing in the waiting room. There was a lot more to say and no more time.

"I couldn't take a chance," she said. "I didn't want you involved. I went back to the program and a few years later married Irv Grazzo. But—"

"Mrs. Wendkos?" a male voice called through the open door. "You all right?"

"Fine," she said. "I'm coming."

She stepped forward and kissed me. It was too fast. It wasn't enough. It brought back memories. And then she was gone.

A woman came in almost immediately after, as I was looking at my face in the mirror.

"Lady," I said, "you're in the men's room."

She was small, feisty and had a heavy Spanish accent.

"No," she said. "You go look at the—"

"*Puerto,*" I said. "Door."

"*Sí,*" she said.

"Okay," I said and left to call off the mariachi band and

head home with Angel, hoping that Rene would find some way to stay in touch or that in a while Melisa could and would come back to see me.

As soon as I stepped out of the women's room, I heard a shot. The band went flat and men were shouting and women screaming. I hurried to the waiting room. Troy was heading toward me but I don't think he saw me, at least not yet. He was just checking the station along with the others. Donahue was questioning the mariachi band, and Rene was slumped over the seat.

Melisa was nowhere in sight. I felt sick. I hoped the band would cover for Angel. I headed for the exit door through the crowd pressing toward Rene. Donahue shouted everyone back, shouted that he was a federal marshal, and showed his gun. He was scanning the crowd for someone who might be there to take another shot at Rene. Someone did. Troy saw me. He saw no gun in my hand and no Melisa. He turned. I don't think he saw the blond man walking slowly toward the terminal exit with a suitcase in his hand.

Rene stood up, and Donahue, to his credit, put his body in front of hers. The bullet had missed. Wright was not the kind to miss, definitely not twice, unless it was intentional.

When Troy turned back to look for me, I was out the exit door and going as fast as my bad knees would let me toward Rocky's pickup parked right in front of the terminal.

People were streaming out as I got in.

"What's goin' on, Jimmy?" he said, looking at the people.

"Drive, Angel, drive," I said.

He did.

"Did you see Melisa?" I said.

"Melisa?"

"I think Barini's got her," I said. "I should have known. I should have at least figured it for a possibility. Tony the giant wasn't supposed to bring me in. I was supposed to get away. I was supposed to lead them to Melisa. They knew Angel. They knew Rene was still alive."

"Rene's alive?" he said, almost hitting a parked car.

"I led them to her," I said, rubbing my forehead, trying to think. "They used our plan, our setup to get Melisa. They didn't know Rene was in the women's room. Wright stayed behind, took a shot at her, missed and ran."

"This is very bad, Jimmy," Angel said. "I don't know. Last night everything looked like pink feathers and good food. Now . . ."

"Angel," I said. "Barini plans to pretend to offer a deal for Rene not to testify, but he really wants Corlis to stay in prison till he dies. So . . . ?"

"Oh no," said Angel. "They're gonna kill Melisa, kill her to be sure Rene will testify against Corlis."

"That's the way I see it," I said. "And I don't know how much time I have before they do it."

"How much time *we* have," Angel said glumly.

We went back to the trailer, where Travis was waiting, ten-galloned and anxious to talk as we got out of the truck.

"That big guy," he said. "The second you were gone he just got up, brushed himself off, ignored me, got in his Lincoln and drove away right after you left. I think he was singing."

I looked at Angel, who looked back at me. It seemed as if I had been right.

We had been taken, and so had Melisa. Then I thought about it as we sat in the trailer with Angel complaining of a headache and the need for food. He told me he had downed a couple of tacos on Olvera Street, but when he was nervous he was hungry. I pointed toward the cupboard and refrigerator as I sat behind my desk. There were no messages.

"Angel," I said, "they knew."

"Who knew what?" he asked, searching for something, anything, to put between two slices of bread.

"They knew about the three o'clock train," I said. "Barini knew. We didn't lead them there. They followed us but they had a gunman ready to kill Rene. The taking of Melisa had just been luck. I think they just planned to take those shots at Rene and miss, but we gave them an opportunity they couldn't pass up. Whoever in the U.S. Marshal's office or the L.A. police is on Barini's payroll passed the train plan on to Barini."

"So what do we do now?" Angel said, fixing himself a sandwich of mayonnaise and thick, ancient slices of salami I had in the refrigerator in a Ziploc bag.

"Now we try to get word to a blond killer that I have something he'd be interested in," I said.

"Call him?" said Angel, taking a huge bite.

"I don't have his number, but I may know a way to have him come and find me," I said. I picked up the phone. I made a call. Dennis answered. I didn't care if someone was listening. I not only didn't care, I wanted what I had to say passed around headquarters and back to Donahue.

"Dennis," I said, "about an hour ago someone tried to kill Rene. They missed but they kidnapped Melisa."

"I know, Jim," he said. "I'm sorry."

"You knew Rene was alive?"

"No, I just found that out after someone tried to kill her in Union Station. It seems the U.S. Marshal's office didn't confide everything to us."

"No one mentioned seeing me there?"

"Were you there?"

"No," I said. "But tell Diehl, tell anyone you want to tell, that I have some solid information on who killed Irv Grazzo."

"Do you?"

"Yes," I said. "The second I finish talking to you I'm going to call my lawyer. I don't plan on telling you or anyone who it is until I know Melisa isn't dead."

"You're going to try to deal with Barini," Dennis said with resignation.

"If it were your son, if it were Andy, what would you do, Dennis?" I asked.

"Good luck, Jim," he said. "I'll go tell Diehl. You know where to find me."

"Thanks, Dennis," I said, and hung up.

Angel was finishing his sandwich, seated quietly in the wooden chair. He hadn't turned on the television and he wasn't fidgeting with a magazine.

"It's my fault, Jimmy," he said, shaking his head. "You were right. I was so busy raking in bucks with my scam I didn't watch her. I could have kept Melisa from being taken in the first place."

"We'll get her back, Angel," I said, going for my holster.

The .38 had weighed heavily in my jacket and torn the lining of my pocket. I put on the holster, placed the .38 on the desk, took out my old tape recorder and called Fred Archer and then waited to see who would get to me first. I had ignored the pain in my shoulder from the giant's grip. It came back strong now and throbbing, and I even felt a deep soreness from Grazzo's punch. It was time for Doc Bohanan's pills. I took two and sat down to wait.

Pain inside and out was with me, and I was mad as hell and remembering Rene's face in the rest room a little more than an hour ago.

"Jimmy?" Angel said, looking at me. "I don't like that look on your face. You're not gonna shoot anyone?"

"I don't know, Angel," I said. "I don't think so, but right now I think I could if I have to. The trick is deciding if I have to."

CHAPTER TWELVE

Wright arrived first. I thought and hoped he would, that Fred Archer had convinced the police not to come for me, that he and I would be in later to discuss what I knew about Irv Grazzo's murder.

Wright stood tall in a lightweight tan suit, probably silk, and a colorful paisley tie. He looked at me and the gun in front of me as I sat behind my desk. He also noted the tape recorder and then he turned to Angel.

"A friend," I said.

"I know who he is," Wright said. "I think he should go for a walk."

Angel seemed to agree. He got up from the sofa and said, "I do need some air, Jimmy. These walks are about my only exercise."

"Don't go far," I said. "And if you hear a shot or more, tell Travis."

"Check," said Angel, going out the door.

When Angel was gone, I pointed to the chair in front of my desk. Wright chose not to sit. I couldn't tell his mood from his face. He was great at hiding what he was feeling when he wanted to. I decided to change that.

"Press the Play button on the tape recorder," I said.

He reached for the tape recorder and pressed Play. Then he listened to himself reciting poetry and admitting to the murder of Irving Grazzo.

When he heard the admission, Wright turned off the recorder.

"Keep the tape," I said. "I've got two more, one I've got hidden, the other is with someone who'll turn copies in to both the police and Barini if anything happens to me."

"I think I can persuade you to get all the copies," he said.

I shook my head no and told him,

"I don't think so. You'd probably wind up killing me or me killing you. You kill me and the tape goes to the police and your boss. I kill you and neither of us get what we want."

Wright stood silently for a moment, deciding, and then said,

> "The Clock strikes on that just struck two—
> Some schism in the Sun—
> A Vagabond from Genesis
> Has wrecked the Pendulum."

"Emily Dickinson," I said.

"You're learning, Rockford."

"Had to learn it a hundred years ago in high school," I said. "I like the way it sounds. You want to talk deal?"

He pushed the tape recorder toward me without removing the tape.

"You and your lawyer are going to the police about Grazzo's murder?" he said quite calmly.

"We are," I agreed. "That's what I want to talk to you about. First, I want you to help me get Melisa. I want her safe. I want her with her mother. Second, I want to know who the cop on Barini's payroll is."

He stood, thinking, and decided to sit.

"You have coffee?" he asked.

"Help yourself," I said, pointing to the coffeemaker. The pot was almost full.

He got up again found a clean cup, washed it again and poured himself some coffee. He took a sip, pursed his lips and came back to the chair to face me.

"Depending on how all this comes out," he said, "I may be buying you some decent coffee."

"Happy with what I've got," I said. "Who's Barini's informant in the L.A. police department or the U.S. Marshal's office and are you going to help me save Melisa?"

He drank the coffee black, looked at me with unblinking eyes worthy of Charlton Heston, and said,

"I was lucky, Rockford, and so were you. When the call came in that you were going to the police with information about Grazzo's killing, I was with Barini. Since it was my problem, I volunteered to come here and take care of it. Barini said that would be fine. If I hadn't been there . . ."

"You would have found a way," I said. "You're a smart man. You know poetry. You dress great. You've got plans. You took a shot at Rene in the train station. You missed. You don't miss. It was an easy shot. You wanted her alive. The way I see it, Barini wants it to look as if you tried to kill Rene and missed. Barini took Melisa to kill her to be sure Rene will testify again."

"Something like that," Wright agreed, putting down his cup, crossing his legs and folding his hands in his lap. "I don't think this is a good deal for me, Rockford. You can't afford to give me whatever copies you have of this tape. You know I'd kill you. You also know I can't take your word when this is over that you'll destroy the tapes."

"You'll have to take my word that they won't go to the police unless something happens to me or we don't save

Melisa," I said. "That's what you've got to work with. Rene will testify even if Melisa is alive and with her."

"But she's sure to testify if the girl has an accident," he said.

I would have sworn that he was enjoying the conversation, the game we were playing.

"Are we wasting time?" I asked. "Is Melisa's time running out?"

He smiled.

"I'd like to propose a plan," he said.

I nodded and he went on.

"You and I go rescue the girl. No one sees me. No one sees you. We leave evidence that the cop on the payroll told his boss where to find her. You get the girl. Barini wants to kill the cop. I tell you who the cop is and you do what you want with the information. Then I have to live with you holding the tapes. 'How frugal is the chariot that bears the human race.' More Emily Dickinson."

"Who is he?" I asked.

"We get the girl first," he said, reaching for the tape recorder and removing the tape. "I put this tape in an envelope, seal it and mail it to a post office box in New Jersey. I'm the only one who knows the box number and I'm the only one with a key. You turn in that tape anytime after today and I get taken, I give the police or the feds the dated copy of my tape. Then you're up on withholding evidence in a murder case. Maybe some other things too. You play chess?"

"Not well," I said.

"What we have here is a stalemate," he said. "At least after we get the girl and the turncoat cop. Agreed?"

"Agreed," I said. "Let's go."

I stood up, put my gun in my holster and watched Wright, who was about to speak when I said,

"No more poetry for now."

He shrugged with disappointment. I think he had thought of something from Keats or someone like that, something he thought fit the occasion.

"How long will it take?" I said.

"No more than two hours including driving time," Wright said, straightening the wrinkles in his jacket and trousers and opening the door.

I went through the door. Wright closed it behind us. Angel was pacing back and forth as far away as he could and still be able to hear a shot. He stopped pacing and a look of relief came to his pink face. He walked cautiously to us, keeping his eyes on Wright.

"Angel," I said, "I'll be gone for no more than three hours. If I'm not back by then, call our lawyer. He'll know what to do."

"Okay, Jimmy," he said. "Melisa . . . ?"

"We'll bring her back," I said.

Wright looked out at the bathers on the beach and then went to his red sports car, opened the passenger-side door and went to the driver's side. He got in and closed the door.

"Jimmy, I don't like this," Angel whispered, his eyes on the car. "You want me to follow you?"

"No," I said. "Just stay here and make that call if I'm not back in three hours."

Angel looked relieved. I know Angel well. He felt he had to offer, but he didn't want the offer accepted. I had let him off the hook, at least for now. I didn't share with him the possibility that Wright might shoot me and get back to shoot Angel before the three hours were up. It was possible, but not likely. It wouldn't stop the tape from going to Dennis.

I got in Wright's car and closed the door. Angel just stood on the cracking concrete watching us leave.

We drove up Palisades Beach Road to San Vincente Boulevard. Wright played classical music tapes and said nothing. He made a turn on Burlingame and we went into Brentwood Park, where the houses ranged from small to mansion and cost nearly as much as Beverly Hills.

"From here, we walk," he said, parking in a stone-covered small space on a dirt road. We got out and he led the way. I looked back and saw that the car couldn't be seen from Burlingame.

Wright looked both ways and quick-stepped across the street and behind a house with a lawn that you could use for a putting green. Behind the house we moved through backyards. About six houses down, we stopped behind some shrubs with flowers. I didn't know what they were called, but I knew I was allergic to them. My eyes watered and Wright looked at me.

"Rockford, if you sneeze, if they spot us, you're dead."

"I won't sneeze," I said. "Can we get away from this spot?"

"Someone's watching through a back window," he said. "We can't see him but he's there. Someone is watching through the front windows. Nobody's watching the side. They have no reason to think anyone is coming for the girl so they're not watching carefully, and neither of them is too bright. The smartest one is with the girl. If he sees me, I have to kill him. I'll think of a story later."

"Let's try not to kill him," I said.

He didn't answer. We moved to the side of the house next door to where they were holding Melisa. Slowly, our backs to the wall, we turned the corner and kept moving along the wall. Then he stopped and pointed to the second floor of the house in front of us.

"There's a skylight over the bathroom on the roof off of the bedroom where they're keeping the girl," he whispered. "We climb up, open the skylight, go into the bathroom and hope we don't get seen. I go first. If the man in the bedroom sees me, I kill him. If he doesn't see me, you try to motion the girl into the bathroom. Since there are no windows, you tell her to tell him she wants to take a shower. He'll let her. We turn on the shower, go through the skylight and I don't put the skylight on so it looks like she got out on her own. You're clear. I'm clear."

While he was whispering, he took out his gun, took a barrel-shaped silencer from his pocket and put the gun back in his holster, which was specially cut to accommodate his weapon with the longer barrel.

"I don't think I can climb up there," I whispered.

"We'll make it," Wright said as he took off his shoes and socks and motioned for me to do the same.

I did and he said,

> "My spectre around me night and day
> Like a wild beast guards my way.
> My Emanation far within
> Weeps incessantly for my sin."

With shoes in hand we dashed from the wall we were standing against to the wall of the house we were planning to break into. We put our shoes and socks on the ground.

"William Blake," he said. "Follow me."

His silk suit didn't seem to stand a chance of surviving. My own clothes would be no great loss. Silently, he grabbed a drainpipe and leaped up to the sill of the downstairs window. Then he put his foot on the window sash slightly higher, gripping with his toes, and reached down for my hand while he clung with one hand to the drainpipe. I outweighed him by about thirty pounds, but he almost lifted me to the sill, where I clung to his hand trying to stay balanced. He took my free hand and placed it on the drainpipe.

I was standing on the windowsill facing the house, clinging to a drainpipe and praying that whoever was inside didn't decide to wander over and take a look outside.

I almost fell when Wright released my hand, but I pressed against the narrow inner wall around the window. Wright climbed gracefully, using the drainpipe and the moorings that held it. I repeated the same process getting to the second floor. He pulled me up. I straddled the window. There were no drapes, blinds or shades on this window. Inside was an office with a desk, phone, files and a bookcase. The lights were out. The room was empty.

Getting to the roof wasn't as bad as I feared. Wright scampered up silently. There was only a gentle slope to the roof, and my hand on the drainpipe was only a few feet down. He grabbed my wrist, motioned for my other hand and I dangled, trying to help him silently by getting a toehold on the brick wall. Finally, panting, I sat next to him on the roof. He wasn't panting. His suit looked clean and unwrinkled. He was already working on the skylight with a Swiss army knife. He worked slowly, and I came close to catching my breath. First he removed the all-weather tape around the skylight. Then he worked on the screws underneath. It couldn't have been more than two minutes later when he motioned for me to come. I did. I looked down through the skylight at an empty bathroom. The door wasn't closed but it was only slightly open. Wright placed the screws in the aluminum gutter and moved back to my side.

He slowly slid the skylight upward, holding it to keep it from making noise. He had left one swivel screw in the top right-hand corner. A television was blaring in the room beyond the bathroom. As long as we didn't make any really loud noise, we were probably safe.

Wright went first. The toilet seat was below the skylight,

and it wasn't even necessary to drop, just let himself down on the toilet bowl and take a quick step back onto the toilet. I came after him. I was taller that Wright, but not in his shape. He helped me down.

When were were standing barefoot on the tile floor, he took out his gun and inched his way to the door. He looked around and motioned for me. I went to the door. Melisa was sitting cross-legged on a bed. She was wearing the same dress she'd had on at Union Station. A heavyset man in slacks and a white dress shirt sat in a chair. His jacket and tie were sitting on another chair. Both of them were watching a *Hogan's Heroes* rerun. The man was clearly absorbed. He even let out a small chuckle when Klink stammered an apology for something to a general.

I put my face into the opening, looked at the back of the man and waved at Melisa. She saw me waving almost immediately, and I put my finger to my lips to keep her silent. When I was sure she could see me, I motioned for her to come into the bathroom.

"I need the bathroom," she said to the heavyset man.

He waved at her over his shoulder. He was wearing a holster. I couldn't see his gun. Melisa came into the bathroom and closed the door. She came into my arms and hugged me, sobbing.

Wright whispered to her.

"Go back in there. Tell Ezra that you want to take a shower. I don't think he'll try to stop you. But convince him or I'll kill him. You understand?"

She nodded.

She stepped back and wiped her eyes, and Wright flushed the toilet. Melisa went back into the bedroom, almost closing the door all the way so that I couldn't see, but I could hear. She said she wanted to take a shower. He didn't care. There was no way she could get out, and he was having fun watching the boys in the stalag put another one over on the comic Nazis.

Melisa forced herself to take her time coming back to the bathroom. A beat after she closed the door and locked it, I knew the lock would never stop someone Ezra's size. Wright motioned toward the shower. I understood. I could afford to get my shirt wet. He was wearing a silk suit. I turned the cold and hot water on full blast.

Getting out was a lot easier than getting in. Wright motioned for Melisa to get on the toilet seat. She did. He motioned her up to the toilet bowl, where she went with his hand on her back. Then he simply lifted her to the open skylight and she scrambled through. He went next, pulling himself up and out like a gymnast who wasn't going to settle for a bronze or silver. When he was out, he reached back down for me. I got on the toilet seat and with a little help from my enemy, I made it out on the roof.

Melisa started to close the skylight. Wright stopped her and whispered,

"Let them think you did this on your own."

"Ezra's going to be in big trouble," I whispered.

Wright didn't bother to answer. We slid to the edge of the roof. Melisa and I were on our stomachs. Wright was squatting. He motioned for Melisa, took her hands and whispered, "Slow and quiet. Use the drainpipe. Wait against the wall."

She nodded and started down with a hand from him. He looked over the side as she went down.

"She's good," he said with admiration. "She's already down. Your turn."

I moved reluctantly, took his hand, went over the side, my toes clutching the wall, and when he was sure I had a firm grip on the drainpipe, he let go. Going down wasn't bad at all. The drainpipe creaked a little. It wasn't built for holding almost two hundred pounds, but it held and I was next to Melisa. I tried not to pant since she wasn't. She took my hand and we watched Wright scamper down after us. The whole escape so far from the time Melisa had stepped into the bathroom and locked the door had been no more than three minutes.

Wright and I didn't bother to put on our shoes and socks. We picked them up, and the three of us dashed across to the side of the house next door. With Wright leading the way, we moved slowly, backs to the wall and around the corner so the downstairs man wouldn't see us.

He didn't, but when we had made the turn, we faced a woman, short, plump and at least seventy, wearing shorts, a flowered blouse and a straw hat with the biggest brim I had ever seen. She was wearing gloves and holding a hedge clipper.

"What are you doing?" she asked loudly.

I put my finger to my mouth and looked over my shoulder toward the house from which had just escaped. Wright and Melisa moved forward with me toward the woman.

"Who lives next door?" I asked.

"Next . . . Alice and Raymond Cupperman," she said with suspicion. "Dr. Cupperman. They're on vacation, a villa in France. Go every year."

"You noticed people going into the house?" I asked.

"They let friends use it when they're gone," she said.

"Well we were out for a walk and saw two men in the front window," I said. "They had guns in their hands."

"No," the woman said, her mouth remaining open.

"Yes," said Melisa. "We got away from there as fast as we could."

"I think you should call the police," I said. "I don't think those are guests of the Cuppermans."

The woman, hedge clipper in hand, straw hat brim flopping, headed for the house and probably 911.

Wright smiled at me and we hurried away. We got to his car without another word and had to walk about twenty yards on small stones in the road that had looked like dirt when we pulled in. When we got to the car, Wright cleaned off the bottoms of his feet with his hands and put on his shoes. I did the same. Melisa just stood at my side touching my back.

Wright told me to get in the back with Melisa and to stay down if anything approached from the back or front. Instead of going back on Burlingame, he continued up the dirt-and-stone road playing soft classical music.

"Mozart," Melisa whispered.

"Correct," said Wright. "Opera?"

"I think *Don Giovanni,*" she said.

"Right again," he said. "Here comes the quartet. Brilliant."

He drove. He listened. Melisa closed her eyes and put her head against me. Eventually we got off the dirt-and-stone road onto a street. I was disoriented, but Wright knew what he was doing. He drove inside the speed limit and he drove for a long time. Melisa was definitely asleep. We went into the valley and to a motel on Sherman Way off the Hollywood Freeway.

"Rockford," he said as Melisa woke up, "you register her. I can't be seen and I don't even want my car seen."

He had parked at the side of the motel away from the office.

"Right," I said, taking Melisa's hand and helping her out of the car.

We went into the office where a young woman in a blue suit, white blouse and name tag telling us her name was *Elizabeth* took my name and cash for one night. I didn't want my credit card on record on some computer where it could be tracked.

"My daughter will be staying the night," I told the woman behind the desk. "I'm going to go get her mother out of the hospital in Fresno. Honey," I said to Melisa, "here's some cash. You can eat at one of the fast-food restaurants right over there or you can order in. I'll be back with Mom tomorrow."

"Okay," she said brightly, playing the game.

We left the office and I gave her the key. Wright was parked around the corner and out of sight.

"I just gave you enough cash to go to that phone at McDonald's, call a cab and go to the Coronado Motel on Victory. Register as Mrs. Goldman. If the clerk looks suspicious or asks, tell them your husband will be picking you up tomorrow. He's in the navy and this is his first leave since you were married."

She nodded, understanding, and said,

"My mother?"

"She's fine," I said. "I'll get the two of you together after I take care of a few things. Wait fifteen minutes in the room before you get that cab. When you get to the room at the Coronado, don't make any calls except to order a pizza."

I kissed her cheek, took her to the room, let her in and handed her the keys.

"Leave the keys on the bed," I said. "Mess up the bed before you go. Don't make any calls from here."

Again she nodded and I said, "It's going to be fine."

I went out the door, closed it and went back to Wright in the red sports car.

"The car needs a wash," he said, pulling away behind the motel and over a rear road to a gas station. We drove through the gas station and out onto Sherman Way. He took the freeway back toward the city and said nothing until he turned off at Ventura and found a deluxe car wash that suited him. It was one of those where you sit in the car while supersoft brushes roll and the gentle soapy water squirts.

"They cater to foreign sports cars here," he said.

I nodded and said, "Thanks for the help."

"Don't mention it," he said. "I'm being blackmailed by you, remember?"

"I remember," I said. "I still thank you."

We had to raise our voices as the blowers started to dry the car and little beads of water quivered on the windshield.

"I hope you sent her someplace safe," he said.

"Sent her . . . ?"

"If you trust me, Rockford, you're stupid. I know you're not stupid."

"I sent her someplace safe," I said.

We came out of the tunnel and Wright, every blond hair in place, stepped out to inspect the wash. He got back in, reasonably satisfied. He took a small leather notebook out of his pocket and wrote a telephone number on it.

"Call that number," he said. "Wait an hour or two. Ask for Barini. Tell whoever answers that you've got the girl. I'm going to tell Barini you weren't home, that I waited for a few hours. Where do you want me to drop you?"

"Place off the highway in Santa Monica," I said. "Sandy Boone Bar and Grill. I'll show you."

"Will Angel be in your trailer?" he asked.

"Yes," I said.

"I'd suggest you call him and tell him to get out fast," Wright said. "Tell him to go someplace safe. He can call you in two days."

I agreed and we drove to the bar. When we stopped, I said,

"The other thing I wanted, the cop on Barini's payroll."

"When the person answers at the number I gave you,

he'll ask how you got the number. Tell him Riordon gave it to you. Riordon will deny it, but the fact that you have the number and know he has it will be enough to make him expendable. Do what you want, but . . ."

". . . keep your name out of it," I completed.

"Have you searched
    the dark waters
for dead memories
    and felt them glide flide
from your fingertips?
Tis better thus."

"Chinese poet, Lao Tumin."

"I like it," I said.

Wright reached over, closed my door and drove away.

I went into the Sandy Boone blues bar. The bartender recognized me. I called home and Angel answered. I told him to get out fast, that the item I went for was safe, and that he should call me from someplace safe in two or three days.

"Check, Jimmy," he said. "When I hang up, I'm gone."

He hung up.

I waited an hour before calling the number Wright had given me. It was an easy number to remember. After I dialed it, I threw the sheet of paper from Wright's notebook in a trash container near the phone.

Patsy Cline sang "Your Cheatin' Heart" while I waited for an answer. It wasn't exactly the blues, but the combination of Hank Williams and Patsy Cline wasn't going to have anyone complaining.

"Yeah," said a man's gravelly voice on the other end of the line.

"My name's Rockford," I said. "I want to talk to Barini."

"No one named Barini here," he said.

"Tell him I've got the girl," I said.

"Hold it," the man said, putting down the phone with a clunk.

In about two minutes he came back and asked where I could be called. I hesitated for a few seconds and said I'd be at the number I was going to give him for exactly five minutes. He said nothing. I gave him the number of the pay phone and hung up. I immediately called for a cab, hung up and waited.

"Your cheatin' heart will tell on you," Patsy almost wept. The phone rang.

"Who gave you the number?" Barini asked with more than a touch of held-back anger in his voice.

"In a second," I said. "The girl escaped. She came to me."

"Cops picked up the idiots at the house. Neighbor saw them with guns. I'm thinking of letting 'em get out of this on their own. All three have records. None of them is dumb enough to tell the cops the truth. What do you want, Rockford?"

"I don't think you want me to talk about it over the phone," I said. "Griffith Park Zoo. In front of the tiger cage. One hour. Alone."

"I don't go anywhere alone," he said.

"Okay, but we talk privately."

He thought for a few seconds and said,

"I'll be there, but so help me on my mother's grave, if you're setting me up, there won't be enough left of you, the girl or the woman to identify. Not even the teeth."

"I'll keep that in mind," I said and hung up.

The cab was there. I took a chance and had him drive me home. I already had an appointment with Diehl so there wasn't much point in the police or Donahue looking for me. I had just made an appointment with Barini, so if his people were watching my place he would probably call them in. At least that's what I hoped. When the cabbie dropped me, I didn't see any cars parked on the highway and I didn't see any in the lot that didn't belong there. Angel and his Toyota were gone. There were four cars at the bar and grill down the beach but it didn't look as if anyone was in them.

Then I made a mistake. I took the Firebird instead of the pickup.

I drove to the Griffith Park Zoo, stopping at an automatic teller machine to get the last of my cash from the bank. There wasn't much to get. Putting together the fifty I had gotten from Gwen Bailey, the twenty I had left in my wallet and the sixty I had left in my account, I could last for a few days if I didn't run into a major disaster. I looked around when I got out of the car in the parking lot and made my way to the tiger cage. I liked the zoo, went when I could with Rocky, who loved the zoo and hated the cages.

"They're safe here, Rocky," I said once.

"But they're not free, Sonny," he answered, looking at a chimp who was looking at him. "Prisoners in solitary confinement are safe. How much of his freedom is a man willing to give up to be safe."

"Chimp had no choice," I had said.

"No choice at all," Rocky had said, leaning on the rail. "And here I am looking at him when maybe I should be busting him out and flying him back to Africa."

"Where he'd probably get eaten within a day," I had said.

"I don't doubt it," he had said with a sigh. "Cute fella. Looks kinda smart too. And he's safe in solitary confinement."

Since that day about four years earlier, I still went to the zoo. It calmed me to sit, eat peanuts, have a Coke and watch the animals, but it was never the same as it used to be after that day with Rocky at the chimp cage. Instead of seeing tigers stalking, I saw tigers pacing in prison. Instead of seeing apes having fun, I saw apes going crazy, jumping, climbing, fighting with each other.

Barini was there with Big Tony. Tony's face was blank. Barini kept straightening his cuffs. Both were wearing suits. Barini's was better, not as classy as Wright's silks, but close.

People were walking by, stopping at cages.

"Pat him down," Barini said.

The big guy moved behind me and said,

"Hands on the rail."

I put my hands on the rail.

"My shoulder still hurts," I said, trying to make it sound like we were even in the pain contest. He didn't answer. He was quick and his big body hid the quick search. In about ten seconds, he stepped back and said to Barini,

"No wire, no tape, no mike. A thirty-eight in a holster under the jacket."

"You move your hands from your sides," Barini said, looking around, "and you're dead right here."

"The way Corlis killed Wendkos," I said. "Can we talk privately?"

Barini thought, looked at the tiger who was lying down and blinking at the wall, and nodded for the Tony to move away. The big man moved to a bench and stood in front of it.

"What do you want, Rockford?"

"You want Corlis to stay where he is," I said. "Leave the girl alone and I guarantee Adrienne Wendkos will testify against him again."

"What makes you think I want my teacher, a man who is more than a father to me, to die in jail?" he asked, folding his hands in front of him.

"Sources," I said. "You've got sources like the man I got

the phone number from and I've got sources that tell me
you want Corlis in prison for life. Not only will he testify
against him, but so will Aspermonte."

Barini stood, considering. He looked over at his man near
the bench and looked back at me. The nearby lion let out a
roar or a yawn.

"If she doesn't testify," he said, "you, the girl, the mother
disappear forever, like Hoffa. Understand?"

"I understand," I said.

"Good, now you tell me who gave you the number and
we never had this talk. The talk we just had was about you
trying to get more money out of me to find the Wendkos
woman. I told you I'd think about it. Again, you understand?"

"I understand," I said.

"Fine, the name."

"Riordon."

Barini looked at Tony and nodded. The big man nodded
back. Barini walked away and Tony approached me, ignoring the crowd of teenagers on a field trip he had to plow
through.

"You bring peanuts?" I asked.

He didn't answer.

"Red meat?"

"I can't kill you," Tony said quietly. "Mr. Barini says no,
not yet, but you hurt me. I don't like to be hurt."

"Only a select few of us do," I said. "My neighbor said
you got right up after I hit you and you weren't clutching
your throat in pain."

"I can take a lot of pain," he said with pride.

"I can't," I said.

We were close now and looking into each other's eyes. I
slipped my .38 out, hoping he wouldn't see.

"I owe you some pain," he said.

"I'd say we were even," I answered. "My shoulder has your finger prints and still aches."

"All I need is one good punch," he said. "Mr. Barini said I could give you one if I didn't hurt you too bad."

"Feel the gun in your gut," I said, grinning at a young couple strolling by pushing a baby in a stroller.

From the look on Tony's face, I could tell that he wasn't impressed.

"You gonna shoot me in the zoo? Witnesses all over the place?"

"Let's make a deal," I said. "You don't punch me. I don't shoot you. I shoot you and Mr. Barini won't get what he wants with me in jail. Think about it."

He blinked, which I took for thought, and then turned away without another word and followed Barini.

I stood looking at the tiger for about five minutes more, found a phone, called Archer and told him to call Diehl and say we were both on our way. He said, "On my way," and hung up.

I got to police headquarters in about half an hour. Archer should have been there by then. I found a place to park on the street and fed the meter.

When I got out of my car, a woman, young, pretty, in a yellow dress walked up to me and said,

"Read this and open your trunk."

She handed me a sheet of paper and walked away.

It looked like a sheet from Wright's notebook. I was sure when I read the neatly written poetry:

> "Pensive at eve on the hard world I mused,
> And my poor heart was sad; so at the moon
> I gazed—and sighed, and sighed!—
> for, ah! how soon
> Eve darkens into night."

The name Coleridge was printed neatly at the bottom of the sheet.

I opened the trunk.

Wright was in about the same position in the same trunk in which he had once placed Irving Grazzo. Wright's silk suit was covered with blood from the bullets that had killed him.

CHAPTER THIRTEEN

THE first person I saw in Diehl's office was Sarah Bright from the district attorney's office. She didn't bother to turn to look at me as she sat in one of Diehl's uncomfortable chairs, but she did take off her glasses and hold them up to be sure they were clean. Dennis was, at my insistence, also in the room, but he wasn't seated. He stood near the door, his arms folded. Diehl was behind the desk. Neither Donahue, Troy nor anyone else was in the small office. There were two open chairs next to Sarah Bright. Archer and I sat.

We had taken ten minutes in the lobby to go over everything that had happened. I abridged. Archer understood. Now we were ready to play.

"I want Donahue," I said.

"You want, you want," Diehl said. "I don't give a damn about what you want."

"My client is willing to come to an agreement," said Archer. "He will do two things. First, he will turn over the killer of Irving Grazzo with sufficient evidence to convict him of the crime. Second, he will give you the name of the police officer in your department who's on Barini's payroll and, possibly, get him to confess."

"And he wants?"

"Melisa and Adrienne Wendkos to remain in the witness protection program for as long as they wish," said Archer. "And witness protection for Louis Aspermonte, who will, if necessary, also testify against Corlis. I'll deliver Melisa when we have a deal. Finally, a private meeting for my client with Adrienne Wendkos Grazzo before she and her daughter are moved to a safe place."

"Is that all?" Diehl said sarcastically.

Archer held up his tape recorder to show this was on the record. We knew there were at least two other tapes running and possibly an intercom.

"That will be all," said Archer.

"Rockford can deliver?" asked Diehl.

"Try him," said Archer.

"Donahue," Diehl said, talking to the room.

He sat back and less than a minute later U.S. Marshal Anthony Donahue came in the door wearing the same suit I had first seen him in. He looked at Sarah Bright, who said,

"We get the murderer and the rogue cop. You get Aspermonte. You get the girl."

Donahue looked at me and Archer. We had to look over our shoulders at him.

"I have to call Washington, but I think we can deal," he said.

"There's a phone," said Archer, adjusting his glasses and nodding toward it. "We can wait."

Donahue sighed and picked up the phone. He got an outside line and made his call, getting his superior with no trouble. He stated the situation, said, "Yes, Al," and hung up, looking at Sarah Bright and saying,

"Deal."

"Credit for breaking the case goes jointly to Captain Diehl and Lieutenant Becker," I said.

"Who cares?" said Donahue.

"Diehl and Becker," I said.

"It's their case," Donahue said, looking at Sarah Bright, who nodded.

"Mr. Archer has a copy of a tape I made of a man who called himself Wright," I said. "Wright confesses to Grazzo's murder."

"When did you make this tape?" Sarah Bright asked.

"Last night," I lied. I wasn't on the witness stand and I hadn't taken any oath. I didn't want to be nailed for withholding evidence in a murder case.

"You wouldn't have anything more than a tape, would you?" she asked.

Her cheeks were a little pink today and she looked in a better mood than the last time.

"I've got Wright and I believe he has the gun he killed Grazzo with in the holster under his arm," I said. "It's probably the same gun he used to take a couple of shots at Rene in the train station. You should have no trouble matching the bullets to the gun."

"And where do you have him?" she asked.

"In the trunk of my car, downstairs, across the street," I said. "Just found him there."

"Keys, Jim," Dennis said. I took out my keys and threw them to Dennis, who hurried out of the office.

"How did he get in your trunk?" asked Diehl.

"How did Grazzo get in yours?" I returned. "Someone put him there."

Everyone was silent for a minute and then Diehl said,

"The cop on the mob payroll," he said.

"Call Riordon in," I said, looking at Archer, who nodded.

Diehl picked up the phone and called. Riordon was in the building. Dennis came back before Riordon arrived and said,

"Body's in the trunk. I told Forensics. There's a gun like Rockford said."

Then Riordon came in and looked around. Archer was going to handle this. Riordon looked around the room. There wasn't a friendly face in sight, and he knew something was rotten in the county of Los Angeles.

"What's up, Captain?" he asked as casually as he could.

"Detective Riordon, my name is Fred Archer. I represent Mr. Rockford. You have been feeding information to a known criminal. You have been violating the law."

"Bullshit," said Riordon.

"Mr. Rockford," Archer said.

I read the number Wright had given me to call for Barini and said, "I told Barini I got it from you. A tall blond man gave you up and gave me the number. My guess is that if you walk out of here instead of confessing and getting some protection, you won't live to see the smog and sun tomorrow morning."

Riordon was putting up a good front. He had almost twenty years in and knew the right drill. I wondered if Riordon had a family, debts, a sick wife or child with big medical expenses. I wondered but I didn't ask.

"I want a lawyer," Riordon said. "I'm not going to be railroaded into being a fall guy for some murder we can't solve."

"Did you kill a tall, blond man who works for Barini?" asked Sarah Bright calmly.

"He's dead?" Riordon asked, beads of sweat starting to twinkle his bald brow.

"Very," she said. "And if you don't cooperate, you . . . you understand?"

"I want a lawyer," he said. "None of this is admissible. I didn't do anything."

"Mr. Rockford will give you a number," Sarah Bright said. "Call it, please."

I gave him the number Wright had given to me to reach Barini.

"No," said Riordon.

"May I?" I asked Diehl as I stood up and reached for the phone.

He nodded. I dialed, listened to the answer and held the phone out for Riordon, who fumbled in his jacket for a cigarette, not caring who, if anyone, he might be offending or what rules he might be breaking. Reluctantly, he took the phone and heard the same thing I had heard,

"The number you have called has been disconnected. If you would like to try another number, please hang up and try again."

Riordon hung up, put a crumpled cigarette between his lips and lit it with a hand that didn't shake but wanted to.

"A lawyer," he said. "Damn it, Diehl, I've been a good cop for almost twenty years. This is a setup. I'll sue the department. Remember Stevens three years ago? The settlement he got? I'll get double."

"Call your lawyer," Sarah Bright said. "My guess is that he or she will tell you to cooperate with the police. I'll discuss some accommodation with him or her."

"Him," said Riordon. "My brother-in-law. What kind of accommodation?"

Sarah took off her glasses, looked at Diehl and Donahue and said,

"I'll have to check with the prosecutor's office, but it's possible the FBI might want to talk to you about Barini, and if you come up with information of value in obtaining his arrest and conviction, there's a chance charges might be dropped or reduced."

"It's possible," Donahue added.

"My pension?" Donahue asked, looking at Diehl.

Diehl nodded no, and looked at Sarah Bright, who said,

"Call your lawyer."

"In private," he said. "I've got a right."

"Lieutenant Becker," said Sarah Bright, "will you please find a phone where Detective Riordon can call his lawyer. You dial the number. You confirm that he is talking to an attorney."

Dennis unfolded his arms and nodded. He touched Riordon's shoulder. Riordon gave Dennis a look intended to show that this was all unfair. Dennis wasn't buying.

"When he's made his call," she said, "please put him in a cell on the charges we have already stated."

"Do it," said Diehl, giving Sarah Bright a look that said she had no right to be telling his men what to do.

When Dennis and Riordon had left, Sarah Bright looked at Archer and at me and said, "Anything else?"

"I'd like to see Aspermonte," I said. "I want Marshal Donahue to make the witness protection offer in front of witnesses and then I want the chance to talk to Aspermonte alone to try to convince him to accept the offer. He's a little gun shy now."

Bright, Donahue and Diehl exchanged looks and waited for one of them to give the word.

"Okay," said Diehl. "Is that it?"

"Nope," I said. "I want to talk to Corlis."

"What the hell for?" asked Diehl.

"I think he has a birthday coming up and I want to wish him a long life behind bars for trying to kill Adrienne Wendkos," I said. "A short, private phone call will do."

"No," said Donahue.

"You can listen," I said to Donahue, who looked at me for a few seconds. "You won't be disappointed."

"I . . ." Donahue began and I finished,

". . . need to call Washington first."

This time he took out a pocket cell phone and left the room.

"That should do it," said Archer with a smile, adjusting his jacket, packing his briefcase and rising. "I assume my client is free to go."

"We'll have to talk to him in greater detail later," Sarah Bright said, packing her suitcase.

"Understandable," Archer said soberly. "We'll be there at a time convenient for both of us."

"Would you like to discuss it over coffee?" Sarah Bright said.

For the first time since I had met him, Archer was without immediate words and action.

"I . . . " he started. "Yes."

"Let's go," she said. And then to Diehl: "Start the paperwork, Captain, and please get me the full report on the body in Mr. Rockford's trunk."

Sarah Bright left with Fred Archer right behind her. He turned to me to shrug, adjust his glasses, smile and follow his adversary out.

"Let's make that lunch," she said, closing the door.

That left me and Diehl.

"You think you're gonna weasel out again, Rockford," he said.

"Captain, I'm coming in like a very mad bear, not a weasel," I said. "You've got nothing to complain about. You've turned up a bad cop and a murderer."

"Who's dead," he added.

"Who's dead," I agreed. "And you and Sarah Bright can help Donahue put pressure on Riordon to find a trail to Barini."

"Maybe," he said, sitting forward.

He was right. Barini was too smart. Riordon had proba-

bly never even met him, but I had a plan to take care of
that.

Donahue came back into the room, his cell phone back in
his pocket, and said, "All right, but I listen and cut you off
the second you get out of line. Corlis may not want to talk
to you."

"Tell him I'm someone who can tell him who's betraying
him," I said.

"We use your office?" Donahue said.

Reluctantly, Diehl got up and left. Again, Donahue used
the cell phone. He didn't have to look up the number on the
other side of the country.

"Warden's office," he said into the phone. "Tell him Donahue, 6121."

There was a wait. I sat. Donahue looked at me.

"Warden," he said finally. "Donahue. I'd like to talk to
Corlis. . . . Tell him I have someone here who can tell him
he's being betrayed by a friend. . . . Sorry to hear that. . . .
I'll hold."

Donahue kept the phone to his ear and said to me,

"He may not want to talk. Warden says Corlis is a lot
sicker, emphysema."

"I'm sure we're all very sorry," I said. "I'll send a card.
How about 'Sorry to hear about your illness. Get well soon.
Your friends.' "

"He'll be touched," said Donahue and then, into the
phone, "Corlis? This is United States Marshal Donahue. I
have a witness here who wants to tell you something. He'll
make it quick."

I took the phone. There was a cough, a rasp and the voice
of a suspicious old man on the other end of the phone.

"Mr. Corlis," I said, "I'll make this fast. You know a tall
blond man, associate of John Barini?"

"Maybe," he said. "So?"

"Mr. Wright . . ."

"Who?" he said impatiently.

"The blond man," I said.

"His name is Vincent Corlapetti, my sister's son," said Corlis.

"He's dead," I said. "Barini had him killed."

There was more than a blink of silence. Donahue was at my ear listening. Then the old man coughed and came back.

"Who did you say did it?"

"No proof, but I'd say Barini. Your old friend Barini doesn't want you out of there. He's just going through the motions. He didn't get Adrienne Wendkos. He didn't get her daughter and he didn't get Louis Aspermonte."

"Louie? What's Louie got to do with this?"

"He's going to testify against you," I said. "Barini didn't take care of him, didn't send him money. I found Louis Aspermonte in a flophouse waiting with a rifle in his lap for Barini or the police. You like poetry?"

"No," said Corlis.

"Your nephew did," I said. "He left this one to me."

I read the Dylan Thomas.

"You were Vince's friend?" he asked.

"I guess in a way I was," I said.

"I'll check it out," Corlis said, wheezing.

He hung up. So did I, and Donahue took the phone.

"Corlis'll check," he said. "He'll find out that he hasn't got a shot at getting past a review board and having a new trial. I'd say Barini's going to be looking under his bed at night and jumping when dark cars roll by."

"And you'll get a promotion," I said, getting up.

"Possible," he said.

"Troy?" I asked.

"I'll cover for his taking the girl," he said. "But I don't think he's got the stomach for this kind of work."

"Aspermonte," I said.

Donahue led the way to the door.

Five minutes later I was on the bench in the squad room. It was noisy. A woman weighing about four hundred pounds was crying out her story to a black detective named Montague. Montague was an amateur weight lifter. I wondered if he could get the woman out of the chair. At another desk, two thin black kids no more than thirteen or fourteen were protesting their innocence. They were sincere. They were believable. They were lying. The detective behind the desk had his hands behind his head. He had been doing this for fifteen years. He would hear them out for about five minutes and then pounce. The room was noisy.

A uniformed officer led Aspermonte in and brought him to the bench. The officer backed away where he couldn't hear us but could see us with a relatively unobstructed view. There was little chance that Aspermonte, at his age, would make a wild dash for freedom.

"Why we meetin' here?" he asked.

"No one can hear us," I said.

"Either way," he said with a sigh, "I gotta go back on the streets today."

"No," I said. "You agree to testify and you get witness protection."

"No lie?" he said, rubbing his one-day growth of gray stubble beard.

"No lie," I said.

He smiled.

"Frankie Corlis'll call out every crook, con and crooked cop in the States to get me," he said.

"I told Corlis you'd be testifying. I told him you hadn't

been taken care of. After a few calls, he'll be after Barini. And remember, you're not the only witness. The key witness is alive, well and willing to talk again. I don't think Corlis's case is going up for review and trial. And I don't think Corlis will be coming out of prison alive."

"Lung stuff," Aspermonte said.

"Emphysema," I said.

"Smokes like Bogart," he said. "Knew the lungs would go. I was just smart enough not to tell him. Okay, a deal. Where will they be sendin' me?"

"I don't know, Louis," I said. "I don't think I should know."

"Hope it's warm," he said. "Texas maybe. Not Florida. Too many connected guys in Florida."

He got up and we shook hands. His grip was tight, and there was a look of something like hope on his face.

"Say hi to Eddie Thibidou," he said. "Tell him thanks."

"I will," I said.

I motioned the officer forward and he escorted Louis Aspermonte away.

When I stepped out of the squad room, Dennis and Troy were standing there waiting.

"We get the girl now, Jim," he said.

"We get the girl now," I agreed.

We took an unmarked car. My Firebird had been confiscated by Forensics for investigation. Nobody would know how long it would be before I got it back. Maybe weeks or even months or maybe it would be taken as evidence for years till it rusted to death. It depended on whether Diehl was more angry at me than he was grateful.

Dennis drove. I sat next to him. Troy was in back. I told Dennis the name of the motel and where it was. He knew the place.

"Lew, Marshal Troy, was telling me that he's thinking of quitting the job," Dennis finally said.

"You can't be your father," Troy said softly from behind. "If you're not as good, you feel like you've failed. If you're better, you feel guilty. If you're just as good, you feel like you should have done something else. No win."

"What are you going to do?" I asked.

"Don't know," he said. "Mom's still alive. Dad died protecting a six-time killer from a bullet. I know a lot about guns. Maybe I'll get out of law enforcement. Maybe I'll open a gun shop in the South, sell weapons, teach people how to protect themselves, shoot straight and keep their guns locked up and close by."

"A worthy ambition," I said.

"What the hell," Troy said with a sigh. "Maybe I'll just apply for manager of a McDonald's back in Boise. Be near my mother and sister."

"I know a homicide cop in Boise," Dennis said. "If you want—"

"No, thanks," said Troy. "Too close to my father's footsteps."

Melisa was where I told her to be. She waited till she was sure it was me before she opened the door and then ran into my arms. She recognized Troy but not Dennis.

"This is Lieutenant Becker," I said. "I guess I'd say he's my best friend. And you know Marshal Troy."

She nodded at the two men.

"We're taking you to your mom now," I said.

She was smiling and wiping away tears at the same time. I sat in back with her, my arm around her shoulder, and Troy guided Dennis to the San Bernardino Freeway to West Covina and Cameron Street not far from the Cal Polytech campus.

"No one followed," Dennis said.

If Dennis said no one followed, then no one followed. We got out of the unmarked car in front of a small house, white, stucco, like all the others on the street of small, dried-out lawns.

Troy led the way, knocked, identified himself and faced a leveled shotgun when the door opened. The man with the gun was average, not tall, not short, not flashy, not shabby. His hair was dark, his body not overweight or under. He did have a white scar across his forehead.

"Donahue here?" Troy asked.

The man with the shotgun stepped back, gun now aimed at me and Dennis as he said,

"Yes."

"This is Rockford," Troy said.

The man with the shotgun nodded. He had heard about me.

"This is Lieutenant Becker of the LAPD."

"Pleased to meet you," said Dennis.

The man with the gun nodded again.

"And you know Melisa," he said.

The man with the scar and shotgun smiled at her. She tried to smile back. A door suddenly opened and the woman I knew as Rene ran out, seeing nothing but Melisa. The two hugged, kissed, wept. Donahue appeared in the door Rene had come out of. He stood watching.

Over Melisa's shoulder Rene said, "Thank you, Jim. All of you, thanks."

"Ten minutes, Rockford," Donahue said. "No more. We've got to move. Mrs. Grazzo has agreed to testify now that her daughter's safe."

"I've got to talk to Jim, Melisa," Rene said, looking at me and stepping back just a bit.

Melisa nodded, showing that she understood, and I followed Rene through the door into the back room. Donahue

closed the door and I saw the man with the scar and Troy go
to the windows. Dennis stood watching.

It was a bedroom. It was decent size. There was a dresser,
nothing special. A bed, nothing special. A love seat, cheap
and red, and a double bed with a pink cover. A bad painting of a bunch of flowers hung on the wall. It was a big
painting.

We were about two feet apart. Neither of us made a move
to sit. She had been crying, but it looked like she had put
on some makeup and put on a solid black, figure-fitting
dress of some silky-like material. She looked beautiful.

"If you want me," I said. "I'll go with you and Melisa."

"No," she said.

"I still love you, Rene," I said. "And Melisa's my daughter."

"You don't know what it's like to spend your life running
and hiding and waking up in the middle of the night when
a car turns a corner with a skid two blocks away. Jim, you
have a life here, friends, a job."

"I can walk away, Rene," I said.

"Melisa's not your daughter, Jim," she said.

I didn't say anything. I wasn't sure I believed her. I knew
I wanted Melisa to be my daughter. She was the only
daughter, the only child, I'd ever have.

"You're just—" I started but she was already shaking her
head.

"Melisa's father was murdered by Frank Corlis. I was in
witness protection, but I ran. I was sure I could become
someone new, maybe eventually meet someone, have my
own new life. I met you. It was so much faster than I had
expected. And then I started to have cramps. I went to a
doctor and found out I was going to have a baby. I was too
far along for the baby to be yours. I ran back to witness protection. I ran back to protect my child, my baby. I loved
you, but I left you."

"Wait a minute," I said. "You're saying this to keep me from wanting to come with you. Melisa told me her birthday. You weren't pregnant when we got together."

Rene turned and went to a black purse on the bed. She found a small wallet inside and took out a folded sheet. She handed it to me.

"I lied to her, Jim," I said. "God help me. I thought she, we, might need you someday, that she might need someplace, somebody to run to. I knew you'd . . ."

She trailed off and watched while I read a birth certificate from the State of Florida, Melisa Grazzo. Grazzo had been assigned to her only a few months earlier. Rene had married him before Melisa was born, when Rene was at least seven or eight months' pregnant. If the certificate were true, and it looked real enough, then Melisa was conceived at least three months before I met Rene, before we first made love, real love.

I folded the certificate and handed it back to her.

"You going to tell her now?" I asked.

"Do you want me to?"

"No," I said. "Can you keep her from hating me for not going with you?"

"She loves you, Jim," Rene said with a sad smile. "I told her a lot about you before you found her on your porch. Nothing has changed that or will. I promise."

"You'll find a way to stay in touch," I said.

"Yes," she said.

"There may be a time when Corlis stops looking for you, Corlis and Barini," I said. "Corlis is an old man, a sick old man."

She shook her head no and said,

"It's not just them. I'm a bad example for all of them, the witness who got away. If I can get away, anyone can get away. None of them will be safe. I'm living proof."

I was out of words. I stepped forward. She came into my arms. It felt good, more than good to feel her breasts against me, to kiss her forehead, to press my mouth against hers. We held the kiss a long, long time. Neither of us wanted it to stop, but we knew it had to end. We came to the decision at the same time and backed away.

I went to the door, opened it and asked if Melisa could come in.

"Three minutes, Rockford," Donahue said. "We've got to move."

When Melisa was in the room, Rene and I took each other's hands and looked at her.

"You and your mom will be safe," I said. "I'll find a way to see you, to stay in touch. I'd like to come with you but you'll be safer without me and . . . your mother will tell you more."

"I still love Jim," Rene said. "We've got to go. Say goodbye to your father."

Melisa came to me again. I put her head against my shoulder for a few seconds and then stepped back.

"Your mother's told you about my dad, your grandfather, Rocky," I said, taking a ring from my little finger. "Here, this was his high school class ring. I think he'd be happy knowing you had it."

She took Rocky's ring and squeezed it in her hands till her fingers went white.

"Now," said Donahue, opening the door.

"I'll find a way to see you," I said to Melisa. "And you know where to find me if you need me again."

And then they were gone. I stood in the tacky bedroom and listened to footsteps and the door closing. A few seconds later Dennis came in the bedroom and softly said,

"We should be going, Jim."

"Right," I said, moving to the door.

"I've got the next two days off," he said as we drove to Santa Monica and my trailer at the Cove. "I think I can swing it with Andy's watch sergeant to get him to let Andy to switch days with someone who's willing. Fishing?"

"Sounds good to me," I said.

"Rocky's river?"

"Rocky's river will suit me just fine. I'll come for you in the morning, about six, in the pickup," I said. "You bring the beer."

"I bring the beer and if you feel like talking about all this, I'll listen," he said. "You know I might walk away from this whole thing with a commendation and who knows, maybe a transfer and promotion. Thanks, Jim."

"What're friends for," I said.

The sun was gone. I got out of the car. No strange vehicles around. No Toyota. I looked toward Travis's trailer and waved, knowing he or his wife was in the darkness behind the window. Mrs. Bailey was in her chair. She waved at me as Dennis drove away.

"Mr. Rockford," she said with a smile, "I could make you guess, but I'm busting to tell you. I showed my script to the man who fixes the roof. He said he had an uncle who was a producer. Next thing I know, this producer gives me a call, says he wants to option my script, ten thousand dollars for a year and a hundred thousand when they make the movie. Man said it was a natural and that I'd have to make public appearances. Said with the writer being an eighty-one-year-old black woman, the publicity would make the picture a success if they could keep the budget down."

"Congratulations," I said.

She looked around with a smile.

"Thought for a minute or two about takin' the money and moving again," she said, "but I like it here. Things to see all the time, ocean behind me. The Lord plays strange games with us, Mr. Rockford, and that's half the fun of living."

"Amen, Mrs. Bailey," I said.

I went back to my trailer. There were calls on the machine, including another one from Roy Palmer, who said this was urgent and I had to call him immediately. The rest of the messages weren't important except for the one from Gandy Finch reminding me he'd be in town next week. I wanted to see Gandy. Usually, Gandy was trouble. I didn't think he'd be this time.

I took my clothes off, showered. The bruise marks on my shoulder were purple now and definitely put there by a strong hand. My stomach where Grazzo had hit me only a few days ago seemed to be fine except when I touched it. I was down to my last hundred and twenty-two dollars and without a client. I should have called Palmer, but I was tired and thoughts of Melisa, Rene and even Wright wouldn't let me sleep. Everyone had a different name, a different life, a different lie. I thought of fish, big glistening fish on the end of a line, flopping and fighting. And then I was asleep. I had the dream I wanted and needed. I was hip deep in the river with Rocky at my side and I hooked a big one, the shiny one I'd imagined before I fell asleep.

"Don't lose him, Sonny," Rocky said. "Stay with him."

I stayed with him and pulled the fish in magically. I held him by the gill, removed the hook and held him up.

"Good work, Sonny," Rocky said. "I'm proud of you."

Rocky in my dream looked exactly like the picture of Rocky on my desk.

"You've got a granddaughter," I said, putting the fish in the box on the shore.

"I know," he said. "I know."

EPILOGUE

The weekend went fast and the fish were biting. Dennis and Andy were both good listeners but I didn't feel much like talking. Andy caught the big one, a trout. We threw the rest back except for one decent-sized one for Dennis and one for me. Those we kept on ice. We grilled Andy's big trout and ate it outside of the tent with a beer. Andy had a Sprite. He didn't drink anymore.

We were back in the pickup and on our way home on Sunday.

"Ready for another backyard barbecue?" Dennis asked.

"Ready," I said.

He was about to ask me if there was someone I wanted to bring with me the way he usually did, but he stopped himself, thought about it and said,

"How about bringing your lawyer, Archer. Next Saturday night," Dennis said as I dropped him and Andy off and waved good-bye.

I was back at the trailer by three. The phone was ringing. I picked it up. It was Angel.

"Jimmy, where the hell have you been?"

"Fishing," I said. "Come on over and I'll bake it and tell you what's happened."

I didn't feel like being alone.

"Fred Archer tells me he thinks it's safe," Angel said. "Is it?"

"Safe as its ever going to be."

"I'm on my way," said Angel. "I'll bring the beer."

I hung up, changed clothes, made sure my .38 was in the cookie jar and hadn't been fired. I cleaned up, scrubbed with Fels Naptha to get the fish smell out, and put on a pair of shorts and a Lakers T-shirt with Magic Johnson on the front smiling that smile I couldn't resist.

I started the fish, and Angel arrived in about an hour. He burst in, full of energy, and said,

"Archer's got the deal. I'm in business. Two thousand bucks and suspended sentence. We celebrate. I brought the beer and one of those salads in a plastic bag."

"We celebrate," I said. "Set up the folding table on the deck after you put down the six-pack and salad."

"Gotcha," he said.

Angel was wearing a brand-new pair of designer jeans and a white Ralph Lauren pullover polo shirt. He even sported a new pair of tan Rockports on his feet. He was back in business.

"I'm actually thinking of going to the papers and television with my story, Jimmy," he said, coming back in from setting the table. "I'll cry, you know, say I'm sorry, say I'm still sure I'm a direct descendant of Velasquez. You wanna bet it drums up more business?"

"No bet, Angel," I said.

Angel bustled around, setting the table outside, putting the salad in my only bowl and singing "With a Little Bit of Luck" in the worst Cockney accent I've ever heard. He got a few of the words right, but not many.

The phone rang when Angel was on the deck. I decided to answer it.

"Rockford," I said.

"Roy Palmer," he said. "Thank whatever Gods may be. I finally reached you."

"What can I do for you, Mr. Palmer?" I said.

"Roy," he said.

"Roy, what can I do for you?"

"A friend recommended you. I'm not at liberty to give his name, but he said you'd be the only person for this job. My wife, Susan, posed for a painting by a fraud named Martinez, Angel Martinez. I understand from a certain source that you have dealt with Mr. Martinez in the past. I want to return that painting. I want you to return that painting and get my money back."

"I hear Martinez paintings are going to be collectors' items," I said. "Their price is going to be going up every year and if you get lucky and Martinez gets killed, their value is going to go up fast."

"It will?" Palmer said.

"It will," I said as Angel came back in smiling.

"All right," Palmer said. "We'll keep the painting, but I want half of what I paid back."

"How much did you pay?"

Angel ignored the conversation and went on singing. He took the fish out after he tested it with a fork.

"Twelve thousand," Palmer said. "I'll take six and keep the painting."

"I charge two thousand," I said. "But I guarantee you get your money in two days."

"Sounds fair," he said.

"I've got your number," I said. "I'll call you as soon as I get the money."

"Rockford," he said, "you just keep two thousand and bring me the other four."

He gave me his address.

"I'll call you tomorrow," I said. "I think I'm going to like doing business with you."

We hung up and I looked at Angel standing in the door.

"Dinner's ready on the patio and the sun is going down," he said.

"I'll be right out," I said. "We've got a little business to discuss."

"I like that," he said.

"We'll see," I said.

He didn't seem to notice my tone.

I took Melisa's photograph out of my wallet and the one of Rene and me at the beach. I put them in the desk drawer after looking at them for a while. I'd get them framed, maybe in the same frame, and put them on my desk, maybe next to Rocky, maybe not.

I came out from behind the desk and went out on the narrow deck to eat fish, drink a beer, have some salad and a nice friendly talk with Angel.

I pulled up the chair I had found Melisa curled in less than a week ago, sat down, opened a beer and raised in a toast with Angel, who was still smiling and doing the same. I'd save the Palmer news till after the sun was down and Angel was in a good mood with a few beers and a smile.

I was back in business.